Willie the Actor

David Barry

Libros
INTERNATIONAL

ISBN 978-1-905988-19-8

Cover design by Mischa Fulljames www.mischart.com

Published by Libros International

www.librosinternational.com

For Patsy

'Commit a crime and the earth is made of glass.
There is no such thing as concealment'
Ralph Waldo Emerson

CHAPTER 1

DECEMBER, 1923

A creaking noise came from deep within the stillness of the building. Eddie "Doc" Tate stopped working on the safe and listened intently. Even though it was a December night, and cold inside the office, tiny drops of sweat glistened on his forehead.

At his side stood Bill Sutton. If his accomplice was nervous it didn't show. Doc stared at him, wondering if it was an act. Maybe his young partner was trying to keep from shitting his pants. But standing there in his expensive overcoat, tuxedo and black tie, Sutton was every inch the young man about town. No one would guess he was a felon risking a five-stretch in the pen. You had to hand it to him, Bill Sutton had balls. Doc had never worked with such a levelheaded guy.

Bill Sutton shrugged. 'It was nothing. Just a...' He left the unfinished sentence hanging in the silence.

The tension on Doc's face eased as he realized what his accomplice meant. The noise from the bowels of the office was just one of a myriad of shifting sounds buildings generate late at night when the senses are keenest. He tugged his bowtie at the corners before continuing, then pressed his ear to the safe, just below the combination. Steel cold against his cheek. *Click.* Another spin of the wheel. *Click.* And another. All other sounds shut out. Relying solely on Bill now to listen out for a prowling night-watchman. Doc's concentration was focused. Nothing could get in its way as the wheels clicked. The wheels of fortune spinning as the sweat ran from under his arms. Counting in his head. Numerals spinning through space.

Bill was deathly still, watching the older man like a boy watching his father. The expression in his eyes said it all. There was a tenderness he felt for the older man that he had never felt for his own father. But then Doc was a great guy, one of the best. A science graduate from the University of Chicago, he had a mathematical mind and was fascinated by any mechanical contrivance, and with this aptitude began a lifelong study of locks and safes, becoming one of the best lock pickers and safecrackers in the business.

Not only that, Doc knew how to enjoy life, ate in all the best restaurants, took in all the shows. And the whorehouses...the smell of perfume and sex...the wild laughter of the women. Not that Doc ever paid for sex. He just enjoyed the company, the brash honesty of the girls, generously showering them with gifts and champagne like a kindly uncle. Yeah, he was a great guy.

Doc wiped the sweat from his forehead with the back of his hand. Then he turned it palm over and pressed his ear back on the safe again. Like a nurse assisting a surgeon, Bill slid another delicate instrument into Doc's outstretched hand. From far away came the distant strains of a Charleston, no doubt coming from some illicit liquor dive. The music made Bill feel restless. He brushed a hand across his dark, neatly parted hair and glanced at his watch. Doc noticed out of the corner of his eye.

'Might as well take it easy.' His voice was relaxed, designed to put his colleague at ease. 'We've got no cause to rush.'

'I've got a date,' Bill said.

Doc frowned, paused in his work and looked up at him. Bill gave his excuses like a dutiful pupil offering a favorite tutor an explanation.

'I know women, whiskey and work don't mix. But don't

worry. This one thinks I peddle insurance.'

Doc relaxed and concentrated on the safe again. He felt the tumbler click into place and permitted himself a tiny smile of satisfaction.

'You don't need me any more,' he said. 'You've learnt about all I can teach you.'

Bill's pale blue eyes brightened at the compliment, and he grinned at his mentor. Although he was thought to be reasonably good looking, Bill believed he looked an average sort of guy, which was an advantage in the line of business he had chosen. No witnesses would be able to single him out by some distinctive feature. It was a cute face, but instantly forgettable.

As Doc pressed his cheek against the freezing metal, breathing in the metallic smell, he heard the final numeric click. He lowered the handle and tugged. The door swung open. He paused, savoring the sweet rows of money. Clean, crisp bundles. Tidy and neat, like they'd been waiting for him. A good night's work. He looked up at Bill and grinned, but his young accomplice was deep in thought, showing little interest in their successful haul. Doc started to empty the safe, Bill frowned deeply and his voice had the faintest hint of a tremor as he spoke.

'You're not thinking of retiring? Not just yet.'

'Thought I'd take a sabbatical,' Doc replied. 'Go to the west coast. Live off the spoils for a while.'

He wiped his prints off the safe, while Bill wiped the tools clean. Doc, who looked more like a Wall Street banker, with his patrician, noble face, and graying hair, sorted the money into neat bundles and divided it equally.

'Beats working for a living,' he said.

'Sure does,' Bill agreed, as they crammed their pockets full of money.

As they were leaving, Doc tripped on Bill's abandoned jemmy lying at his feet and mouthed 'Fuck.' He was too much of a pro to vocalize it. When doing a job, Doc liked to keep his emotions in check. Sheepishly, Bill bent down and picked up the crowbar. As he straightened and their eyes met, he felt himself blushing for this oversight.

'Always leave your tools behind you when you finish a job,' he said, quoting his mentor. 'Except your jemmy. If you have your jemmy with you, no door is locked against you.'

Doc smiled. No harm done. He felt good. Another easy job. And they probably had about ten, maybe fifteen, thousand bucks apiece. He slid his hands into a pair of white gloves, which he rarely removed when he wasn't working, and patted Bill affectionately on the back.

'Like I said, you've learnt about all I can teach you.'

They walked cautiously through an open-plan office, passed rows of uniformly-spaced desks. The neon light from a hotel across the street threw red patterns across the desktops. A door banged. Neither of them knew if it was from inside the building or not. They stood rooted to the spot. Bill could see the neon from the hotel shining on his partner's face, giving his eyes a crazed look. He could feel the tension emanating from the older man, oozing and seeping like a stale odor of fear. Doc had never done any time. Now that he was older, maybe his nerves were going and that was why he needed to get away.

Bill heard his partner exhaling slowly, as though he'd been holding his breath. Then Doc whispered urgently, 'Come on. I don't think it came from this office. Let's get out of here.'

Like two prowling cats, they padded across the office to a door at the other end, leading to a staircase. They stopped before opening the door...listening for sounds...noises... footsteps. Doc eased the door open. The hinges squeaked loudly. Both men froze. If there was anyone on the ground floor, they must surely have heard the noise. But the two burglars knew that the sound was magnified by their fear. Doc eased the door closed and was relieved when it swung into place silently.

They started to walk down the stairs, their footsteps echoing eerily on the uncarpeted stone steps, and Bill felt a rush of adrenaline hitting him. Any moment now he expected a night-watchman to emerge from the shadows. He felt a slight loosening of the bowels and cursed himself for this sudden attack of nerves.

'Made it,' Doc whispered as they reached the door on the ground floor. They had broken in this way, so getting out was a cinch. Doc had disabled the alarm, so now all they had to do was step out on to the street and they were home and dry. Unless they walked straight into the arms of a cop on the beat. The icy night air hit them as they stepped outside, and the jarring clang of metal made them both jump.

'Gimme tha' bottle, asshole!'

'Fuck you!'

Two drunks arguing in an alley. A trash can knocked over. The argument became more incoherent and there was a splintering sound of broken glass.

'Nah loog watcha fuckin' done.'

Bill and Doc walked hurriedly to the corner of the block and crossed under the El as a train clattered and thundered overhead. Clash of metal...grinding of steel...making them tense, and the acrid smell of soot and smoke followed them down the street. Gritting their teeth, shoulders hunched, they walked silently for ten minutes, both deep in their respective thoughts. A chill gust of wind blew down Tenth Avenue as though it had been lying in wait for them and Doc raised his coat collar and wrapped it around himself. They passed a bank and he noticed the look that came into his partner's eyes as he surveyed the building.

'Stick to the devil you know,' Doc told him, without breaking his stride. 'These days, bank vaults are too sophisticated.'

'There's always the acetylene torch,' Bill said.

'You know me, Bill, I've never been one for welding. This is where my talents lie.' Doc wiggled his fingers in front of him. 'Even I have to admit defeat when it comes to some of those fancy bank vaults.'

'But think how much money we could take from just one bank.'

Doc shook his head. 'Too risky. Remember last July when we did three offices in one night. Thirty grand apiece. That sort of money is not to be sneezed at. And it's less risky than a bank.'

Bill knew that without Doc his days were numbered. Doc had taught him a great deal and he was an expert lock picker himself, but there was no way he could develop his talents to pick his way into safes like his partner.

Doc sensed his colleague's thoughts. 'It's only a sabbatical, Bill. Maybe a year at the most. Then, when I get back, we'll clean up and retire while we're still young.'

They reached Broadway and walked towards Times Square. Crowds jostled and staggered along the sidewalks and yelled yuletide greetings in voices slurred with bootleg liquor. A group of sailors was arguing drunkenly over where to go next, the whites of their uniforms bathed in bright neon. A cab tooted angrily as one of them fell back a few steps into the street.

A flapper hoisted up her skirt to reveal a garter from which she took a miniature flask. She unscrewed the top, brazenly toasted the air and yelled 'Merry Christmas' at the top of her voice. Somewhere a jazz band played as though they were in a race against time, and some drunks were singing "Yes we have no bananas", which jarred contrapuntally with the band. Bill bumped into one of the revelers and nearly dropped the crowbar he still carried concealed beneath his coat. He wanted to get rid of it. The steel was cold and his hand was starting to ache from its weight. They crossed Times Square and walked another couple of blocks, until they reached a police precinct. Doc stopped, indicating a parting of the ways.

'I'll see you around, Bill.'

Bill felt awkward. He felt something was slipping away from him, as though a great moment in his life was ending.

'But you and me, Doc...' he began, then corrected himself. 'You and I, Doc, we make a great team. And I've got no form.'

'That's just a question of time, Bill,' Doc said, and took a step back, widening the distance between them.

In Bill's stomach, a small wave of panic rose and fell. 'You think it's true there's a jinx on me?'

Bill didn't like to think about it, but it was always there at the back of his mind. All the guys he'd worked with before he met Doc. The first guy he'd committed a felony with was Charlie McCarthy, his school pal. They used to rob grocery stores together. Charlie's light had gone out when he'd run across the railroad tracks one night, escaping from the law. He was sixteen years old. Then there was Brannigan, who got badly beaten up by a pimp in a whorehouse. He nearly died. And it would have been better if he had. He'd be a vegetable for the rest of his life. Then there was Scott...the list was endless. Nearly everyone he'd worked with up until now had met with a violent end.

A policeman walked between them and turned into the precinct. He turned and looked back, staring at Bill's hand, so obviously concealing something under the coat.

Maybe this was it...the jinx. End of the road. Up the river to Sing Sing. The Big House on the Hudson.

He decided to bluff it out, hardly daring to glance at Doc beside him. He grinned at the cop and shrugged, hoping he'd think it was just a bottle of booze under his coat. The cop bought it. He gave Bill a tolerant wave of the hand, smiled and bade him Merry Christmas in a warm and liquor-soaked Irish brogue.

'A close call,' Doc whispered

'He thought it was a liquor bottle.' Bill chuckled and relaxed. Maybe the jinx was baloney. Perhaps his luck had changed.

The older man stared at his partner for a moment, smiled and winked at him. 'You'd better get rid of the jemmy now.'

Bill returned his mischievous smile. 'Sure,' he said and

marched boldly up to the precinct steps. He took out the jemmy, placed it on one of the window ledges of the police precinct, and walked hurriedly back to where Doc was standing. Except Doc had disappeared, had vanished into the crowds. He scanned the street, trying to see if he could place the tall, distinguished-looking man's retreating figure, but it was impossible. He felt lost and lonely. A peroxide blonde woman, in a flapper dress with a long pearl necklace, and the worse-the-wear for drink, threw an arm around him.

'Hey, honey, you've got a cute little face. Whadda yah say we party someplace?'

Whiskey breath hit Bill head-on and he reeled backwards. 'Thanks for the offer, but I'm already spoken for.'

'The cute ones always are. Oh well, Merry Christmas.'

She gave him a slobbering kiss on his cheek before lurching off to find someone else. Bill could feel the smear of a large lipstick imprint on his cheek and wiped it away with his handkerchief. He stood for a while feeling lost and cold. A sheet of newspaper fluttered at his feet, and he read the headline 'MEXICANS SMUGGLE RUM INTO TEXAS', without taking it in. The sound of a band playing a rousing Charleston reminded him he had a girl to meet. He turned up his coat collar and walked purposefully to meet his date. At least he could find some comfort in the arms of a sweet girl.

CHAPTER 2

NOVEMBER, 1929

As the gates of Sing Sing closed behind him, Bill took a deep breath, savoring the frosty air that blew down the Hudson. There was a light covering of snow on the ground and a damp mist hung over the river further downstream. He shivered and blew warm air on to each hand before setting out for the station. Not once did he glance back at the penitentiary. Clutching a small brown suitcase containing his scant belongings, he walked with his shoulders hunched, partly because of the cold, but mainly to avoid eye contact with the respectable citizens of the small town of Ossining, because he was aware that ex-convict was written all over him.

On the train, he went into the smoker, lit up a cigarette, and stared out of the window at the beauty of New York State, covered in a fairytale glitter of frost, as the train clattered along the Hudson Valley. He waited for a feeling of elation to sweep over him now that he was free and heading for Manhattan. But all he could feel was an aching emptiness, bordering on a deep depression. He was free, but it seemed he was chained to his recent past.

Time and time again he had cursed himself for his stupidity. If only he'd heeded Doc's advice to stay away from using the oxy-acetylene method to break into a safe – a sure way to get caught. Access to the small Brooklyn Bank had been fairly simple. But the safe was solid and modern and he didn't think even Doc's skills could have opened that beauty. It had to be either gelignite or the acetylene torch. And he chose the latter, hiring it from a scrapyard in New Jersey. It hadn't taken a great deal of detection to trace the equipment and he'd been arrested early one Saturday morning while he lay in the arms of a sweet girl from Chicago. And then it was up the river to Sing Sing.

How could he have been so brainless? He inhaled deeply on his cigarette. Across the aisle from him, a heavily-set man whistled the same two bars of "Swanee" over and over. It should have grated on his nerves but it didn't. Anyone, he decided, who has suffered the stir-crazy ravings of convicts at night, with monotonous regularity for five years, should be able to tolerate a little tuneless whistling.

As he stared out at the scenery flying by, his thoughts wandered to the craziness of the last summer. The temperature had soared in July, staying close to a hundred for nearly a month. That terrible heatwave...his cell a furnace. Yet he didn't dare leave it. He could feel the tension building up....*The prison walls seething hot...the air rancid and fetid...about to burst, festering with hatred and frustration, building up and up, until... After a brooding, heavy silence the explosion came. Mass hysteria suddenly unleashed ...crashing and splintering of furniture...clanging of metal...obscenities screamed...Warders kicked unconscious by frenzied mobs.*

Bill kept his cell door closed, shut away in the airless nine-by-five, standing with his back to the wall, hoping he could melt away into the fabric of this hellhole. His legs turned to jelly and his stomach churned. The cell door crashed open suddenly and a prisoner, blood seeping from a gash in his head like a battle-scarred warrior, lurched inside brandishing a heavy lead pipe.

'Sutton! We're gonna make the cocksuckers pay,' he roared.

He closed his eyes, the futile, desperate action of a child trying to make the threat go away. But he couldn't escape the screams and cacophony coming from the corridors of hell outside. He braced himself for the pain, the slam of the lead pipe against his skull, the crushing and tearing of bone. He waited…Any moment now… Any con not a part of this frenzied mob was against them…that's how this crazy con saw it.

But he knew he could never be a part of this riot…never lose his sanity this way. As much as he hated the tough regime, the treatment at the hands of the brutal guards and the disgusting pigswill food, it just wasn't in his nature to resort to violence. He would rather die first. He opened his eyes, expecting to catch the bludgeoning swing of the lead pipe before it crushed him. But the convict had disappeared. It had worked. His childlike action had made the monster vanish.

Bill smiled as he remembered this close call with death and drew deeply on his cigarette. That July had been his first experience of mob rule. And his last, he hoped. Soldiers were brought in to quell the riot. Thankfully, he had managed to keep out of it. And when his review came up before the Parole Board, it counted in his favor.

As the train got nearer to Manhattan, his mood began to lighten and he thought about the lights at Times Square and of all his old haunts, the clubs and dance halls and theatres.

Before heading out to Brooklyn, he opted to spend some time aimlessly walking around Manhattan to raise his spirits. When he emerged from Grand Central, a strange sensation, like a warning sign screeching something unintelligible, hit him right between the eyes. Nothing he could put his finger on, just a strange feeling that something was seriously wrong. No one seemed to be rushing about anymore. Everyone seemed dazed, tired. He seemed to be adrift in a city of sleepwalkers. And he couldn't work it out…this black depression, a dark and somber mood that hung over the city like a threat.

Beneath an underpass, on a vacant lot, he saw what looked like an army of hoboes camping in a shanty town, warming themselves by scrapwood fires. He noticed that many of them were reasonably well-dressed. It confused him. Just what the hell was going on? He wanted to stop and ask but was afraid he might offend someone. With some reluctance, he continued walking, thinking about what he'd seen. Guys in decent clothes huddled round fires trying to keep warm, like a strange army of survivors from a war fought in city suits and collars and ties. Without realizing it, his pace quickened automatically, wanting to distance himself from a scene he found too disturbing, like something out of a weird dream.

His heart pounding, his breathing erratic, he hurried along East 33rd Street. In spite of the freezing temperature, he was sweating and his shirt clung to his back. He stopped to rest, leaning against the wall of a building. Gradually his feeling of panic subsided and his breathing became regular again.

He thought about the city he loved; in particular, Manhattan. It no longer seemed so familiar. The district was sleepwalking and had become a stranger, distant and remote. Of course, he expected a few changes after an absence of five years, but this was too strange to take in.

He examined his own feelings. Maybe it had nothing to do with New York. Perhaps it was him: ex-convict attempting to crawl back into society on his first day of freedom. Maybe Sing Sing had institutionalized him and he couldn't adjust. Maybe that was it.

Suddenly, he heard a scream. Piercing in its intensity, it cut through the traffic noise. He turned and saw that further along East 33rd, about a block away, a crowd had gathered. Sensing that something terrible had happened, his first instinct had been to cross the street to avoid it. But, dazed and fearful, his legs moving involuntarily, he was drawn slowly towards the circle.

As he got nearer, he saw beneath the feet of the crowd a huge red stain running across the sidewalk and into the gutter. It almost stopped him short, but he felt a compulsion, a burning curiosity, to know what was going on. At the edge of the sidewalk a woman was crouched over a fire hydrant, crying and clutching her stomach. The crowd stood still and silent, stunned by what they had witnessed.

Bill edged closer, shoulder-to-shoulder with them. He almost gagged when he looked down and spotted the body on the sidewalk. What was once a human being was now only the pitiful and bloody remnants of a carcass, a piece of meat, split open like a flimsy bag. The silence was eventually broken by the awestruck voice of a small man with a drooping moustache.

'For the love of sweet Jesus,' he said. 'I was walkin' here seconds before he hit the sidewalk. I mighta broken his fall.'

Someone giggled. It was a nervous giggle, but the man rounded on the crowd indignantly, as though everyone had laughed.

'It ain't no laughing matter. Guy's welcome to end it all, but not if it jeopardizes innocent people walking along the sidewalk minding their own business.'

A foul smell of excrement caught in Bill's throat, as he breathed deeply to steady his nerves. Maybe the guy next to him had shit his pants. He stepped backwards and turned his head away. He watched the heavy traffic crawl by as cabbies and drivers slowed down to stare at the accident. A dowdy woman in a headscarf spoke in a high-pitched voice, 'He must have fell at least forty floors.'

Normally loquacious New Yorkers merely mumbled and grunted an affirmative. A large heavily-built man wearing denims and a grubby windcheater disengaged himself from the crowd. He looked dazed and shocked, unable to make a decision about what he should do next. Bill walked up to him.

'What's going on?' he asked.

The man regarded Bill like he must be a simpleton.

'Guy threw himself outa the window. Up there, see. Then splat!'

'I don't mean that,' Bill said. 'I mean what's going on in general? I've just seen what looked like a group of realtors or bankers sleeping rough like hoboes.'

The man's jaw dropped open. He stared at Bill for a moment before speaking, 'You mean you ain't heard... 'bout the Wall Street crash? Millions of dollars wiped out. Kaput! Made paupers outa rich guys.'

His eyes narrowed as he regarded Bill with growing suspicion. 'Say, where you been? You been stuck in an elevator or something?'

His eyes dropped to the suitcase Bill was carrying, and he nodded with a self-satisfied smile. 'Oh, I get it...'

'Yeah, well thanks,' Bill said abruptly, and hurried away. He heard the distant wail of a cop car and instinctively walked faster. As he reached the next block and crossed the street, dodging in and out of the traffic, a cab tooted angrily and he heard the squeal of brakes. He felt he was running away, trying to distance himself from Manhattan's suffering. But there was no escape.

Two blocks further on, he saw a long queue of men and women waiting at a temporary soup kitchen. They looked in a daze as they patiently shuffled along to collect their food. At the back, a tall unshaven man stepped out and accosted Bill as he walked by. 'Say, pal, you got any change you can spare?'

Bill looked into the man's eyes and saw the resigned expression of someone who had nothing left to lose. He fumbled in his pocket, then handed him two dollars.

'Be lucky,' he said, realizing it sounded trite.

The man stared down at the bills, not believing his luck. He'd been expecting a dime, hoping for a quarter maybe, but two dollars! His hand balled into a fist over the money and he shoved it quickly into a trouser pocket. Avoiding Bill's eye, he said, 'I'll stand you a drink someday,' then returned to his place in the queue.

'I'll keep you to that,' Bill told him before hurrying on. He hadn't much money left now, just about enough to get to Brooklyn. And he was starting to feel insecure about the shoebox that lay buried behind some rhododendron bushes in Prospect Park.

At 28th Street, he caught the subway to Brooklyn. His parents lived in the Park Slope section of Brooklyn, not far from the park. He decided he couldn't face seeing them right away and would leave it for a few days. He was dreading the embarrassed silences. They would avoid talking about his experience as though the last five years hadn't existed. The only reference his mother would make, he guessed, would be to ask if he was able to attend Mass regularly.

Another reason he wanted to delay seeing them was because he felt guilty. They had given him a good upbringing and he had brought them nothing but shame. But maybe in a week's time, things might be different. He could sort himself out. Get a job. Prove to them that he intended to live a decent life.

As he reached the entrance to Prospect Park, he felt a sudden dryness in the throat and his stomach churned. Memories of Bessie, the first real love of his life, returned to tease and taunt him. He remembered the idyllic summer nights they had spent in the park, making love in the shadier corners, in their own small world.

Although it was ten long years ago, he recalled every detail of their affair as though it had happened only yesterday.

It was the first time he had been in trouble with the police. Bessie's father owned a ship repair yard and she provided Bill with the inside information he needed to steal the firm's wages by breaking into her father's office. It had been easy pickings; the easiest ever. It was an old safe that was unlocked with a key. But the most surprising thing of all was the amount of money it contained. They had been expecting a haul running into hundreds of dollars, but...

'We've hit the jackpot!' Bill said as he counted the last note. 'There's sixteen thousand bucks here.'

Bessie pursed her lips and whistled expertly. 'I can hardly believe it.'

'Me neither,' Bill replied.

They were holed up in a small hotel in Albany. Bessie had a cheap wedding ring on her finger, and they had checked in as a married couple, using a false name. The money was spread out over the bed and they sat on the edge. Bill rose suddenly, pulled Bessie to her feet and held her close. She could feel his erection through her thin cotton dress.

'Hey, Mr. Sutton,' she teased. 'Is it me or the money that arouses you?'

'Both,' he smiled.

She giggled as they fell back on to the bed and tore and tugged at each other's clothing, frenzied and feverish, giddy from the enormity of the crime they'd pulled off.

'I love you, Bessie,' Bill panted. 'Will you marry me?'

'I thought you'd never ask,' Bessie tittered.

'I take it that's a "yes"?' Bill decided, as he slid a hand up her stockings to the cool, smoothness of her thighs.

'Oh, Bill honey,' Bessie moaned. 'You betcha.'

But their elopement was short-lived. They froze as a fist pounded the door.

'Open up! Police!'

Bill's last memory of Bessie was of her frightened, fearful expression, like a deer startled in a forest. It was the last he saw of her. She was taken away, back to her father, and he spent what he hoped was going to be his wedding night in a police cell.

Bessie's father, who couldn't face the disgrace it would bring on his daughter, decided not to press charges provided Bill agreed never to see his daughter again. He was twenty-one years old and, faced with the prospect of at least a five stretch in the penitentiary, saw no alternative but to agree.

Troubled by memories of Bessie, and wondering if she ever thought of him, Bill walked carefully along the treacherously icy winding path until he came to the spot where Bessie and he had made love all those years ago, behind a large cluster of mature rhododendrons.

Somehow it had seemed a fitting spot to bury the money,

because he saw it as a magical lucky place. He glanced around to see if there was anyone about, but the park was deserted. It was too cold and too slippery to be out walking.

He went quickly behind the cluster of shrubs and bushes, found the small trowel he had buried close to a rhododendron, and began to dig. He dug for ten minutes, until he made a hole about a foot deep. And there it was - the remains of what was once a shoebox, now just remnants of soggy cardboard blending with the earth. But its contents, a bundle done up in a waterproof bag, was safe. The string around it was rotted and Bill broke it apart effortlessly. From inside the bag he removed bundles of money, no longer crisp, but at least intact. A little over ten thousand dollars. This would see him all right until he found himself a job, because now he had every intention of going straight.

That evening Bill wandered the streets on the Upper East Side of Manhattan. He needed a place to stay, but each time he approached several smart-looking hotels, he lost his nerve and couldn't bring himself to check in. He was finding it difficult to adjust to being a free man, a man of some substance. He felt disoriented walking in a strange world in which he didn't yet belong.

He crossed Park Avenue into East 63rd Street and stopped outside a small hotel, flanked by two enormous apartment buildings. The hotel was thin, like a meager filling between two thick slices of bread, and the discreet sign over the entrance said almost apologetically: *The Barnes Hotel.* Bill warmed to the place. It was the sort of place one might describe as "homely". He looked down at his rather sorry-looking case. What the hell, he decided. At least it contained $10,000. Enough to afford him somewhere far more luxurious than this small hotel.

Feeling more confident, and knowing it was just a question of time before he could make the adjustment to a more urbane lifestyle, he went inside and checked in. The look he got from the desk clerk was cursory, though a trifle guarded and suspicious, but he seemed to pass muster. And the room he was given, he was pleased to discover, was comfortable and tastefully furnished.

Yet no sooner had he sat down and switched on the radio than he felt edgy and impatient. Now that he was free he couldn't face being cooped up, however pleasant his surroundings were. And he felt suddenly very horny. It was funny but, when he was inside, he'd adapted to a life of celibacy without giving sex a thought. But now he was here on the outside...

He thought about a hooker but decided against it. Apart from the partying with Doc at some brothels, he'd never been with a prostitute. And he didn't intend to start now. Pouring cold water on to his spicy thoughts and shifting his mind to what sort of employment he might get, he went out and spent a long time walking along Broadway and gazing at the flashing signs of Times Square like some out-of-towner. He felt restless and lonely, yet he didn't feel like making contact with any of his old friends for a while.

He knew it was going to be difficult getting a job following the crash. There were thousands of desperate men looking for work. But he was determined and he figured that, if he was going to stand any chance, it would have to be some distance away.

The next day he made a point of getting up early, breakfasted in the hotel's small dining room, and went out with the intention of buying a brand new automobile. He hadn't gone far from his hotel when he saw some men standing around outside an apartment block, generating a certain amount of excitement. Another suicide? He didn't think he could take another corpse. But there was no way he could give it a miss. His natural curiosity just got the better of him. Corpse or not, he had to know what was going on.

He pushed through the crowd and, right away, something told him it was going to be his lucky day. Parked by the sidewalk was a beautiful gleaming Pierce Arrow, the latest model. A dapper man, smartly dressed in a double-breasted pin-striped suit and a bowler hat, was posed with one foot on the running board, and drawing the crowd's attention to a handwritten notice placed on the windscreen.

'$100 WILL BUY THIS CAR
MUST HAVE CASH
LOST ALL ON THE
STOCK MARKET'

'Come on,' the hapless investor called out, 'someone's got to have a hundred dollars. Brand new, she runs into four figures. And this baby's less than six weeks old.'

Bill was transfixed. This guy was a survivor. So what if he'd lost everything, he'd get by. His demeanor was that of a gentleman pugilist, squaring up to life's hard knocks, telling it to take a running jump. Surviving would be a challenge.

'Come on,' he urged. 'Just one hundred bucks buys this little baby.'

He patted the car the way a man with lust in his eye pats a floozy's backside.

'I'm wiped out,' someone in the crowd said.

'Me too,' another said.

Bill quickly counted out $200 in tens and pushed his way to the front. 'Like you said,' he told the man, 'she's worth a four-figure sum. Take two hundred for her?'

The man looked confused and hurt at first, as though he thought this was a cruel joke. When he saw the serious expression on Bill's face and, more importantly, the wad of notes in his hand, the relief in his face was expressed by a wide grin.

'Cash secures this beautiful baby,' he said. 'Thank you, sir. She's all yours.'

He took the notice off the windscreen and the crowd began to drift away.

After the deal was done, Bill checked out of his hotel and set off for Jamaica, Long Island.

It was freezing cold, but the sun was hard and bright, the sky clear and vivid. As he sped across the East River, the sun glinting on the water, the heady smell of the leather upholstery and the vibrating rhythm of the engine gave him a pleasant, horny feeling, causing him to smile as he speculated that it was maybe the luxuries of life that stimulate the libido. He felt about as relaxed as any man driving an expensive automobile can feel, like a conquering warrior riding his chariot through a cheering awestruck crowd. His bargain automobile gave him a positive outlook and he suddenly felt optimistic about finding work.

As soon he got to Jamaica, he checked into another hotel and immediately began his search for work. He soon discovered ex-convicts don't get a second chance. His first interview was at a large plumbing equipment warehouse. The manager was an efficient, no-nonsense guy with a pencil-thin moustache, who had a habit of brushing it with his forefinger every few minutes. It was his pride and joy.

At first the interview seemed to go Bill's way. The manager seemed satisfied with the answers to his questions and Bill could see he was making a good impression. Until he was asked, 'What was your last employment?'

Of course, he could have lied. But then would follow the demand for references. His only chance lay in being open and honest. 'I'm afraid I spent the last five years in Sing Sing Penitentiary.'

Bill watched the manager's face as he digested this information, slowly at first, in pin-dropping silence. Then the Number-One-efficient-guy routine snapped back into action again. He leaned forward in his chair, shuffled papers on his desk, and avoided looking directly at Bill. 'I'm sorry, but we have no vacancies.'

'But I thought …' Bill began.

'You thought wrong,' the manager said, scraping his chair backwards and getting to his feet. 'We have no vacancies.'

Bill remained seated. 'If you'll just give me a chance, I'll prove to you...'

He was cut short.

'If you'll excuse me, I have a very busy schedule.'

And that was that. He was out the door faster than a jack-rabbit. Of course, he could have abandoned his quest for work after being turned down in similar fashion in six interviews over two days, but he was determined to give it his best shot. So every day for a fortnight he diligently studied the wanted ads in the papers and attended dozens of interviews; but whenever it seemed he was close to rejoining society as a respectable wage-earner, there came that inevitable question, 'What was your last employment?'

And when he was forced to admit to being cooped up courtesy of Uncle Sam for the past five years, there followed the certain brush-off.

On his final and fourteenth day at Jamaica, he got up early, determined to have one last attempt at finding honest employment. He bought the morning papers as usual on Jamaica Avenue. As he walked along, he noticed an armored vehicle stopping outside a bank. Two uniformed guards rang the bell and were admitted by the bank guard. He watched every move. He watched as passers-by ignored this common ritual. And he was intrigued at how easy it was to gain admittance to the bank, providing you were wearing the right uniform. It was like a shot of adrenaline.

His thoughts honed in on the finer details of bank robbery. He was so focused he forgot just how cold it was. The freezing temperature and the white of his fingers suddenly brought him to his senses. He turned away from the bank, telling himself not to be such a fool. He owed it to his parents to go straight. He had no intention of committing any more felonies. He was firm in his determination to lead an honest life, in spite of how things were stacked against him as an ex-con.

As he drove back to Manhattan, a small niggling doubt at the back of his mind chipped away at his resolve. The way those security guards had entered the bank was so easy.

He caught himself daydreaming about what uniforms he could hire in order to pull off a bank job. Eventually, he gave in to the temptation and convinced himself that, as it was merely an intellectual exercise, he would plan a bank robbery, purely for his own amusement.

Back in the Manhattan, he parked his car on West 39th Street and strolled along Broadway, intending to visit some of his old haunts and seek out old acquaintances. He crossed over the busy street and dodged between a streetcar and a horse-drawn brewer's dray. There was an anti-prohibition message scrawled across it, and he pondered how things had changed since he'd been inside: the volume of traffic for a start and, as if to consolidate his thoughts, a car horn blared loudly and he leapt on to the sidewalk. He smiled grimly, realizing he still had some adjustments to make, and walked on.

Outside one of the theatres, he saw dozens of attractive showgirls waiting to get in the stage door. He wondered how long they'd been queuing in the freezing cold, and it reminded him that there were now too many people chasing too few jobs.

'Hey, Bill! Bill Sutton!'

One of the girls in the queue waved at him. It took him a moment to recognize her. She said something to the girl next to her and stepped out of the queue.

'Hello, Adeline,' he said, as she came towards him. 'It's good to see you.'

She grabbed his arm and moved him further from the queue. He could smell the perfume on her neck and he desperately wanted to hug and kiss her as the memory of their brief time together returned. Her blonde curls looked cute beneath her bright blue cloche hat, the color emphasizing the blue of her eyes. He remembered the way he always kissed her gently in that same spot on her neck just beneath her hair, the place she said always gave her goose pimples and sent shivers down her spine.

'You're looking great, Adeline,' he said. 'After your audition, what do you say we...'

She drew back and didn't let him finish. 'You've got a nerve, Sutton. You walk out of my life five years ago, and now you think you can pick up where you left off.' Her eyes narrowed suspiciously. 'So what happened?'

He looked away from her for a moment, composed himself, and then stared straight into her eyes. 'I had to go back to the old country to attend an uncle's funeral.'

'Five years ago? It must have been one hell of a wake. Pull the other one, Sutton.'

He shrugged and gestured helplessly. 'You know better than to ask, Adeline.'

'Oh, sure! Well, I'll see you around, Bill.' She walked back to the queue.

'Remember the Dutchman's joint?' he called after her. 'I'll wait there for you.'

She ignored him and returned to her place in the queue, deliberately avoiding any eye contact with him. He waited, balanced on the edge of the sidewalk, looking helpless and lost, like a little boy. Eventually, her curiosity got the better of her and she turned to look at him. He gave her a tender smile and an apologetic gesture, before crossing the street. She looked away again and bit her lip.

The girl next to her said, 'I'll bet a dollar to a dime you'll be there.'

The Dutchman's speakeasy was in a large basement beneath a garment factory and the decor was of a stylish Gay Nineties bar. Bill had been hoping that it might be reasonably quiet at this time of day but, as he looked around, he saw how crowded it was. Every table seemed to be taken. The air was a thick fug of blue cigar smoke. A black pianist on a small stage was playing ragtime and men with loosened ties sat at the bar sipping foaming beers and knocking back whiskey chasers as though it was some sort of convention or race to see who could get loaded the quickest. Scantily-clad girls moved enticingly between tables, serving drinks, laughing and flirting with customers, and milking them for decent tips. Screams of raucous laughter came from a table in the centre of the room where a celebratory party was in full swing. The joint was doing such a roaring trade it looked as though Wall Street had been just a minor glitch.

As his eyes became accustomed to the gloom, Bill spotted a free table tucked away in a far corner and he made a beeline for it. As soon as he had sat down, a waitress appeared out of a dark corner, her teeth gleaming through her smile. He ordered a bottle of champagne and her eyes lit up. The grin became a sexy smile. Just for him. But as soon as he asked her to bring two glasses, the light dimmed, the smile faded, and she left to get his order.

He unfolded a copy of the *Brooklyn Daily Eagle* while he waited, and scanned the headlines. He read about Jimmy Walker being re-elected as Mayor of New York and about the Fascists controlling Italy. After the waitress had brought his order, he turned to the wanted ads section of the paper and sighed deeply, wondering if there was any point. A shadow fell across his newspaper and he looked up. Towering above him was the bulk of Johnny Goldstein, a swarthy man with bovine eyes that would light up whenever his face cracked into a smile.

'Bill! How yah doin'?'

Bill had always liked Johnny and indicated for him to take a seat. Johnny shook his head and remained standing, 'Can't stay, Bill, and I notice you're expecting company. So when d'you get out?'

'Week ago.'

'Any plans?'

Bill pursed his lips and shook his head, 'Not a thing. I'm in a tight spot, Johnny. I need a job.'

Johnny turned his palms upwards, 'You've found the right guy. I'll put a word in for you. The Dutchman could use a reliable collector.'

Bill frowned. Although he had met him just once, he knew Dutch Schultz mostly by reputation and was reluctant to have much to do with him. The man was fearless, ruthless and unpredictable.

'Well, I don't know, Johnny...'

Johnny grinned and shrugged, 'It's easy money, Bill. And, while it ain't strictly legit, the Dutchman has it all under control. So how about it?'

Bill leaned back in his chair and relaxed. What had he got to lose? 'Sure. Why not?'

'The Dutchman's out of town today. Come by here same time tomorrow and I'll see if I can fix you up.'

'Yeah ... thanks, Johnny.'

Cries of laughter came from the centre table and a champagne cork popped. Johnny glanced over, grinned at Bill and jerked a thumb in its direction. 'That's how our old mayor celebrates when he's re-elected. In style. See you tomorrow, Bill.'

Their business concluded, Johnny Goldstein turned abruptly and walked towards the exit. Bill sat staring into space and thought long and hard about working for Dutch Schultz, weighing up the pros and cons. The Dutchman had a fiery temper and was an arrogant egomaniac. He trusted no one and had few friends. On the other hand, he was known to have police connections and probably had most of County Hall on his payroll, so his Harlem "numbers" racket was unlikely to get busted. And Bill would be little more than an errand boy, collecting the lottery takings from the salesmen, so it was unlikely he would have much to do with the higher echelons of the Dutchman's organization. It could be easy work and easy money.

'Penny for them!'

Deep in thought, Bill hadn't noticed Adeline's arrival. She indicated the second glass opposite him, 'You expecting company?'

He gave her a cheeky grin. 'Looks that way. So how'd it go?'

Adeline sat down opposite him and, bubbling over with excitement, threw her coat off her shoulders on to the back of the chair. She talked enthusiastically about her audition, as Bill poured her a glass of champagne, but only half a glass for himself. He had never liked alcohol much, only in very small doses.

'I think I'm in there, Bill. I know they liked me. I could tell. You know, the way they looked at me in that special way, like they thought I was the person they'd been hoping would turn up.'

Bill clinked glasses with her. 'They must have taste.'

Adeline smiled; a twinkle in her eyes. She made up her mind right there and then that she was going to sleep with him. She guessed he operated outside the law. She accepted that. He more than made up for it in other ways. He was generous, caring and considerate. In fact, unlike most of the other men she had known, he had been the most considerate lover. But only for two months, until he had suddenly vanished out of her life.

'It's been almost five years to the day,' she said. 'How was it being cooped up with nothing but men?'

'I'd sooner not discuss it.'

'You must be...' She paused and gave him a sensuous smile. 'Well, let's just say you could use a little female company.'

'And I'm enjoying the company,' he said.

'Mmm,' she purred contentedly as she sipped her champagne. 'So what's it to be, Bill? Your place or mine?'

'It'll have to be yours. I'm not fixed up yet.'

She gave him a questioning look.

'Only just got back from the old country,' he lied, grinning.

'Oh sure,' she said, and raised her glass to him. 'Welcome home.'

A week later Bill lay in bed watching Adeline, as she sat in front of a mirror and hurriedly applied her make-up. She had been offered a small speaking role in the Broadway show she had auditioned for the day she had met him and she was about to leave for the first rehearsal. Although nervous and on edge, she applied her make-up with the skill of an artist.

'I hope it goes well today,' Bill said.

'I always get nervous on the first day. I get more nervous performing in front of my peers than I do to an audience.'

'Wouldn't that be the same for all the other actors?'

'I guess so. But it doesn't make any difference. I still get nervous.'

Bill opened a fresh pack of Camels and lit his first cigarette of the day. He lay back, inhaling contentedly, and blowing occasional smoke rings to amuse himself. After their lovemaking, both in the night and the morning, he felt deliciously relaxed. As he watched her putting the finishing touches to her face, his mind began to wander. He thought about Adeline's appearance and how easily she could alter it. Something buzzed in the back of his mind, like a signal or a warning, and he couldn't work out what it was. Eventually the thought expressed itself in a flattering remark.

'You sure go to great lengths to alter that natural beauty,' he said.

'I'm a performer, Bill. So I gotta look like one.'

She took a last look at her reflection, pursing her lips to smooth the lipstick, then took a dress from a wooden hanger in the wardrobe and stepped into it. She came over to Bill and turned her back to him. 'Would you?'

He put his cigarette in the bedside ashtray, climbed naked out of bed and zipped up her dress.

'Thanks, honey,' she said. 'Now I really do have to rush or I'll be late. See you tonight.'

With barely a glance back at him she threw on her coat, gave him a cursory wave, and dashed out. Bill listened for the slam of the apartment door and then sat on the edge of the bed, finishing his coffee and cigarette. From another apartment he could hear muffled voices and from the street below came the steady sound of horses' hooves pulling a squeaky cart,

35

before fading into the distance.

On Adeline's side of the bed, in a silver frame, was a sepia-tinted photograph of her parents, stern and upright, standing in front of a picket fence. They reminded Bill of his own parents. There was such little laughter and gaiety in their lives.

He had been to visit them only two days ago and awkwardness hung in the air like a fog. Not once was the past five years mentioned. And he'd been right about his mother asking about Mass. Avoiding her probing stare, he muttered something about attending whenever possible. She knew he was lying and her disapproving look bore into him, making him feel small and dirty.

He'd never been able to lie to her ever since, as a small boy, he had stolen fifty cents from her purse. After he owned up, he burst into tears. She forgave him and sent him to confession. Although lying to her was impossible, the stealing became easier after that. He and his friend, Charlie McCarthy, broke into the same grocery store six times, each time emptying the cash register which sometimes contained as much as five dollars in small change. They became the richest kids in the neighborhood.

He finished his cigarette and screwed it into the bedside ashtray. For the first time in his life, a thought crossed his mind concerning his parents. Like Adeline, he was an only child. Unusual for a Catholic family. He wondered if his parents had tried to have other children and were unsuccessful, or had they become celibate. As he stared at Adeline's parents' photograph and saw how the camera had captured the severity of their lives, he thought it might be the latter. But he knew the truth would always elude him because there was no way he could ever talk to them about it.

He looked at his watch and thought he might get started on his rounds in Harlem. He had begun working for the Dutchman three days ago. He was paid a hundred dollars a week and it was easy money. But he was little more than an errand boy, working for a man he despised. Still, at least he was able to convince his parents he was now earning an honest living as a rent collector. And he thought his mother accepted this half-truth.

He slipped his underwear on and carried his coffee cup into the living room. He stopped to survey the mess. Adeline was a naturally untidy person and magazines lay abandoned wherever she happened to have been distracted from them. An old copy of *Variety* stared at him from the floor, with the headline 'WALL STREET LAYS AN EGG', which made him smile wryly for the second time that week. He thought about cleaning and tidying the apartment before going out, but decided against it. Why bother? Adeline wouldn't notice.

He went into the bathroom to wash and shave and stood gazing at his reflection in the cabinet mirror for a while. More of Adeline's make-up lay scattered on a shelf nearby. He stared thoughtfully at a small container of rouge, a wad of cotton wool, and a black eyeliner. He looked at his reflection again, and slowly it began to dawn on him how he might change his appearance.

He picked up the wad of cotton wool, tugged bits off, and pushed them into his mouth, hard up against his gums. Next he experimented with the rouge, rubbing a small amount on his nose and cheeks, giving him a florid complexion. The reflected face that stared back at him certainly looked different. Like a more rotund person with a drink problem. It wasn't perfect, but he knew he'd hit on something.

His thoughts strayed back to that juicy bank in Jamaica, Long Island. And as his plans began to take shape, a quiver of excitement pulsed through his body like an electrical charge. It was a challenge and he was certain he could pull it off. He grinned at his reflection in the mirror. It was a cheeky, audacious grin, and there was a certain boyish innocence in his expression, as though he was plotting a little harmless mischief instead of scheming to rob a bank. For now he knew without a shadow of a doubt that he was going to rise to the challenge of bank robbery.

CHAPTER 3

MARCH, 1930

Bill sat at the table drinking coffee, and watched Adeline as she checked the contents of her handbag. She took the top off a lipstick, held a compact in front of her and gave her lips another shiny coat. Finding it difficult to concentrate under his questioning gaze, she turned her back on him, but caught his eye in the small mirror. Her eyes darted away again and she stared steadfastly at her own reflection. They both heard the minute hand of the electric wall clock in the kitchenette click as it reached the hour. It accentuated the awkward silence between them.

He had to know what was going on and decided it was time to put things to the test. He rose from the table, came around behind her, slid his arms round her waist and pressed his groin in between the cheeks of her backside. She reacted like she was being violated.

'Not now, honey. You'll crease this dress.'

Her voice was harsh and strident and he was struck by the ugliness of the sound. How come he'd never noticed it before? When he saw her Broadway show, she was playing one of those broads who deliberately made a show of appearing loud and dumb, so he accepted her stage voice as part of her character and convinced himself it was all part of an act. But, recently, he found her voice unattractive and it grated on him.

She moved quickly sideways from his embrace, picked up a

pack of Camels and lit up. She blew out a cloud of blue smoke and waved an arm about to disperse it.

Bill sighed loudly and slumped back into his chair. Adeline feigned not to notice his petulance. She knew the embrace had been a test and was annoyed by his smugness. Armed with this knowledge, she knew he could now wallow in his self-satisfaction, having blamed her for everything.

Out the corner of her eye, she saw him reach across the living room table for her copy of *Variety*. He wasn't remotely interested in showbusiness news, so she knew he was now trying to avoid a confrontation. He turned the pages noisily, which grated on her nerves, raised his coffee cup to his lips and slurped.

'Do you have to?' she said, unable to suppress her irritation.

'What?'

'Make such a noise when you eat and drink.'

'I wasn't aware that I did.'

'Well, you do.'

Angered, she grabbed her coat from the coat rack by the door, and pulled it on roughly. Bill watched her. It wasn't the first time she'd given him the brush-off, but lately it had been happening with increasing regularity. These days their love life was non-existent. True, they rarely quarreled, and still behaved with a certain amount of affection towards each other, but the fire had gone out of the relationship. They were more like brother and sister.

'Where are you going?' he asked.

'The theatre,' she replied without looking at him, and struggled to smooth the fur collar of her coat down at the back.

There was something burning inside her, Bill could see it, and he felt anxious. Times had been good between them, but seeing her like this scared the pants off him. Certain women, he realized, were capable of anything when it came to relationships. His old mentor, Doc, had always warned him about mixing a life of crime with a certain type of woman. Not that he'd committed any crime since his parole. But that was just a question of time.

Adeline brushed down her coat and stood waiting at the door. There was a challenge in her expression. Defiance. She was waiting for him to protest the obvious.

'Isn't it a bit early to go to the theatre?' he asked.

'I'm meeting Patricia for tea, and then we'll go together.'

The way she avoided looking at him, and the studied casualness of her voice, told him she was lying. The slight hesitation, the gathering of the wits, the smoothing out of the voice, and the avoidance of eye contact was a pattern he recognized in himself.

Awkwardly, she turned and opened the door. Then, as though she had just remembered something, she turned back and stared at him. Her eyes were fiery. 'You never ever confide in me,' she said, accusingly. 'You never talk to me about your business. You've never once told me where you really were in those five years or the reason for your disappearance. It's as though you don't trust me.'

'And you resent that?'

'What do you think?'

He shrugged, gave her a regretful smile and a palms-up gesture of apology. The response it elicited was bigger than he expected. He had never before seen such venom in her expression. She hated him.

'If I'm not good enough to trust...' she snapped, then turned on her heel and exited dramatically, like a character in a Broadway melodrama.

As the door slammed shut, a shadowy image of his cell at Sing Sing surfaced in his mind. The silence in the apartment was heavy and brooding and his thoughts darkened. He felt claustrophobic. The tension was a ball in his stomach and he felt angry with Adeline and imagined his fist smashing into her face. He dug his nails into his palms and tried to calm down. He was shaking angrily. Gradually the violent moment subsided as he banished any brutal thoughts from his mind. Be rational, he thought. Keep calm. Work it out. He thought about

Adeline's parting words, which at first seemed enigmatic, until he realized just how revealing they were.

She'd been transferring her own guilt on to him.

He thought about the last couple of months. The clues had been there all along. More and more regularly she'd been having lunches with girlfriends...or so she said...and not coming home before going to the evening performance at the theatre. Or, there was a last minute understudy rehearsal she had to attend. And then the late arrival home, reeking of alcohol, and armed with the excuse that the party would be good for her career.

He lit a cigarette and inhaled deeply. He watched the smoke curling lazily upwards and examined his feelings towards her. If, as he suspected, she was having an affair, could he really blame her? He'd been too caught up in his own scheming and planning to notice there was anything wrong.

Their relationship had sunk into a vague oblivion, both taking each other for granted. And the strange thing was, the more he thought about it the more he became aware that he wasn't in the least bit jealous. In fact, he was almost relieved and pleased that maybe Adeline had found the man of her dreams.

Head tilted back, Bill smiled passively and thought about Doc's advice about women and whiskey. He thought of the robberies he and Doc had pulled off, all of them successful. They were halcyon days, and he missed his old partner. It was strange how he'd never heard from him. Maybe the safecracker had retired and was now basking in the sunshine down in Florida. A life of ease down at Palm Beach, sipping cocktails by the pool.

Bill indulged himself, lazily watching the drifting smoke from his cigarette, as the fond memories came floating back. He knew Doc would not have approved of his plans to do a bank job. He started a conversation in his head with his old partner where he justified his actions by telling his mentor that he was going to use his advice, and plan everything down to the last detail, so that nothing could possibly go wrong.

He needed an accomplice, someone trustworthy. He couldn't pull off a bank job on his own, that was for sure. He'd already put out a couple of feelers, but so far the only two men who'd been suggested to him were Italian. Not that he had anything against Italians, as such. He'd never held a racist thought in his head. It was just that the Italian involvement in organized crime tended to make the police heavy-handed when it came to questioning them. And there was only so much of a beating a man could take before he talked.

A weak sun cast a little warmth over the chilly city, and Bill decided to drive over to Central Park before going to Harlem to begin collecting for the Dutchman. Since he'd been cooped up in the penitentiary, there was nothing he liked better than the freedom of a long walk.

As he walked, occasionally nodding and smiling at passing mothers with their children, he began humming a dance tune he'd heard on the radio recently. He was feeling much better about Adeline now. At first he'd sat in the apartment brooding about things. But now he made up his mind that he would find a place of his own to live and, first thing in the morning, he would tell Adeline that he was leaving. He suspected that she'd be relieved and, if that was the case, there was no earthly reason why they couldn't part as friends.

He felt so much brighter now. Perhaps it was because winter was fading and the optimism of spring was taking over. He strolled along East Drive towards Pilgrim Hill and stopped. His attention was caught by a familiar figure some fifty yards ahead, walking in the same direction. It looked like Jack Bassett, an ex-convict from Sing Sing.

It was difficult to tell from the back of the man. He had the same athletic build as Jack Bassett and the same cautious gait, like a prowling cat, and his sleek dark hair, but he was too far off to be certain. He was carrying a rolled-up newspaper and he slumped down on to the nearest empty bench.

Even from this distance, Bill could see the man's body was

loaded and heavy with depression. But he couldn't tell if it *was* Jack. Not for sure, because the man had opened the paper and had his face buried in it. Bill continued walking until he reached the bench.

'Jack?' he enquired tentatively.

Peering over the newspaper was a pallid, sun-starved face. Startled at first, his face lit up when he recognized him. 'Bill! Where did you spring from?'

'I might ask you the same thing.'

'You know I was paroled last August …'

Bill sat down next to him. 'Sure. A couple of months before me. I meant to keep in touch, but somehow …'

'Same here. Best laid plans and all that.'

They fell into an awkward silence. Bill took a pack of Camels out of his pocket. He caught Jack staring at them and offered him the pack. As Jack lit up, Bill watched him inhaling deeply, savoring it with a kind of desperation.

'So, how've you been?' Bill asked, after lighting up himself.

Jack shrugged. 'You know what it's like. There aren't enough jobs to go round and, if you're an ex-con…'

Jack let the sentence hang in the air and stared into the distance with a melancholic, fixed look.

'So, how are you making out?' Bill asked.

Lost in his own thoughts, Jack took a while to answer. Eventually, he cleared his throat and turned to look at Bill. His expression was open and honest and, right away, Bill knew he had found his accomplice. Although he'd never worked with Bassett, he was certain he was trustworthy and reliable.

They had met in prison and become close friends. Jack was an intelligent man, an ex-college graduate, who wanted to be a writer. Back in 1920, he stole an automobile, hoping to sell it to pay his bills, but he was caught and sentenced to two-and-a-half years in Sing Sing.

Then, with only six months left to serve, he escaped. He was caught after five days of freedom and received another ten-year sentence. Bill often wondered why someone of Jack's intelligence had escaped while he had so little of his original sentence left to serve. He never summoned the courage to ask.

After the attempted escape, Jack kept his head down and become a model prisoner, was a champion player in the Sing Sing inmates' baseball team, and earned himself a review with the parole board and an early release.

'When I was paroled, things went okay for a month or so. I worked for Waxey Gordon for a while rum-running, but it got too dangerous. If I was caught, with my record, I'd be looking at a twenty-year stretch. I had a couple of narrow escapes. And it didn't take me long to realize it's always the little guys who get caught, never the Waxey Gordons of this world. And Kitty begged me to go straight.'

Bill raised his eyebrows. 'Kitty?'

Jack chuckled. 'You think I look this tired because I'm unemployed and walking the streets forever searching for work. It's what married life does to you.'

Bill returned Jack's smile. 'So you decided to settle down and become an honest man.'

'Only that's easier said than done.'

'The settling down or the honesty part?'

'Both,' Jack said, with an ironic laugh. 'So, how about you?'

Bill told him about his work for Dutch Schultz and Jack shook his head disapprovingly. 'I've heard a lot of things about that man. All of them bad.'

'It's a temporary position.'

'Until something better comes along?'

Bill smiled openly and patted Jack's shoulder. 'It already has. And I've planned this one down to every last detail.'

Jack felt a nervous tick in his cheek and he frowned. 'Something tells me this is dangerous. More dangerous than bootlegging.'

'On the contrary,' Bill said. 'I think this is marginally *less* dangerous as it only involves you and me.'

'You mean we don't have to tangle with the likes of this Schultz fellow?'

Bill smiled confidently. 'Exactly. We don't have to deal with any hoodlums.'

Despite the fear starting to swell inside him and the memories of being cooped up like a caged beast for nearly ten years, Jack also began to feel an excitement, a similar kind of nervous expectant excitement he felt at the start of a really good ball game. His mouth felt dry and he wet his lips before speaking, 'So tell me, what have you in mind?'

A woman pushing a pram stopped to lean over and adjust something around her baby and Bill waited for her to move on before he spoke. He told Jack about the bank on Jamaica Avenue and how he planned to rob it. Jack listened without moving, his face expressionless. After Bill finished speaking, he took a final puff on his cigarette and threw it on to the ground. He stared at it for some time before he spoke. When he did, his voice was almost inaudible, speaking purely for his own benefit.

'I guess we have no choice,' he said.

Later that night, Bill sat on the sofa in the living room reading *Nicholas Nickleby*. He had read it during his second year at Sing Sing and it had become one of his favorites.

But now, as he attempted to concentrate on the demise of poor Smike, his attention wandered. He kept listening for the sounds of footsteps in the hall outside. From far away he heard the familiar rattle of the El. He sighed and looked at his watch. It was nearly 2am. He wondered if Adeline intended returning or if she was planning to stay out all night. He lit another cigarette, abandoned the book, and picked up a copy of the *Herald Tribune.* On the second page, a headline caught his eye.

'YOUTH BURNED ON PYRE
OF ALCOHOL CONTAINERS'

Drawing deeply on his cigarette, he read the story with unease.

'Yesterday, in Steeger, Illinois, the body of a youth was found by the police, burning on a flaming pile of alcohol drums. Evidence led them to believe that the lad was killed for encroaching on the preserve of a gang of bootleggers.'

Bill flicked through the paper. Every page seemed to be filled with reports of horrific murders and organized crime. There was even a story about two New York detectives being gunned down at point-blank range.

He pushed the paper aside and thought about Dutch Schultz. He knew the Dutchman was a ruthless killer. He'd heard rumors from reliable sources that his employer had some union bosses of the city's waiters and cooks eliminated before forcibly taking over the union himself and extracting millions of dollars from the membership.

While aware that he was only a small cog in the Dutchman's empire, Bill still loathed the man. On the few occasions they had met, he knew the gangster wasn't so much sizing him up as trying to strike terror into his soul. He had a sneering, tough expression, and there was something mad and fearful in his dark eyes that reminded Bill of an evil gargoyle. He trusted nobody. Bill was made to feel that if he put a step out of line, or was disloyal in any way, then dark forces would be unleashed and his employment would be terminated with fatal consequences.

But working for the Dutchman suited his purposes for the moment. Although he still had a sizable amount of his $10,000 left, he was a lavish spender and generous to a fault. And, like most well-planned jobs, the bank robbery would take some financing.

He had already given Jack $500 to make his life easier and enough to rent an apartment in the theatre district of Broadway so that the address could be used to give credibility to his well-researched plan. He also needed to buy another automobile. Stealing one to do the job was too risky.

A key grated in the lock and Bill's nerves grated. Adeline swept in, slamming the door behind her. He could tell she'd been drinking and there was a defensive look in her eyes.

'You're still up,' she demanded.

He nodded and ground out his cigarette in an overfull ashtray.

Trying not to catch his eye, she went purposefully towards the bedroom door. 'I'm going to bed.'

'Wait!' he said. 'We need to talk.'

She stopped and looked at him, her eyes glazed through alcohol, but still piercing in their intensity. 'Can't it wait till morning? I'm all in.'

'I know what's going on,' he lied. 'I know all about him. You did well to pick a Broadway director.'

Her expression told him that his guess had hit the bullseye. She swayed ever so slightly, collected herself, tottered around a table and sank into a chair. She banged her elbows down, ruffling the damask tablecloth.

'How did you find out?' she moaned. 'Oh, don't tell me. You hired a private detective and had me followed. Or maybe you got one of your criminal pals to spy on me.'

'I guessed,' he said.

She looked across at him, amazement spread across her face, as though no one was capable of such deduction. 'You guessed?'

He nodded, giving her the trace of an understanding smile. 'Well, things between us haven't been exactly …' He coughed lightly, giving himself time to choose the right words. 'Well, let's face it, for some time now, we haven't been lovers. And you don't seem to like it whenever I touch you. You react as though you've been burned.'

She went to speak, and he held up a hand. 'Look, hear me out. I quite understand. I'm really not blaming you. I just want for you to be happy. We can still be friends, can't we? I really don't want us to end up as enemies.'

She stared at him for a long while, thinking it over. Then she threw him an affectionate smile as tears that appeared from nowhere ran down her cheeks. She got up from the table and hurried over to sit next to him on the sofa.

'Oh, Bill,' she said, burying her head on his shoulder. 'I'm sorry. I've hated myself for what I was doing to you. I'm so glad you understand.'

He slipped his arms comfortingly around her shoulders.

Bill sat at his desk, examined a Western Union wire and smiled contentedly. He raised a cup of hot black coffee to his lips and blew on it. Over the rim of the cup, he could see the apartment window. Rain was lashing against the grubby pane and dirty grey rivulets streamed from top to bottom. It was such blinding rain, he could barely see the buildings across the street.

The apartment was a touch on the seedy side and he wondered why Jack had chosen it. Maybe his partner felt they might have to abandon it once the job was done and there was no sense in renting a fancy, lavish apartment since the only important thing was to have an address in the theatre district.

He took little sips of coffee and stared thoughtfully at the letter-headed paper by his typewriter. He'd had it printed out-of-town: 'The Waverley School of Dramatic Art', with the address and phone number of the apartment printed underneath.

There was a light tap at the door, followed by a key in the lock, and Jack let himself in. His light-grey hat was dark from the wet and his raincoat dripped water on to the threadbare carpet. He took them off and hung them on a peg next to a Western Union uniform. Bill noticed that he seemed flushed, almost excited, though he rarely made a display of emotion. He found revealing his feelings was in some way self-indulgent.

'I can't believe we're ready,' he said. 'This time tomorrow we'll be rich.'

Bill showed him the wire. 'This little beauty gets us inside the bank.'

He had sent the wire to himself, steamed it open, typed the bank manager's name on a blank, inserted it in the envelope and re-sealed it.

Jack grinned at him and nodded at the pile of Waverley School paper by the Underwood. 'I think you could have become an actor yourself.'

'Well, tomorrow I'll be giving my best performance,' he said, and glanced at the uniform. He mumbled his own reassuring mantra, 'Uniforms are official. Uniforms can open doors.'

Something about the uniform made Jack feel uneasy. He frowned, pulled up a chair and sat next to Bill. 'Just one thing bothers me. Returning the uniform to the costumiers after the job. I'm not sure about that.'

'We've been through this, Jack. Believe me, it's the best way. By the time the Jamaica cops have alerted all the other precincts and the story's hit the papers, that uniform'll be back at the costumiers. The Waverley School of Drama hired that uniform over a week ago for their school production. If you don't return it, they'll be on to us for certain. But chances are, once it's back in their stock, they won't give it another thought.'

Jack nodded grudgingly. 'Sure. I know you're right. It's just as I was the one who went to collect it, means I'm going to have to return it.'

'It's the best way, Jack. That way, they won't notice anything unusual.'

'Let's hope you're right.'

Bill took a sip of coffee and frowned thoughtfully. 'There's something else we need to talk about. If any of the bank staff decide to play hero, shoot to miss, Jack, fire just above their heads. It should be enough to stop them.'

'Sure. Like you, Bill, I ain't gonna walk that last mile.'

'It's not that. If we shot anyone, I could never live with

myself. And, as soon as the job's over, get rid of the gun.'

Jack stared at his partner, an objection forming on his lips.

'If the cops get on to us,' Bill continued, 'we don't want to be near any guns, theirs or ours.'

The tension disappeared from Jack's shoulders, and he gave Bill a devil-may-care grin. 'They won't get on to us, Bill. So, who needs a gun?'

Jack went through to the kitchenette, got himself a cup of coffee and a pint bottle of bourbon, before returning to the living room. He poured a slug of the spirit into his coffee and offered to pour some into Bill's.

Bill shook his head. 'You know me. Never was much of a drinker.'

Jack took this as a criticism of his own habits.

'I don't have a problem with it, Bill. You know that.'

'I know. It's just that whiskey and dames don't mix in this business. Doc Tate taught me that.'

'Shame he didn't stick to his own advice.'

'What do you mean by that?'

Unaware of just how close Bill had been to Doc Tate, Jack treated the news as a juicy morsel of criminal fraternity gossip, something to be enjoyed in the telling. 'You mean you haven't heard? He was sent down for twenty at Alcatraz. Some floozy shopped him. He died in some crazy fight there. Knifed in the guts, I believe.'

Shaken by the news, Bill got unsteadily to his feet, went over to the window and stared at the raindrops running down the window pane like teardrops. He felt a curious numbness, like a dull ache that he'd lived with all his life.

Jack, sensitive to the sudden change in his partner, cleared his throat quietly before speaking. 'I'm sorry, Bill. I thought you knew. Sure you won't have that tipple now?'

He shook his head adamantly. 'Especially now.'

Bill always sought refuge in books and that afternoon he was drawn to the public library. He loved the atmosphere of this sanctum, with its comforting, slightly musty smell and the peace and quiet broken only by echoing footsteps and muffled voices. He sat at a table and tried to lose himself in a large volume on ancient Greek history, but his thoughts kept returning to the news about Doc.

Random images came at him like scraps of half-remembered truths...*Doc strolling along Broadway, white-gloved and debonair. Locks being picked. A safe door swinging open. Doc at a speakeasy, laughing over some ribald story...*then some harsher images intruded...*a blade sinking into flesh. Doc's face soundlessly screaming with pain, like an old movie without the piano accompaniment, his head smashing into the callous stone of the exercise yard...*

With a sigh, Bill closed the book. He was about to get up from the table when someone brushed close behind him. He looked around and saw her in the same instant that she recognized him. Her face lit up and he was dazzled by the radiance of her smile and the joy of meeting him. He pushed back his chair and rose hurriedly.

'Bill?' she asked, the smile fading slightly, doubting her first instinct. 'Is it really you?'

He was struck by her beauty, and the sudden unexpected reunion threw him into a quandary. She'd been a pretty little ten-year-old kid when he'd eloped with Bessie.

He'd been friends with her older brother, Oscar. Now here she was, looking up at him, her big brown eyes aglow and an amused smile playing on her mouth. He wanted to embrace her.

'You don't remember me, do you? Louise Leudeman.'

'Of course I remember you,' he said. 'How could I ever forget you? It's good to see you, Louise. It really is.'

They stood looking at one another, smiling foolishly. She awkwardly transferred the pile of books she was carrying into her left hand and offered him her other one.

'And it's good to see you,' she said, as he shook it. 'Fancy bumping into you like this, after all these years.'

From somewhere close by, there came an irritated shushing sound. They both looked at each other and stifled a giggle, like naughty children caught out in some minor mischief.

Bill leaned closer to her. 'What do you say we go somewhere for a coffee?' he whispered

She nodded and smiled. 'Yes, I'd like that.'

Seated opposite one another in the diner, Louise looked at Bill with such warmth and affection that he found it difficult to speak. They made stilted small talk to begin with until Bill fell silent. For the first time in his life he felt terribly shy and he couldn't work out why. But he was comfortable with the silence, enjoying the anticipation of getting to know her again. And, because he knew Louise to be a gentle soul, he thought that his timidity might work in his favor.

She laughed suddenly and shook her head.

'What is it?' he asked.

'To think I had a crush on you when I was fourteen.'

'Did you?'

'You know very well I did.'

From the warmth of her gaze and the almost-whispered sensuality of her words, he felt an overwhelming sensation of love. He was being drawn like a magnet towards her softness. He was certain, more certain than he'd ever been, that she was the only one for him. He was almost tempted to declare his love to her. He told himself not to be so ridiculous. He hardly knew her.

He looked away briefly. His eyes quickly traveled around the diner and he began to feel good about everything. The other customers, even the obese woman in the far corner shoveling a gargantuan portion of apple pie into her mouth, seemed beautiful. From behind the lunch counter, a radio was softly playing 'Star Dust', which heightened the feeling of romance that was growing inside him. His eyes met Louise's again.

'I was eight years older than you,' he said.

'You still *are* eight years older than me,' Louise replied, a teasing look in her eyes.

Bill laughed. His voice was low and husky, 'But that was nine years ago. You were just a kid back then. And now - well now - you've grown into a beautiful young woman.'

He could feel himself blushing. Louise noticed his embarrassment and it pleased her that he was flattering her, but with a degree of shyness. She found it an utterly endearing trait and knew she'd been right to have had a crush on him all those years ago.

'Not that you weren't beautiful back then,' he went on, more to cover his embarrassment.

She frowned. 'Why did you run off with that girl?'

He found the sudden change disconcerting.

'Bessie?' he said. 'We wanted to get married.'

'I think she was a bad influence on you, stealing from her father like that.'

'The robbery was all my idea.'

'We all do things we regret when we're young and foolish,' she said with a faraway look in here eyes.

He wondered what things she might have done to regret. He couldn't imagine her doing anyone any harm, or even so much as harboring bad thoughts about someone.

She tipped a small spoonful of sugar into her cup and stirred it thoughtfully. As their eyes met again, she said, 'When they arrested you, I cried my eyes out for days and days. I thought you'd end up in prison.'

'Yeah, well,' he began awkwardly, 'her old man wanted it kept quiet. That's what saved me from a jail sentence.'

She gave him a gentle, compassionate smile. 'You're a good man, Bill. To think you very nearly became a convicted criminal.'

He fidgeted with his cigarette packet and stared into his coffee cup. 'I'm all straightened out now, thank God.'

'What line of business are you in?'

'I'm a manager in Mr. Schultz's organization.'

'And what is it you manage?'

'Oh, he owns many properties.' Bill forced himself to look into her eyes. 'When I say I manage them, I suppose I'm nothing more than a glorified rent collector.'

He coughed lightly, and pointed to her coffee cup. 'Refill?'

She glanced at her watch. 'I have to get going. I said I'd meet Oscar at work. He's in the garment industry.'

'Give him my very best regards when you see him.'

'I will.'

Birdlike wings fluttered in Bill's stomach at the thought he might lose her. He felt awkward and nervous. All those things a much younger man feels when he wants to ask a girl out on a date.

He thought his voice might come out sounding leaden and stupid and was surprised when it sounded perfectly normal. 'If you're not too busy, how about dinner some night?'

Louise looked at him for a moment and he feared she was going to turn him down. Then she smiled, took a diary out of her handbag, and made a great show of flicking through the empty pages. 'Well now, I find myself unexpectedly available later tonight.'

Bill considered it. Early tomorrow morning he and Jack would be setting off for Long Island and he was already starting to feel nervous about the job. 'I have to meet a potential client for Mr. Schultz tonight.'

Louise flicked over a page in her diary. '*And* I'm free tomorrow night,' she said with a small laugh.

Bill grinned back. 'Tomorrow it is then. We'll push the boat out. I hope to have clinched a good deal by then.'

'As long as it's not another robbery,' she teased.

He went suddenly cold until he realized she was joking. He laughed and shook his head. He looked at her innocent expression, the purity of her smile, and he almost felt guilty about lying to her.

They parked just around the corner from the bank. Bill had bought a Dodge for their getaway. Nothing too conspicuous, but he knew the car to be fairly reliable. He had bought it in Newark and, all being well, that's where he planned to sell it after the job.

Jack wore a grey fedora and brown-rimmed spectacles with plain glass in them. Bill was dressed in the Western Union uniform but hadn't put his hat on yet, which lay on the floor under the passenger seat. He was clutching a small black briefcase and sported a moustache. He had also used matching crepe 'hair' to join his eyebrows in the middle and his face was fatter-looking from the cotton wool in his cheeks.

Jack drummed his fingers on the steering wheel and glanced at his watch. 'Seven-fifty,' he said. 'The guard should arrive within the next ten minutes.'

Bill nodded towards Jamaica Avenue. 'The main street's already busy. That's a good sign. Everybody's going about their business. No one'll pay us any attention.'

They had been out here every day for a week to observe the employees arriving at the bank. The guard was the first to arrive at eight. The staff and the manager arrived close to eight-thirty, ready for the bank to open at nine. They were always punctual.

Their biggest fear was that an armored vehicle and security guards might arrive unexpectedly. But, if that happened, they had already decided they would abort the robbery and return the following day.

'You nervous?' Bill asked.

Jack breathed in deeply through his mouth and exhaled loudly before speaking, 'I'll be okay. Strange though it may seem, I feel more excited than nervous.'

Bill smiled. 'I know what you mean. For the first time in years, I feel really alive.'

He thought about his meeting with Louise the previous day. He had felt alive then, too. But somehow this was different. This was excitement stretched to the limit...*this was the greatest challenge in the world. This was a lifetime of stress crammed into one glorious moment, the emotions fizzing like a firecracker about to explode. He was an athlete poised at the starting line, under orders...adrenaline pumping, blood surging...like a cock stiffening...*

Jack coughed lightly. Bill checked his watch and put on his Western Union hat. 'Okay. Let's go,' he said.

This was it. The moment had arrived. Make or break time.

As prearranged, Bill walked several paces ahead of Jack and rounded the corner into Jamaica Avenue. The bank's front entrance was just a few yards away. Bill stopped and searched through his briefcase for the telegram. Jack overtook him, walked to the other side of the bank and stood looking into the window of a delicatessen.

Sure enough, the bank guard, a beefy man with a large midriff, arrived dead on eight o'clock. Bill waited for him to let himself in and then ambled slowly towards the door. He caught Jack's eye from the opposite side of the door and he could sense the tension emanating from him, like an animal about to pounce on its quarry.

Heart pounding out a tattoo on his ribcage, Bill took a deep breath and felt the adrenaline rushing through his body as he raised his finger and rang the doorbell.

He heard the bell ringing loudly deep inside the bank. He waited. A car horn blared angrily and Bill's nervous system suffered a jolt.

Presently, the guard's face appeared in the glass halfway up the door. Bill showed him the telegram. The guard looked at it for a moment and then at Bill who kept his expression deadpan. It was less than a second, but waiting for the guard's decision was like the Coney Island rollercoaster drop, stomach churning. But the uniform seemed to satisfy him and he began to unlock the door.

Bill threw his partner a glance. Jack's face was like granite, tough and cold. It flitted across Bill's mind that his partner might resort to using his gun if he had to. But it was only a fleeting concern because they were already past the point of no return as the bank door swung open.

'I've got a wire for the boss,' Bill told the guard. 'I need a signature.'

Trying to keep his hands from shaking, he handed the guard the telegram, a receipt book and pencil. As soon as the guard's hands were occupied, awkwardly holding the telegram and trying to sign his name in the receipt book at the same time, Bill unclipped the clasp on his gun holster and pulled out the revolver.

'Okay,' he said, pointing the gun at the bewildered guard, 'just obey orders and you won't get hurt.'

At that moment, Jack barged in, pushing the guard backwards and brandishing a Colt.45 in his face. The guard shakily raised his hands as Bill slammed the door shut and locked it. 'Those chairs, line some of them along that wall.'

The guard's face was strained and seemed unable to comprehend what he was being told. But Bill figured that keeping him occupied would help him to remain calm and he needed him to be reasonably composed for when the employees arrived.

'Those chairs,' he repeated, waving the gun towards the far end of the lobby, 'bring them over here and line them up against that wall. Do as you're told and you won't get hurt. But if you don't...'

'Okay, I'll do it.'

As the guard walked over to pick up the first chair, Bill threw a glance at his accomplice who gave him a thin, strained smile, and glanced at the bank clock. It was only five after eight. They had at least twenty minutes to wait until the first employees started to arrive. It took the guard three or four minutes to fetch six chairs and put them against the wall, out of sight of the door, just in case anyone should decide to stand on tiptoe and peer into the bank. As soon as the last one was in place, Bill instructed him to sit down on it.

'Take the weight off your feet,' Jack couldn't resist adding.

The guard slumped heavily on to the chair nearest to the door. He stared up at Bill, trying to memorize his face. Bill stared back at him and pointed the gun at his stomach, forcing him to look away.

Jack looked at the clock again. The hands had made little progress. Time was dragging its heels. Each minute was the longest minute he and Bill ever remembered experiencing. The silence was taut, like a time-bomb about to explode. They could hear life going on as normal out in the street. The traffic sounds, the clip-clop of a milkman's horse and the faint ring of a bicycle bell. Each exterior sound seemed to accentuate the silence inside the bank. After what seemed an eternity, the doorbell rang.

'Let them in, and then lock the door,' Bill instructed the guard. 'And don't try anything stupid.'

The guard got up and unlocked the door. 'It's a lovely day, Fred,' one of the employees said as he entered.

'That's what you think,' the guard complained.

The employee, a small, thin man wearing an ugly-patterned tie that clashed with his shirt, halted in his tracks when he spotted the guns. His mouth dropped open and his eyes reflected the fear of a cornered animal. The guard had already bolted the door behind him.

'Sit down, do as you're told, and you won't get hurt,' Bill ordered.

Ugly Tie sank on to one of the chairs. He looked like he was about to wet himself. The bell rang again and Jack nodded to the guard to open up. Two more employees entered, both women. One of them, a mousy-looking girl in a purple cloche hat, opened her mouth to scream when she spotted the guns.

'Don't make a sound,' Jack warned her. 'Keep quiet and you won't get hurt.'

Bill gestured with his gun at the row of chairs. 'Sit next to your colleague, there.'

The girl in the purple hat staggered towards the chairs, assisted by her colleague, an older woman dressed in a long, navy-blue overcoat and a dark beret. They both sank into chairs, their faces ashen. Bill wondered if the girl in the purple hat was going to throw up.

Another ring on the doorbell and two more male employees were let in. Jack instructed them to keep calm and to sit on the chairs with their colleagues. Now all the workers were present, with the exception of the manager.

Another minute passed in silence. They were like statues, hardly daring to breathe let alone move. Bill noticed Ugly Tie moving and craning his neck as though he wanted to loosen his collar but was scared to move his hands. Purple Hat was staring at the floor, shaking with fear. The doorbell pierced the silence heralding the arrival of the manager. Bill nodded at the bank guard and threw Jack a cursory look of relief. They were almost home and dry. Here was the man who knew the combination of the safe.

The manager was a small, tubby man with thinning, grey hair. His face barely registered any emotion when he saw the guns as though the robbery was a commonplace event. He looked the heroic type, the sort of man who was one hundred percent loyal to the bank that employed him. Bill could see by the calm, contemptuous look in his eyes that threats wouldn't mean a thing to him. He would risk death rather than open the vault. Bill cocked the hammer of the revolver and aimed it at the row of employees, just above their heads.

It was a terrible risk. Supposing it went off? And what if he killed one of them? Jesus! It didn't bear thinking about.

He raised the barrel slightly, to a point on the wall about a foot above Ugly Tie's head. 'All I want you to do is to open your safe,' he told the manager, without looking at him. 'If you refuse, nothing will happen to *you*, but I promise you that the lives of your employees here will be jeopardized.'

'I guess I have no choice,' he said wearily, with a tiny, submissive shrug.

The manager's words echoed in Bill's head, reminding him of the day he recruited Jack's help in the robbery.

'That's right,' he said. 'You have no choice.'

Jack kept his gun aimed at the staff and Bill lowered his and

CHAPTER 4

SEPTEMBER, 1930

'Where are we going?' Louise asked for the fifth time that morning, as they headed over the Queensboro Bridge. Bill smiled enigmatically before singing loudly, and a trifle tunelessly, 'my sweet embraceable you,' and followed it with a delighted chuckle.

'Don't be so irritating,' she told him, though she secretly enjoyed playing along with his game.

'If I'm not mistaken, we're headed towards Queens,' he said teasingly, and glanced in her direction.

'That doesn't answer my question.' She squeezed his leg just above the knee with her finger and thumb. His leg shot forward involuntarily. With his other leg he pushed the accelerator down and the car surged forward towards the rear of a bus.

He braked sharply. 'Careful! You'll have us in the East River in a minute.'

'You did that on purpose,' she admonished him. 'And made out it was my fault.'

Bill laughed. 'I told you, it's a surprise. You'll just have to be patient. You don't want to spoil the surprise, do you?'

'I guess not,' she replied. She clasped her hands together and the finger and thumb of her right hand automatically spun the wedding ring on her finger. She was deliriously happy. Almost too happy. Sometimes it made her wary, but she couldn't figure out why. It was like watching a rainbow-colored bubble drifting gently on the air knowing it would eventually pop.

'Are you happy, Mrs. Sutton?' Bill asked her.

'You know I am.'

He followed her reply this time by whistling "Embraceable You", a little more in tune than his singing. She relaxed back into her seat and chased any doubts, any pessimistic thoughts, from her mind. She ran a hand over her stomach and was reassured by Nature's little miracle happening inside her, although there was nothing showing at the moment and her stomach remained disappointingly flat to her.

They drove on in silence for a while. Bill sensed a change of mood, a certain sadness enveloping Louise, or perhaps she was just being thoughtful and serious as she contemplated the birth which wasn't until the New Year.

But he was suddenly unsure of himself. He was, after all, asking her to believe a great deal when he hit her with his surprise. It would take the acting skills of a Barrymore to convince her. So he needed to keep her spirits up, get her thinking about the baby and how he relished the role of father. He glanced at her out of the corner of his eye and could see she was frowning hard, staring at the road ahead.

'Penny for them?' he said.

'I can't help thinking about your poor mother. She would have loved to be a grandmother, I'm certain of it. It was all so sudden.'

'It hit my father pretty hard. He misses her terribly. They lived for each other.'

It crossed his mind that his parents had lived for themselves to the exclusion of all others, even their own son. Then he realized how unfair the thought was. He was the one who had let them down by turning to a life of crime. A fate they hadn't deserved.

'I'm glad your dad attended our wedding.'

Bill grunted bitterly. 'He didn't want to...'

'Don't be hard on him,' Louise broke in. 'Maybe he felt it

was too soon after your mother's funeral.'

'And if he knew you were pregnant prior to the wedding, wild horses wouldn't have dragged him along.'

They fell silent, lost in their respective thoughts about life, death, relationships. It took another thirty minutes to reach their destination and they drove for the most part in silence, sometimes commenting on things they saw along the way: a man walking a beautiful Afghan hound; children roller skating; the gradual changing color of the leaves on the trees, giving the onset of the bleaker months ahead a false feeling of warmth.

Bill eased the Pierce Arrow gently into a tree-lined cul-de-sac. He drove towards the last house in the street and turned into the driveway. Louise surveyed the house, a pretty, white clapboard detached building, neat and pristine, with a sloping front lawn and a side garage.

'Who lives here?' she asked, her voice an awestruck whisper, almost daring herself to guess the answer. Was this the surprise? Surely it couldn't be.

He beamed at her. 'I think the Suttons live here now.'

'Bill...' she began and faltered. She could hardly believe it. But something flashed through her brain, like a hazy and intangible warning.

Bill chuckled happily. 'It's better than an apartment and it has a small garden round back. It's much better to bring up a child in a neighborhood like this.'

She frowned, staring at the dashboard unable to bring herself to look at the house in case it might vanish in front of her eyes.

'What's wrong?' Bill asked, though he guessed what was coming and mentally prepared himself for the questions she would inevitably ask.

'This house...Are we renting it?'

He shook his head. 'It's ours. I bought it.'

'But how...I mean, how could we afford it? Surely not on what Mr. Schultz pays...'

Grasping her by the hand, he interrupted her, fixing her with an earnest look. 'This was all part of the surprise. I so wanted to tell you. For weeks now, I've kept it to myself.'

'What is it?' she said, staring into his eyes, targeting the deeper recesses of his mind for reassurance.

For it to be convincing, he had to believe it himself.

'A relation of mine in the Old Country left me money in his will. A small fortune. I was his only living relative.'

He pictured the relative as a landowner; checked hacking jacket, muddy riding boots and jodhpurs, astride a chestnut gelding, riding down to the village bar and ordering a pint of stout.

He smiled at Louise. 'I met him just the once. Wonderful old boy, he came over here on a visit and we got on like a house on fire.'

He was standing on the dockside as the boat berthed. And there was the man waving from the deck, a windswept, Celtic flush on his large, moon-shaped face, wisps of gingery hair on a balding head.

Doubt still clouded Louise's expression. When she spoke, her voice was timorous yet probing. 'You say he was a relation. What was he? An uncle?'

Bill grinned confidently. 'You tell me. Let's see now. I think he was a cousin to my mother. Her grandfather had several brothers and this old boy was the son of the youngest. So what does that make us?'

'Distant cousins, I guess.'

'Well, whatever our relationship, I guess I was just lucky, being the only living relative.'

'And he left you all this money? Enough to buy this house? I suppose if your mother was still alive she might have been the beneficiary.'

'I guess,' was all Bill could manage. He had already succumbed to guilty feelings where his mother was concerned. Had she not died, he could not have concocted this story. The only way Louise could have discovered the lie about the mythical relative would have been through his mother. And he didn't think his father knew enough about her side of the family, having been born in New Jersey.

All things considered, he had to admit that his mother's death had been very convenient. But now was not the time for remorse. Now it was time to believe wholeheartedly in his story, to convince Louise it was the truth.

'I'm sorry, I know I should have told you.' he said, 'but I really wanted it to be a surprise because I love you so much, Louise.'

She let her eyes wander towards the house which was real enough, a solid presence, solid enough in itself to convince her that here was something she could believe in. She relaxed and she gazed at him with a trusting smile, her nose wrinkling slightly, an expression he loved so much. He grinned back at her, generating warmth and honesty, and he just knew his story was going to be accepted.

'Here's to William O'Rourke,' he added for good measure.

'Who?'

'Our benefactor.'

'Even though I never met you, I think I love you, William O'Rourke,' Louise added.

Bill grinned at her. Even though the man didn't exist, right now he believed that he did! He patted Louise's knee. 'Come on. Let's go take a look around our new house.'

They got out of the car and walked arm-in-arm towards the front door. Across the street, from the darkness behind the window of an almost identical house, an elderly woman watched the couple enter their new home and commented to her husband that he looked like a successful lawyer or businessman and what a handsome young couple they were.

A week later, when Bill met Jack at the Dutchman's speakeasy, his partner was gazing into the eyes of a petite blonde girl in a shimmering, tight dress. Bill could see that, unlike other girls in this joint, she had a naturally beautiful complexion, and the only make-up she wore was a delicate shade of pink lipstick.

He took all this in at a glance as he strolled over to their table while "Way Down Yonder in New Orleans" was pounding out from a band that seemed in a hurry to finish. From behind him, a high note from the trumpet seemed to herald his arrival at the table just as Jack spotted him.

'Bill! Come and meet Gloria,' Jack shouted over the night club din. 'Gloria, this is my business partner, Bill.'

Gloria thrust a delicate pale hand at Bill and he shook it. Her bones felt small and fragile as he applied gentle pressure and he eased up on the handshake. There was something doll-like about her, in a very beautiful and natural way.

Bill sank into a chair and lit a cigarette. While he ordered himself a beer from a waitress, Jack melted under Gloria's gaze, kissed her lightly on the lips. He wanted to vanish inside the kiss. But there was also restraint in his passion, knowing that this was the sweet anticipation of greater things. Bill caught the end of this exchange and a fearful warning alerted him, like the crash of the drummer's cymbal.

Jack slid a hand lovingly on to Gloria's, leant across her, and told Bill, 'Gloria's in *Strike Up The Band.*'

'Congratulations,' Bill said. 'I hear it's a great show.'

'It sure is,' she acknowledged. 'But I'm only in the chorus.'

'Honey, don't put yourself down,' Jack urged, sliding his other hand underneath hers. He looked at Bill, his eyes sparkling with the pride of a lover. 'Gloria may only be in the chorus, but wow! You can't take your eyes off her. What a knockout performance!'

Bill smiled in spite of the niggling doubt he had about his partner's serious involvement with yet another girl. 'I'm sure Jack's right,' he said. 'I expect you'll be discovered one day, and - who knows - you may even have your own show.'

She shrugged and looked down. When she spoke, it was with a trace of wistfulness. 'I expect every chorus girl thinks she's going to be a star. If you don't make the big time by the time you're...'

She checked herself, gave an embarrassed laugh, and shook her head.

'I'm sure you're being hard on yourself,'

'Just being a realist,' she said with a shrug. She smiled at him, displaying a perfect row of sparkling teeth.

He liked her honesty and could appreciate what Jack saw in her. Although she was stunningly attractive, she also had a head on her shoulders, he felt. But now it was down to business. He looked pointedly at his watch so that Jack noticed.

'Honey,' his partner began, with an apologetic shrug.

'I know. You have business to discuss. In any case, I have to be at the theatre early. There's a routine we have to tidy up.'

She picked her handbag up from the side of her chair and rose, pecking Jack on the cheek, all in one brisk movement. 'See you after the show, Jack. Hey, I'm really excited. I've never been in the Plaza before. Nice meeting you, Bill.'

'And nice meeting you,' Bill replied, lost in his own thoughts. As soon as she had gone, he rounded on Jack. 'You got a room booked at the Plaza?'

Jack gave him a lascivious grin. 'You bet. Us hard-earners deserve a little luxury in life.'

'And what about Kitty?'

'She thinks I'm out of town.'

The band was ending its number, every musician competing for a final riff instead of ending clean. The drummer won, marginally beating the clarinetist, with a flourishing roll on the snare. Bill's beer arrived. He took a pensive sip, wiping the foam off his top lip with his tongue. Jack watched him closely, thinking that his partner seemed a trifle moody.

'Something bothering you?' he asked.

'Band's about to strike up again,' Bill replied. 'Mind if we go somewhere quieter to talk?'

'You've just got your beer.'

'You know this stuff doesn't do anything for me.'

Jack nodded. 'Okay.' He paid the bill and they left the

Dutchman's joint. It was late afternoon and was still light outside. It was the end of a working day for most people and Bill and his partner dodged in and out of the teeming hordes of office workers heading for home.

'Where we going?' Jack asked.

'Thought we'd go where it's quiet. The apartment.'

They didn't have far to walk from the Dutchman's to their apartment. Since the bank job out on Long Island, Bill had given the place a bit of a facelift, a coat of paint here, a coat of paint there, and some fancy furnishings and pictures on the walls.

'If we're using this place as an office and somewhere to lie low,' he'd told his accomplice, 'we may as well make it more habitable.'

'I'll make the coffee,' Jack offered as they entered the apartment. Straight away Bill opened the desk drawer and pulled out a sheaf of notes, details of their next potential bank job.

'You cased that joint yet?' Jack called out from the kitchenette as he filled the percolator.

'Got all the details right here. I figured I'd use a mailman's uniform this time.'

Jack hurried back into the room, a puzzled expression on his face. 'How the hell does a mailman get into a bank? I mean they have a mailbox for delivering the mail.'

Bill grinned at him and placed one hand above the other, with a three inch gap between. 'Mailbox, this big.' He widened the gap between his hands another three inches. 'Package, this big.'

Jack laughed, 'Hey! That's pretty neat. And maybe you need a signature as well.'

'A signature is essential,' Bill replied seriously, assuming the demeanor of an over-conscientious mailman.

Jack pulled a bentwood chair away from the desk, turned it to face him, and sat astride it, arms folded across the back. 'Okay. So, where is this bank?'

Bill sat in an easy chair facing Jack. 'First things first,' he said. 'We need to talk.'

'Oh?' Jack questioned warily, guessing what was coming. 'What about?'

'Your love life.'

He saw that Jack was about to protest and continued hurriedly, 'This is not a moral issue. I couldn't care less about someone else's infidelities, but we're treading on dangerous ground here. Does Kitty have any suspicions about your philandering ways?'

Jack shrugged, and exclaimed emphatically, 'Jesus! I hope not.'

'I need you to level with me, Jack. Not long after that job on Jamaica Avenue, I was out with both of you at the Silver Slipper and you kept staring and flirting in a most obvious way with the cigarette girl.'

'Hey! Now, wasn't *she* a bit of all right?'

'Kitty blew her stack that night. The scene was embarrassing.'

Jack tried to look contrite, but the expression failed him. It was more an expression of male solidarity, one man to another. *You know how it is with women.*

'And if Kitty's that jealous over a minor flirtation....' Bill continued.

Jack interrupted him, 'That was the booze talking. She'd had a skinful.'

'But if she finds out about any of these other broads, Jack. Hell hath no fury and all that.'

A tiny smile reached the corners of Jack's mouth. He looked pleased with himself. 'There *are* no other broads. Only Gloria.'

'So what happened to the hatcheck girl and that redhead you met at the Algonquin Hotel?'

Jack grinned sheepishly. 'They're through. I'm in love, Bill. I can't stop thinking about Gloria, morning, noon and night.'

Bill frowned and scratched thoughtfully at his chin. This was more serious than all the other philandering. He stared at Jack, who was grinning at him, suffused with that special glow reserved for someone newly in love.

After a long pause, he spoke in his gravest voice, 'You have to end this relationship with Gloria.'

Jack reacted like he'd been jabbed with a needle. 'Jesus, Bill! This is not some one-night affair. It's serious...it's not like we...'

Bill hushed him with a raised hand and said, 'Let me finish. I don't care how much she means to you. You're married to Kitty. And she knows about the bank job. You're playing with fire, Jack. If you trade Kitty in for the latest model, who knows what might happen.'

As soon as these words escaped from Bill's mouth, he regretted them. His partner went on the attack as he suspected he would.

'And what about Louise? Are you telling me...?'

'She has no knowledge whatsoever of our activities,' Bill cut in. 'Even if she did find out, I know I could rely on her loyalty.'

'Oh?' Jack said, with a trace of sarcasm. 'And how is Louise different from Kitty?'

'It's simple, Jack. Stay loyal to a woman, love her, and she'll return the compliment. No woman'd betray a man who loves her and remains faithful to her. Even you know that.'

Jack stared at the floor, thoughtfully biting his bottom lip. Eventually, he locked eyes with Bill, playing for sympathy. 'You mean I have to get rid of Gloria? Just like that?'

Bill decided it was time to throw down his ace. 'You're a reliable partner, Jack. I trust you. But...I'd hate to have to look around for another.'

He left it at that. He allowed the silence to do its work, to let the enormity of his words to sink in. He became aware of the Broadway sounds: a piercing whistle and shout as someone hailed a cab; a paper boy selling the latest edition; a squeal of brakes.

Jack stared into the distance for a long while. He knew his partner was right. He also knew that Bill was serious about terminating their relationship if it came to the crunch. He couldn't allow that to happen. Jesus! Not with his lifestyle. He had a luxurious and expensive apartment on the Upper East Side, two cars in the underground car park, and some expensive habits to support. He couldn't possibly allow this partnership to be terminated.

'Okay,' he agreed, after a long pause. 'I'll let it simmer with Gloria for a while, then let it cool down. How's that?'

The coffee started to percolate, sending an appetizing roasted aroma into the room. Bill stretched his legs and stood up, 'Why don't you keep your date with Gloria at the Plaza? Then, tomorrow morning, make sure you have a serious pillow talk with her, happily married man, and all that. You like her, but...'

'But it's just one of those things,' Jack concluded.

'Exactly. Make her feel important, but explain that she shouldn't come between you and your wife. I'll pour us some coffee. Then we'll talk about this beautiful bank.'

While Bill was out in the kitchenette fetching the coffee, Jack pondered the situation. It was one hell of a dilemma. Would he be able to throw Gloria over in favor of Kitty? He had serious doubts about that. He decided to do as Bill advised for the time being in the hope that things would work out in the future.

One thing was for certain, if he remained with Kitty he was still going to see Gloria on the side. He had to have her. He just had to. Whatever the cost.

CHAPTER 5

MAY, 1931

The Browning automatic pistol was standard army issue, and Bill had bought one each for himself and Jack through an ex-soldier who had been an armorer during the Great War.

Bill had his Browning aimed at the manager of the Bronx County Savings Bank and saw that the guy was staring at him with a mixture of fear and loathing. He was a heavily built man with a florid complexion and he suspected that he was the sort of man who, given an opening, would have a go. But nobody argues with a gun aimed at their head.

Jack waved his Browning back and forth along the row of subdued employees, as he struggled to shut the clasp on his dispatch case which was bursting with five and ten dollar bills.

Bill could see him struggling. He knew his partner didn't want to risk walking along the street leaving a trail of money behind him but it was time for them to make themselves scarce. It was almost bank opening time and they didn't want to risk trying to escape through a queue of early-bird customers waiting outside. Eventually, Bill heard the click of Jack's case and breathed a sigh of relief.

'Let's go,' he urged.

Using the same *modus operandi* as the Jamaica Bank, Jack warned them, 'We're leaving. We have a third member of our gang waiting outside. Anyone attempting to follow us in the next five minutes will be shot.'

As they backed towards the door, Bill could see by the expression on the manager's face that he didn't believe Jack and he was already poised to come after them and raise the alarm. And if a cop happened to be walking along the street...

'He means it,' Bill snapped. 'So don't even think about it. Our accomplice always aims for the kneecaps, so if you want to spend the rest of your days in a wheelchair...'

It was the psychological advantage he needed. The manager's expression was inscrutable, but his face had drained of color and Bill knew he would now think twice before running after them. Jack had the door open and they slid through, slamming it behind them. A man carrying an expensive-looking brown leather briefcase was waiting for the bank to open.

'Be open any minute now,' Jack assured him before they both melted into the early-morning crowd and headed for their car.

Jack walked a few paces ahead of Bill. He thought of all that money he was carrying. What a haul! And Bill's mailman bag was bursting with crisp new twenties. They must have somewhere in the region of $100,000, Jack reckoned.

The thoughts of all that money and seeing Gloria that evening gave him a snug feeling in his groin and he felt the warmth surge into his penis, as it grew erect. By the time he got to the car, he had an amused expression on his face which Bill noticed as he slid into the passenger seat.

As they pulled away, in the opposite direction from the bank, Bill threw his mailman's hat over the back seat, struggled out of the jacket and asked Jack what he found so amusing.

Jack, unwilling to admit to getting a hard-on, tossed his glasses and hat on to the floor by his partner's feet and said with a light, nervous laugh in his voice, 'It's just too damned easy, Bill.'

'It'll get harder,' Bill said, 'when they start to figure out our

MO. Once the papers give it a hammering, and the cops put two and two together...'

They drove in silence for a while. The atmosphere in the car became heavy with Jack's troubled thoughts and Bill knew that he was trying to formulate some sort of strategy. Bill remained silent, letting his partner work it out in his own way.

When Jack eventually spoke, his voice was perfectly controlled. Although it was always Bill who seemed to be the brains of their two-man outfit, always the one to make the decisions, now it was Jack's turn to take the lead. 'I've been thinking, this mailman's uniform we hired, we need to get it back before this thing hits the papers. It's a way of tracing the robbery back to us. Once the cops start asking questions about where the uniforms are coming from, they just might hit on where we get our supplies. So, I think we ought to find another apartment and create another theatre school.'

'Sounds like a good idea,' Bill agreed.

'And I've had another idea about hiring uniforms. I think we ought to hire a whole production. Different uniforms, including some female costumes. That way the one we want is part of a job lot and is more likely to go unnoticed.'

Bill turned and grinned at his partner. 'Now that really is a great idea, Jack. I really should have thought of that before.'

'We could even make up names for the actors with all their different measurements.'

'Sounds good to me.'

'I mean,' Jack said, swerving to avoid a car that had broken down on the 3rd Avenue Bridge, 'that's the second time we've used the uniform stunt to get into a bank. I think the banks'll be more cautious in the future.'

'Just what I was thinking,' Bill agreed. 'That's why I think we ought to go for some other establishment.'

'Such as?'

'Jewelry store.'

Jack gave his accomplice a cursory look, trying to ascertain if he was being serious.

'I've already cased Rosenthal & Son,' Bill continued. 'You know; the one next to the Capitol Theatre.'

Jack's voice rose an octave. 'Are you serious? That's on Broadway and 51st. Talk about shitting on our own doorstep.'

Bill chuckled confidently. 'Doesn't really matter where we commit a robbery. We're not gonna get caught, are we? And that's all we have to worry about, staying one step ahead of the game. Just keep telling yourself we're not going to get caught, because everything we do we plan down to the last detail. That's one of the reasons we've been successful so far.'

Bill said it like an employer motivating an employee and he slapped Jack's leg.

But Jack wasn't convinced. 'And another thing, we lose a large percentage of our haul when we sell to a fence.'

'I've been inside Rosenthal's and, believe me, those rocks'll fetch a small fortune. Just think of what we lose to the fence as money we might have had to pay the IRS if we were gainfully employed.'

Jack felt more relaxed as they came into East Harlem and he threw Bill an impudent grin. 'Yeah, and we all have to pay our taxes.'

His grin froze when he glanced in the mirror and spotted the cop car following them. 'Jesus Christ! The cops are behind us. Don't look round. Keep looking ahead.'

As they drove down Second Avenue and crossed East 116th, the police car drew level with them. Jack glanced out of the corner of his eye and could feel them staring. He could sense Bill's fear; a sour body odor filled the car. Or maybe it was his own fear he could taste. He risked a look towards the cop car.

He felt they were about to signal that he should pull up. If that happened, it was all over. But suddenly their light began flashing and their siren began wailing. They accelerated away from Jack and Bill's car at speed and screeched left around the next corner.

Bill let his breath out slowly. 'That was lucky,' he said.

'Let's hope it stays that way,' Jack added. 'There are some

things you just can't plan down to the last detail.'

Two weeks after the Bronx bank robbery, Bill and Louise strolled up Fifth Avenue towards the New York Public Library. They were drawn to the library for sentimental reasons for that was where they had met over a year ago. Not only that, this late in May it was getting to be quite a scorcher and Louise, whose baby was due any day now, was overheating and the library was cool and comforting.

Louise posed beside one of the lions at the entrance while Bill took a snapshot of her with his Box Brownie. He loved her pregnancy, seeing it as the most positive event in his life, and he had photographed her every step of the way. And, in spite of her protestations against being photographed as she got bigger, she was secretly pleased and flattered that Bill cared so much and shared her excitement.

After the photograph had been taken, Bill slipped his hand into hers and they entered the library, Louise puffing as she reached the top step. Just as they stepped inside to the coolness of the building, Louise's waters broke.

'Honey,' she said, 'I've just gone into labor.'

'My God!' Bill exclaimed. 'Think you can make it down the steps? '

'Sure. It's okay. Don't panic.'

Out on Fifth Avenue, Bill whistled for a cab. 'Mount Sinai Hospital and step on the gas,' he told the cabbie dramatically.

Events became a blur to Bill as the cab sped along Fifth Avenue to the hospital. He marveled at how calm and in control Louise appeared. He was a bag of nerves. He felt waves of panic surging inside him and everything seemed unreal. Time arrested yet speeded up, a dance with a constantly changing tempo.

The checking in at the hospital seemed so slow, the staff appeared frustratingly unconcerned. Louise was whisked off into the labor room and he was left kicking his heels in the waiting room. He lit a Camel, inhaled deeply and settled down to wait.

After half an hour, which seemed interminable, and while he was on his third cigarette, a nurse appeared and informed him that Louise's contractions were at ten minute intervals. He looked blank and she explained that he might have a long wait, so why not pop out and get some coffee. He thanked her and said he'd sooner wait.

The next hour was a torment. He fretted about Louise, imagined all kinds of pessimistic scenarios. Supposing there were complications? He'd heard of women dying in childbirth. Try as he might to banish these thoughts from his mind, they kept coming back to haunt him.

The hands of the wall clock seemed to be moving slower than normal. He felt this was worse than the hour they'd spent at the banks waiting while the employees showed up.

The nurse, a mousy brunette in a pristine, stiffly-starched uniform, returned and smiled sympathetically at him. 'I told you to get some coffee,' she said.

'What's happening?'

'Nothing to worry about,' she assured him. 'Contractions are now five minutes apart.'

'Meaning?'

She shook her head, she couldn't believe how dumb he was being. 'Meaning you still might like to change your mind and get a coffee. It'll be some time yet.'

'Any idea how long?'

The nurse shrugged. 'I think if you disappeared for a good forty-five minutes, you wouldn't be missed.'

As reluctant as he was to wander far, just in case his child was born, he felt relieved that he could legitimately escape from the tedium and worry of the stuffy waiting room and get some fresh air.

'Okay,' he told the nurse. 'I really could murder a coffee.'

Glad to be out walking, he headed towards Park Avenue and found a diner in one of the side streets. He drank two cups of strong black coffee and glanced at his watch. He'd been gone almost half an hour. He hurriedly paid for the coffee and dashed back to the hospital waiting room.

Time crawled at snail-pace again. Through the glass door of the waiting room, Bill observed the more hurried pace of the corridor outside, trolleys clattered and squeaked and staff in white coats rushed purposefully along, stopping occasionally to read some notes, unsure of where they were supposed to be heading next.

Another man arrived in the waiting room. He had shiny, jet black hair, a swarthy complexion and five o'clock shadow. Bill tried to engage him in conversation but he merely grunted and looked away. Bill assumed he must have been nervous or shy. Either that or anti-social.

The clock's small hand had gained another hour though to Bill it seemed more like a day. He got up, lit another cigarette, stubbed it out, and sat down again. The nurse returned and he looked up expectantly. She avoided his look and addressed the dark-haired man.

'Mr. Gresham. Congratulations. Your wife has given birth to a six-and-a-half pound boy.'

Bill stared at the man with feelings of resentment and jealousy. Had he been waiting as long as him, been out for a breather then returned during the time he had gone for coffee, or had his wife been admitted during that time and given birth right away? If it was the latter, then it seemed unfair. Surely something was wrong. What was happening to Louise?

Sensing his concerns, the nurse turned and reassured him, 'Won't be long now.'

Bill waited another hour and a half, and a sinking, leaden feeling made his body ache with a tiredness he'd never known. Again his mind imagined all kinds of complications as time inched by. He observed that it was almost six hours since Louise had been admitted to the hospital.

He was about to get up and light his tenth cigarette when

the nurse returned and announced, 'At last, Mr. Sutton, you're a father. You have a beautiful baby girl. Congratulations. If you'd like to follow me, I'll take you to see her.'

He followed her along the corridor to a private room. Although Louise had protested that a ward would be perfectly acceptable after the birth, he had insisted on a private room. Hang the cost!

Louise was propped against the pillow, her face pale and wan, dark bags under her eyes. But her eyes were bright and cradled in her arms was a small neat bundle. Bill approached cautiously.

The nurse said, 'I'll leave you to get acquainted with your daughter,' and slipped out of the door.

Bill peered at the tiny wrinkled face of his daughter in wonderment. She looked so small and vulnerable and he was overcome with such paternal devotion that he felt moistness behind the eyes.

'Why don't you hold your daughter?' Louise suggested quietly.

Bill gently took the bundle, anxious that he might be too rough or clumsy. She felt warm against his chest and he experienced a proud blushing sensation as he looked down into her eyes. They twinkled back at him and, although it was fanciful, he could almost swear that she knew instinctively he was her father.

'You're not disappointed it's not a boy?' Louise asked, her voice tremulous with concern.

Bill smiled at her. His grin became wider, as he looked down at his daughter. 'I know now that it was a girl I wanted all along.'

'We said if it was a girl we were going to call her Jenny,' Louise said. 'Jennifer Sutton.'

'No, not Jennifer, Jenny,' Bill emphasized, 'our little Jenny wren.'

From somewhere on Fifth Avenue came the distant and

familiar wail of a siren as a police car hurtled to yet another crime scene.

Holding his bundle of innocence, Bill felt the stirrings of guilt brought about by the sound as he gazed into his daughter's eyes. Just for a brief moment it seemed the baby had vision. The cool eyes stared back at him accusingly as though she knew her father was a professional criminal.

Weeks before Jenny's birth, Bill gave up collecting for Dutch Schultz. He made out he was taking a few weeks' vacation after the baby was born, to spend some time pampering Louise and admiring his offspring. But he still had to pretend to Louise that he had a steady job, so ten days after Louise had been home from the hospital he left the house at midday, telling her that he was now needed back at work. Louise knew that what he did for Mr. Schultz was not nine-to-five, the hours being fairly flexible but he would still have to leave the house on a fairly regular basis and do something to occupy himself while he was out.

On his first day back at the bogus job, he decided to stroll through Manhattan to his and Jack's new apartment on West 42nd. To kill time, he drove over the Williamsburg Bridge, along Lower East Side, parked near Madison Square and walked towards the Empire State Building.

He had wanted to be there on May 1st, when President Hoover had declared it open, but the birth of his baby was imminent and Bill knew it was dangerous to subject Louise to the stifling crowds in her heavily pregnant condition. Now, as he craned back his neck and gazed up at the mighty edifice, he marveled at this feat of engineering, now officially the tallest building in the world.

It made him proud to be a New Yorker. And, as he continued towards his apartment where he intended fine-tuning their plot to rob Rosenthal's jewelry store, the irony of the situation was wasted on this proud citizen.

He'd been at the apartment for five minutes when the phone rang. It was Kitty Bassett. Her voice was clipped and angry. 'I have to speak to you,' she demanded. 'Urgently!'

'What about?' he asked, though he had a pretty good idea what was bothering her.

'I'd sooner not discuss it on the phone.'

'Okay,' he agreed. 'Let's meet - say in half-an-hour - at Jake's Café. It's on the corner...'

'I know it,' she barked. 'Half-an-hour. I'll be there.'

The line went dead. Bill stared at the receiver thoughtfully. This was bad news. If Kitty had found out about Jack's affairs...

He grabbed his hat from the coat peg near the door and stood at the mirror to check his reflection. He folded the brim of his fedora down and brushed a few particles of dandruff from the collar of his double-breasted pinstriped suit. The face that stared back at him was beginning to look gaunt, but then, the baby had woken him several times in the night over the last four days. All the same, the business with Kitty was deeply disturbing and a great frown marked his forehead like indelible pencil marks.

On his way over to Jake's Café, he worked out what he could tell Kitty. Whatever he told her, it would have to be a convincing performance. This would be a test of his ability as an actor.

He smiled wryly as he walked along Broadway. He was no actor. Who was he trying to kid? Con artist was nearer the mark. On the other hand, he thought, a con artist had to give a more convincing performance than most actors.

When he got to Jake's Café, Kitty was already installed in one of the booths. He slid into the seat opposite her. She looked up at him and he could see that her dark brown eyes were no longer so stunning. He guessed that she hadn't slept much and had probably been weeping.

Whatever her problems, Bill noticed that she still managed to put in an elegant appearance: the long ivory cigarette holder delicately held between brightly painted fingernails; the expensive-looking red cloche hat covering her dark brown hair; with kiss curls appearing from beneath the hat and plastered to her cheeks, the red of her hat perfectly matching the color of her fingernails and lipstick; and the tight black Chanel dress showing off her stunning figure.

The waitress appeared and Bill ordered pastrami on rye and black coffee. He looked at Kitty. 'Anything to eat?'

She shook her head. 'I couldn't. Just another coffee.'

Once the waitress departed, Bill smiled at Kitty. 'So what's the problem?' he asked. 'You sounded distraught on the telephone.'

The hand holding her cigarette holder began to tremble involuntarily and Bill wondered if she'd been drinking. Tears welled up in her eyes, but she brushed them quickly away and drew deeply on her cigarette.

'I really love Jack,' she said plaintively, her voice soft and girlish.

'And I know Jack loves you,' Bill replied. 'So what's the problem?'

She took the cigarette out of her holder. 'He's having an affair,' she said, grinding it into the ashtray as though she would have liked it to have been his face.

'Jack..?' he said, '…an affair? That's ridiculous.'

Kitty stared at him, searching for any signs of insincerity. 'Why is that so ridiculous? Men do have affairs, you know.'

'Jack and I are very close,' he said. 'I'd know if he was having an affair. Believe me, Kitty, Jack loves you and is one hundred percent loyal to you. I mean...what makes you think...?'

He let his question hang on the air unfinished, shrugged, and turned his hands palms upwards, throwing the ball into her court. Obviously she must have some evidence and he needed to know just how much information she had and how bad it was.

'Girlfriend of mine saw them driving off together. She said he was with this little blonde girl.'

Bill chuckled and shook his head. 'Oh, that must have been

Gloria your friend saw him with.'

'Who the hell's Gloria?'

'Now don't go jumping to conclusions. Jack's got a friend - Harry McCarthy's his name - and Gloria's his girl. Harry's doing a five stretch in Sing Sing and Harry asked him to look after Gloria, take her to the penitentiary on visiting days, and generally keep his eye on her.'

Kitty's eyes narrowed shrewdly. 'Well, if that's all it is, why didn't he tell me about it?'

'Harry's been mixed with some pretty tough boys and they might try and get back at him through Gloria. I guess Jack didn't want to worry you.'

'You mean he could be in some kind of danger?'

'I think Harry's being cautious, that's all. He just wants to know Gloria's in good hands.'

Kitty, who had no illusions about what a flirt and a charmer her husband was, exclaimed, 'Huh!' as she twisted another cigarette roughly into her holder. 'She'll be in good hands all right if Jack's looking after her.'

'Look,' Bill said, lighting her cigarette, 'I know Jack turns on the charm where the ladies are concerned, but I know he loves you, Kitty. He's as much as told me. And, if you're concerned about Gloria, don't be. If Jack were to cross Harry... You see, Harry's obsessively jealous. He'd go crazy if he thought Jack and Gloria were...Well, I just don't think Jack would.' Bill grinned as he stared into her eyes through the blue plume of smoke from her cigarette.

'Honor among thieves and all that.'

Kitty sat upright, posing with her cigarette holder, as the waitress arrived with their order. Bill immediately tucked into his sandwich.

'I'm starving,' he said, which was another lie. He wasn't in the slightest bit hungry. He just wanted Kitty to see that his appetite wasn't in any way dimmed by her worries, showing her that she was wrong to harbor doubts about Jack. Life: a normal everyday routine.

Kitty shook her head thoughtfully. 'The fool, the stupid fool. Jack should have known if he was seen with this Gloria, I'd have thought the worst.'

'I expect he wanted to save himself any arguments,' Bill mumbled through a mouthful of pastrami.

Kitty eyed him suspiciously. 'How d'you mean?'

'Well, put it this way, Kitty, if you thought Jack was in the slightest danger - and I don't think he is - you'd have argued him out of looking after Gloria.'

'I guess you're right,' she admitted, with a faraway look in here eyes. She refocused on Bill and her gaze was searching, like the stare of a cat.

'You wouldn't lie to me, Bill?'

Bill gave her a look of exasperation. 'I promise you, Kitty...I swear to you that as far as I know Jack is not having an affair. And if he is, believe me I'd be the first to know.'

'Thanks,' she said, as her eyes drifted off to that faraway place again.

Bill found it difficult to interpret these distant looks. Either his story was working its magic or she was plotting something. Whatever she was thinking, he knew that she would confront Jack about Gloria. And Jack wouldn't have a clue what she was on about. After all, Bill had concocted this story out of thin air on his way to meet Kitty. Now, he desperately needed to tell Jack the same story. Fortunately, he knew his partner was at this very moment playing billiards in a club on the Upper West Side and was planning on coming over to their apartment afterwards. But just in case something went wrong...

Bill snatched a look at his watch and pushed his half-eaten sandwich to one side. 'I have an appointment to meet the Dutchman and he doesn't like to be kept waiting. I'm sorry. I have to go. And don't worry about Jack. Everything's above board. You have my word on it.'

He threw a dollar bill on to the table, waved at Kitty, and departed. Out on the street a sweet smell of fresh doughnut mixed with gasoline drifted on the hot air. He managed to hail a cab in less than thirty seconds and instructed the cabby to take him to Jack's billiards club. As he sank back into the seat, he wondered if it was now too dangerous to do the Rosenthal store in three weeks' time. He also wondered if it was time to find another partner.

CHAPTER 6

JUNE, 1931

The Rosenthal store robbery started to go wrong when the elderly store manager began shaking like he suffered from Parkinson's disease. He attempted to spin the combination dial of the safe but his hands shook violently.

He stammered as he tried to remember the combination, but the fear of having a loaded gun aimed at him had turned his brain to jelly. Bill doubted the man could spell his own name if asked. His eyes were watery as he turned to Bill and said, 'I've forgotten the combination.'

Bill knew he was telling the truth. The man was in shock. As were the other three employees who sat in a row, frozen like alabaster statues.

'Anyone else know the combination?' Bill snapped.

They were so scared they were incapable of speech. Eventually it was the black porter who spoke. He seemed calm, indifferent almost. 'Mr. Rosenthal's the only other person who knows the combination.'

'And what time does the boss get here?' Bill demanded.

'Not much before ten.'

It was almost nine. The store was due to open any minute now. And they had no way to get inside that safe. It seemed they might have to abort this robbery and come away empty-handed. So far, everything had gone according to plan, Bill reflected. The porter had arrived at the store at eight. And then, just before half-eight, he and Jack barged their way in using the Western Union telegram trick that had worked so well on their first bank job.

It had all been plain sailing up until now. And, having come this far, Bill felt bitter about calling off the hold-up.

He stared at the porter. He could feel the man's eyes burning into him. The guy was infuriatingly unruffled, peering at Bill as though it was a staring game to see who would break first, until something clicked in Bill's head and he was suddenly grateful for the porter's composure.

'Where would Mr. Rosenthal be right now?' he demanded.

The porter shrugged. 'At home, I guess.'

'Right! Phone him. Tell him the manager called in to say he's ill and hasn't shown up. Say there are a couple of early customers here and no one can open the safe.'

The porter hesitated. Bill started to raise his gun to the man's head when Jack came to the rescue using the same technique his partner had used at the Bronx County Savings Bank.

'Do it,' he snapped, aiming his gun at one of the employee's legs. 'Otherwise one of these gets a bullet in the knees and spends the rest of their days in a wheelchair.'

Calmly, the porter gave a small nod of acquiescence before going over to the telephone, with Bill following closely behind. He began to dial his boss's number. Everyone in the store listened to the dial whirring as the tension heightened. One of the employees, a young girl of nineteen, began sobbing, heaving and gulping air.

'Shut up!' Jack yelled angrily.

She was silenced, letting great rivers of tears flood down her cheeks, while her body shook quietly. They could hear the phone ringing at the boss's end. After three rings, it was answered. Keeping his cool, the porter told his boss everything Bill had told him to say. As he spoke, he did nothing to arouse the store owner's suspicions and spoke without any sign of agitation. He called out the combination as his boss recited it while Bill wrote it on a sheet of paper by the phone. The porter calmly thanked his boss and hung up.

'Okay,' Bill told him. 'You did well.'

He exchanged a brief grin with Jack. It had been that easy. Saved at the last minute by the credibility of the black porter. He went over to the safe, spun the dial, and opened it. It was filled with jewelry of all kinds, but Bill only took the diamonds which were less identifiable and more difficult to trace.

Using the third accomplice routine, they departed hurriedly and melted into the Broadway crowds.

Two weeks later Bill marched along Broadway towards Bill Dwyer's saloon. He crunched into a juicy apple and was humming "Twelfth Street Rag". He had donned his best chalk-striped blue suit, with a navy fedora worn at a slightly jaunty angle, and he was feeling on top of the world. The attaché case he was carrying contained a valuable load and today was payday.

He had arranged to meet his old boss, Dutch Schultz, who was going to fence the diamonds. The daily papers had been full of the robbery and Bill discovered the diamonds were really hot. So hot, in fact, that the insurance companies were offering huge rewards to get them back,and an amnesty for their return. Bill was wary of using the usual fences, which was why he'd chosen the Dutchman. He knew Schultz would only give him a fraction of their value, but at least he could be relied upon not to turn him or the diamonds in.

Dwyer's saloon was quiet and gloomy with only two customers seated at the bar. Bill ordered a beer and headed for the men's room to wash the apple-stickiness from his hands. As he pushed open the door, he was greeted by a hacking smoker's cough from behind the partition that divided the urinals from the washroom. He was about to turn the faucet on at the sink, when a rasping man's voice caught his attention, though it was more what he said.

'The Dutchman's had it coming for a long time.'

'Wait till he sits down,' another man said. 'Then let him have it.'

Bill looked up at the partition dividing the washroom to a large gap at the top. Maybe the two men thought it went right to the ceiling, and that they couldn't be overheard. And because one of them had coughed just as he had entered, they had no idea he was there. But he had to get out fast and warn the Dutchman. Not only that, they might hear him leaving and come after him.

He pulled open the door and darted through, at the same time pulling out his wallet. He strode down the bar and threw a dollar bill on the counter.

'Be right back,' he told the bartender. 'Left something in the office.'

He wasn't certain from which direction Schultz would be coming so he dodged into a shop doorway just half a block away from Dwyer's where he could keep his eye on the premises. He wondered if the two men had heard him leaving the washroom. If that was the case, they weren't going to stick around. But he didn't see anyone come out of the saloon, so he guessed that they hadn't heard his flight from the men's room and were now waiting to kill the Dutchman.

He waited five minutes before he saw the Dutchman walking along on the opposite side of the street. Dodging in and out of the traffic, he hurried over and grabbed Schultz by the arm. 'Come on. Let's get out of here,' he urged.

He dragged Schultz a couple of paces before the gangster resisted, stopped and yanked his arm free. There was chilling look in his eye.

'What's going on?' he demanded.

'I was in the washroom at Dwyer's and I overheard two men plotting to kill you. They said they were going to let you have it soon as you sat down.'

Schultz's hand reached inside his jacket and Bill could tell he had a gun holstered. The gangster made to cross the street, then stopped.

'Who were they? D'you know?'

'I didn't get a look at them.'

Schultz hiked his shoulders like he didn't care. 'How many customers in there?'

'Two guys at the bar.'

'And just the two guys in the washroom?'

Bill nodded. He guessed what was coming.

'I'm going in there to get them,' Schultz growled and stood poised on the edge of the sidewalk waiting for a gap in the traffic.

'Wait a minute!' Bill called. 'They're expecting you. They'll be ready. As soon as you go inside, they'll start shooting. Someone must have known you were coming to Dwyer's for a meeting. Someone in your organization.'

He could see the Dutchman thinking hard, the cogs in his brain fitting into place. Then his face darkened. 'The dirty, no-good fuckers,' he snarled. He thought about this betrayal a while longer, then his face broke out into a malevolent grin while his eyes betrayed a streak of cruelty and coldness that sent a grave-treading shiver down Bill's spine.

'They'll beg for death by the time I'm through with them,' the Dutchman added. He waved the thought aside like a small insect. 'Okay, let's take a look at those rocks.'

They took a short walk to one of Schultz's offices on Fifth Avenue. It was a large single room and Bill guessed that this was a private sanctum for occasions such as this, free from the prying eyes of henchmen and hangers-on. In an organization like Schultz's, he was bound to make many enemies as Bill had just discovered. But Schultz was not the sort of man one should double-cross, as Bill had just witnessed, and he could imagine that his ex-boss's retribution would be brutal and sadistic.

Bill sat in front of the large paperless desk. The office walls were covered with sporting photographs, mainly of boxers. Behind Schultz's desk, there was one of Jack Dempsey in action when he took the world heavyweight title from Jess Willard. He glanced around the opulent office which seemed more like a gentlemen's sporting club than a place of business. There was even a stuffed deer's head on one of the walls and he wondered if it was a trophy Schultz had shot himself.

'Okay,' the Dutchman demanded as he sat in his creaking leather chair, 'let's see what you've got.'

Bill opened the attaché case, took out a biscuit tin incongruously decorated with a cute black-and-white kitten wearing a red ribbon, opened the lid and delicately unfolded the cloth bundle within to reveal the sparkling collection of diamonds. As he pushed them across the desk, he fancied Schultz's eyes glittered greedily from their prismatic reflection.

From the daily papers, Bill knew their value to be $130,000 and he waited to see what his ex-boss would offer. Mesmerized, Schultz stared at them hungrily before snapping out of his reverie.

'We both know what they're worth, Sutton,' he said, 'but that's retail. These might be difficult to offload. I'll give you thirty-five thousand now, and five percent on everything I raise above fifty thousand.'

Bill knew the gangster to be ruthless but it seemed a fair enough offer in the circumstances and he wondered if it was because he had just warned Schultz that his life was in danger.

'Okay,' he agreed. 'It's a deal.'

From his desk drawer, Schultz took out a bundle of money and pushed it across the desk. 'It's all there,' he said. 'I counted it.'

Bill nodded and dropped it into his case. He realized the Dutchman had already prepared this amount so the reasonably generous offer couldn't have had anything to do with his life being saved.

Bill clicked the case shut and started to rise. 'Thanks, Mr. Schultz.'

Schultz stopped him with a hand gesture. 'Just a minute, Sutton.' He reached into his desk drawer, drew out another bundle of notes tied with a rubber band and threw it across the desk.

'Here's an extra fifteen thousand dollars,' he said.

Bill smiled at the gangster as he picked up the notes. 'Thank you. That's very generous of you, Mr. Schultz.'

The following day, Bill was at the apartment when he got another disturbing phone call from Kitty. She was sobbing uncontrollably.

'You lied to me, Bill,' she croaked. 'You and my fucking husband. I hate him. And I hate you too.'

A suffocating feeling of dread deadened Bill's mood. He'd been feeling high all morning. Jenny was awake longer now and Bill adored her. He was so hopelessly in love with her and Louise, he was sure he must be the happiest man in the world. Last night he could have sworn his daughter smiled at him even though Louise had told him she probably needed winding.

But deep down he remained convinced it was a secret smile especially for him. Life was wonderful. And the Dutchman's surprisingly uncharacteristic generosity of yesterday had raised his spirits. Everything was going great guns.

Now this! Right now Bill could have happily strangled Jack. He made up his mind that this was the end of their working relationship and he would terminate the partnership.

His mouth felt dry as he tried to speak. 'Kitty,' he began, 'I know you think I lied...'

'I don't think it,' Kitty's voice crackled on the line. 'I know it, you fucking rat.'

'Look,' Bill said weakly, 'all I said was what I believed...'

Kitty interrupted him. Her voice was brittle, 'Oh, you believed in Harry McCarthy, did you? Well that's funny, because I phoned Sing Sing - said I was *Mrs.* McCarthy, wanting a visit - and there's no one there by that name. And when I confronted Jack about it, he told me the truth. Said he was in love with this Gloria.'

Kitty burst into hysterical weeping again. Bill went cold. How could Jack do this? Even if Kitty was suspicious, short of catching them in each other's arms, there was nothing she could prove.

'Kitty, listen to me,' Bill pleaded. 'Don't do anything foolish. Anything you might regret later.'

All he heard was great shuddering sobs. 'Kitty! Can you hear me?'

She stopped crying at last, and shouted angrily, 'That bastard! I loved him. I really loved him. How could he do this to me?'

'These things happen in a relationship, Kitty. I think we need to talk, face-to-face.'

'What the fuck for, Bill?'

'We need to talk it through. Things might look different in a little while.'

'I don't think so,' she spat. 'I'm never going to get over this. He really took me for a ride, that bastard. And so did you.'

'Please, Kitty,' he begged. 'Just meet me. I'll try to explain...'

'What's to explain?' she said in a resigned tone.

'Just meet me, Kitty,' he said, as forcefully as he dared. 'Fifteen minutes in Jake's Café.'

'I don't see the point.'

Bill's voice rose urgently, 'Kitty! Promise me you'll be there.'

Silence from the other end of the line.

'Kitty!'

'Okay,' she relented in a dazed voice. 'I'll be there.'

A click and the line went dead.

Bill glanced at his watch, inhaled deeply on his cigarette and finished his coffee. He'd been at Jake's Café forty-five minutes and there was still no sign of Kitty. He wondered if he should go round to her apartment and have a word with her, see if he could calm her down. He decided against it.

There was a hardness about Kitty that made him feel uneasy. It had always been there. He had noticed it in her demeanor, her sharp though cautious movements, the way she suggested spending some of Jack's money in an overly casual way, trying not to reveal a mercenary nature, and the way her eyes developed an icy glaze when Bill became over familiar with Jack, cracking the occasional joke with him or empathizing in a way that left her on the periphery.

In spite of this surely, if she really loved Jack, she wouldn't betray him to the police. That she might be capable of getting her husband jailed for twenty years or more didn't bear thinking about. There couldn't be many women who could do that to their husbands. On the other hand, Jack had betrayed her and she might feel she had a score to settle.

The thoughts bounced back and forth in Bill's head, but he came to no satisfactory conclusion as to what to do, except to return home to his beautiful wife and baby daughter and pray that Kitty would do the right thing.

He stubbed his cigarette into the ashtray, paid his bill and peered through the window before leaving the café. Across the street, a black Chrysler saloon was parked directly opposite with two men sitting in the front. Bill waited until a bus passed by in the opposite direction to the way the car was facing. He used it as cover and dashed out of the café, ran alongside the bus and raced around the corner at the next block.

As he hurried along the street, he kept glancing over his shoulder to see if he was being followed. He was becoming paranoid. There was nothing unusual about two men waiting in a parked car. And if Kitty had shopped him to the police, the place would have been crawling with cops. After three major armed robberies, they wouldn't send just two detectives to take him in.

The day was blisteringly hot and, by the time Bill reached

his car, he was sweating profusely. Suddenly he found Manhattan claustrophobic and oppressive and he longed for the freedom of the suburbs. He checked his mirror before setting off and drove cautiously.

He wasn't taking any chances. Every time a car came up close behind him, he felt he was being tailed and he kept peering nervously in the mirror. It wasn't until he was heading out across the East River that he began to relax.

The thoughts of Louise and Jenny and the domestic bliss that awaited him, comforted him and sweetened his mood and he began softly whistling "I'll Build a Stairway to Paradise".

By the time he reached his street and spotted their house at the end, he had shoved all thoughts about Kitty to the back of his mind. He was home and safe.

Louise spotted the car and came to the door to greet him. 'You're early,' she said. 'I wasn't expecting you for hours.'

'Mr. Schultz said to take the rest of the day off.'

'That was kind of him.'

'Mmm-hmm,' he grunted, slid his arms round her waist and nestled a kiss into her neck.

'You'll have the neighbors gossiping,' she whispered.

'Let them,' he said, then drew back from her and looked into her eyes. 'I love you, Louise. Never forget it.'

She frowned. 'What a funny thing to say. Why should I forget it?'

'I just want you to know that I'll always love you.'

'That's good,' she replied and pecked him on the nose, 'because I love you too. Now then, your daughter's asleep in the backyard, in the shade of the apple tree. I expect you want to say hello to her.'

'I'm hot and sweaty,' he said. 'Think I'll freshen up first. By then she might be awake. She can watch her daddy weeding the flower bed.'

Louise giggled, a slightly puzzled expression on her face.

'Wouldn't it be more sensible to freshen up after the gardening?'

Bill tugged his shirt away from his chest to demonstrate how sticky he was. 'I need a shower, Louise; otherwise you and Jenny won't want to know me.'

After he had showered and changed into a pair of denims and an old checked shirt that he wore for gardening, he went out the back and peered into his daughter's pram. She looked beautiful, she was perfection itself. There was no other baby in the world like his Jenny. She had a tiny button nose and a very slight breeze stirred her silky, golden wisps of hair. He stroked the downy hair and couldn't resist the urge to lean over and kiss the top of her head. The sensation was exquisite, like kissing rose petals.

Louise's shadow appeared across the lawn. 'You must be thirsty. I've brought you some lemonade.'

Bill took the cool glass and toasted her with it. 'Here's to the happiest family in the world. You having any?'

Her eyes sparkled as she smiled at him. 'I'll be out in a minute. I just want to finish the apple pie I'm making.'

He beamed at her and watched the alluring sway of her figure as she returned to the house. He glanced into the pram one more time before kneeling down beside the flower bed. He picked up a small fork and dug into the sun-hardened soil, humming absently the same phrase of a tune, over and over.

Louise was kneading dough when the doorbell rang. That was odd. They weren't expecting anyone, and it wasn't as though they'd got to know any of their neighbors yet, at least not on a social basis. She wiped her floury hands on a tea towel and went to open the front door.

She didn't get a chance to speak or even take in the policeman who pushed her aside, followed by another. They both had their guns drawn. They were flushed with fear of conflict.

'Where is he?' one of them yelled, as she was slammed against the wall. Outside, she could see police cars, lights

99

flashing, and other police and men in suits trying to crowd through the front door.

'Your husband?' the same policeman snapped, a frenzied look in his eyes. 'Where is he?'

Louise was incapable of speech. She cringed back against the wall, unable to form a single coherent thought.

A cop went through to the kitchen and spotted Bill in the back garden. 'There he is!'

Bill, vaguely aware that there was a commotion going on somewhere and thinking it was a neighbor playing a radio too loud, turned just as the shadows loomed across the lawn. There were four uniformed cops and three detectives, all with guns aimed at him.

'Put the cuffs on him,' one of the detectives ordered.

As he was dragged to his feet, Bill tried to focus on Jenny. In desperation, he tried to glimpse the innocent face of his beloved daughter, knowing it might be the last time he would see her like this, cozy and snug beneath her blanket.

He was pulled violently away, so that he was thrown round with his back to her. His hands were yanked roughly behind him and he felt the handcuffs snap shut, pinching the skin on one of his arms. Behind the row of cops, he saw Louise staring at him, deeply shocked, her face drawn and vulnerable. It was a look that would haunt him.

Three detectives questioned him at the police station. The first, a bull of a man the others referred to as Murphy, started the interrogation by slamming a nightstick on to the interview room table. His forehead glistened with perspiration and there were dark patches of sweat under his arms. His bulbous nose was purple and cratered like the moon and there was something faintly obscene about his fleshy lips.

'There's a lot of justice in a nightstick,' he said. 'Bear that in mind, Sutton.'

'I'd like to know what's going on,' Bill stated innocently. 'What am I charged with?'

Murphy stared at him for a considerable time. The sneering expression was one he wore regularly, a distinctive look adopted for interrogation purposes, the nostrils of his nose slightly dilated as though he was trying to keep from smelling something deeply repugnant on the suspect. Slowly, he raised the stick and pointed it at Bill.

'It won't work, Sutton,' he said. 'Your accomplice, Bassett, was picked up in Buffalo. And he's confessed. There's the small matter of the bank on Jamaica Avenue, the Bronx County Savings Bank and Rosenthal's jewelry store.'

Bill knew that if Jack had confessed, then they must have worked him over. There was a limit to what a man could take, and he wondered when it would be his turn. 'Look, I know my rights. You're supposed to book me or let me go. And if you book me, I have a right to a lawyer.'

Fists clenched, the youngest of the three detectives darted forward, fighting back the urge to hit Bill.

'Scum like you,' he hissed, leaning forward and sending a spray of saliva into Bill's ear, 'don't have any rights. To have rights, you gotta pay your taxes.'

He seemed genuinely and personally aggrieved on this matter.

There was a loud guffaw from across the table. Murphy was laughing but there was little humor in his eyes. 'I don't s'pose he made a payment to the IRS from the bank jobs. Whadda yah think, Matt?'

The detective called Matt shrugged. He was thin-faced with receding hair and a cleft chin that would have looked more attractive on a chubbier face. 'I think we're wasting time,' he said. 'I think we should hear his confession.'

There was something obscene about his suggestion, made with the same heavy-breathing tone of a pervert.

'You're right,' Murphy agreed. 'But first let's ask Sutton who fenced the jewelry. It was one of the questions your partner couldn't answer. Said you dealt with it, Sutton.'

'I don't know what you're talking about,' Bill replied.

Murphy flipped. 'Right! Take him down.'

The other two grabbed Bill and pulled him to his feet. Murphy threw open the door for them and they dragged him out, along the corridor to another door that led to a flight of steps going down into what appeared to be a cellar.

At the bottom, Bill saw the large gallery beneath the precinct, targets lined against a wall with spotlights over the targets. Bill guessed the shooting range would be soundproofed. The place had an eerie atmosphere and smelled vaguely musty and antiseptic.

'Okay. Take the cuffs off,' Murphy told the younger of the detectives.

Bill felt the handcuffs being unlocked and wondered what was going to happen. Did they intend letting him go, maybe let loose in the shooting range and use him for target practice?

Once the handcuffs were off, two of the detectives stood either side of him and Murphy stood in front, his legs splayed wide, blocking off any means of escape.

'Right,' he said. 'Get undressed.'

The back of Bill's throat tasted vile, like he was about to throw up. He must have reacted too slowly because Murphy socked him in the stomach, just below the belt. The pain shot across his lower abdomen. He doubled over, clutching his stomach, and tears sprang into his eyes.

'Don't keep us waiting. Get your shirt and trousers off. You can leave your underwear. We ain't perverts. We are merely expediting the course of justice.' Murphy must have been proud of this last statement because he followed it with a laugh.

Bill's hands were shaking as he fumbled with his shirt buttons. As soon as the bottom button was undone, one of the detectives tore the shirt from his back. He hesitated as he started on his pants' buttons.

'Shed the pants,' Murphy said impatiently, clenching his fists.

Hurriedly, Bill did as he was told. He stood before them,

feeling frail and vulnerable, his pallid white skin lustrous in the darkness of the gallery. His hands were thrust behind him again and he felt the handcuffs being put on. Then Murphy's meaty hand, stubby fingers like uncooked sausages, shoved him backwards.

He hadn't noticed the thin, narrow table behind him. They laid him on his back along it, like a hospital patient awaiting an operation. There were some lockers behind the table at the back of the shooting range and Bill heard one of them being opened. Despite the coolness in the shooting range, rivulets of sweat ran down his body as the fear and anticipation of what was about to happen clouded his mind.

The younger detective covered Bill's throat with a piece of material that might have been a scarf and pulled it tight over the edge of the table in a stranglehold. The thin-faced detective stood at the other end of the table and held his legs. Murphy stood alongside him, rhythmically tapping a rubber hose against his palm. Bill could smell the rancid sweat from the detective's body and he started to gag. The younger detective didn't want him to choke on his own vomit and eased up on the stranglehold fractionally.

'Now,' Murphy said, 'let's see how much he remembers.'

Quick as a lightning flash, Murphy brought the rubber hose down hard across Bill's stomach. The pain was unbearable. Bill ground his teeth together to keep from screaming.

No sooner had his nervous system marginally recovered from the shock than Murphy brought the hose down hard again in the same place. The pain burned through Bill's body like fire. There was no let up. With all his strength, Murphy hit him again and again on his chest, his stomach, shoulders and thighs, harder and harder each time, sending agonies of searing pain through his entire body so that his brain seemed to scream inside his head. Every time the rubber came in contact with his body he wanted to cry out, ask them to stop, plead with them for the pain to end. But he knew it was useless unless he was willing to confess.

The worst of the pain abated and Murphy leaned over, his face unbearably close to Bill's. 'Had enough, Sutton? Ready to own up to the robberies and sign a confession?'

'I ... I don't know what you're talking about,' Bill stammered.

Murphy straightened up and gave the cleft-chinned detective at Bill's feet a world-weary shrug. 'They always confess in the end, Matt,' he said. 'So why go through hell when the end result is the same?'

'Beats me,' the detective replied.

'No, it beats him,' Murphy said with a nasty laugh.

'Here, take over.'

He handed the hose to the detective named Matt and swapped places with him. A thin smile played at the corners of the thin-faced detective's mouth as he came and stood alongside Bill, holding the hose in one hand while stroking it tenderly with the other, enjoying the anticipation of the beating he was about to deal out.

Suddenly, he went berserk, thrashing Bill's body with the power of a sadist's lust. Bill writhed in agony at each stroke and the pain was so intense and burning he believed his body would split open and shed his guts on to the table and floor. Like a sudden rush of water cascading over a rock, he felt himself falling, plunging downwards like a plane spiraling out of control.

The body hit the ground and burst open like a water-filled balloon, spilling blood and entrails on to the sidewalk. The street was awash with blood. The sound of a woman heaving and puking. The smell of excrement. And the pain. The unbelievable pain. Burning like fire. Burning and burning. Then nothing.

When he came round, he was lying on a bunk in a cell. He tried to move but shards of glass shot through his body. Every part of him ached. He tried to lift his head a fraction but a grinding pain ran up and down his body as his nervous system screamed with agony.

He began shivering violently. He was freezing cold and he realized he was naked but for his underwear. He lay shivering, unable to move, and, every so often, the shivering stopped as the blazing pain of his torture took over. He burned in agony until the fire was quenched by freezing water and he shook like a heroin addict in the grips of cold turkey.

Eventually, unable to stand the coldness and vulnerability of his nakedness, he raised his head. A stinging pain shot through his whole body but he managed to raise himself on to his elbows. He stared at his stomach and legs for a moment, seeing them as something unreal, belonging to someone - or some*thing* - else. Most of his body was already turning a shade of purple from the bruising. Hardly an inch of flesh was white.

On the floor, at the edge of the bunk, his denim pants and checked shirt lay in a heap. He remembered these were his gardening clothes and thoughts of Louise and Jenny drifted into his head. He wanted to weep. But the pain was too intense for self-pity.

He turned sideways on to the edge of the bunk and managed to swing his legs on to the floor. With a superhuman determination, he reached for his denim pants and winced as he pulled them on, his body protesting at the effort needed and, as he struggled into his shirt, every part of his torso felt raw, like open wounds, and his breath caught in his throat. By the time he had finished dressing, he was sweating feverishly and trembling uncontrollably.

He leaned back against the cell wall, hardly daring to move because of the pain. At least he was dressed now and felt slightly less vulnerable. He tried to free his mind, to dissociate it from the brutal agony of his beating and, for a brief moment, his mind was distracted from the physical suffering as he noticed something different about his denim pants. What was it? There was something missing. His belt! They had removed his belt in case he attempted to hang himself. But they might as well have left it, he reflected grimly. As far as he was concerned, suicide was never an option however bad things became.

He stared into space, his head buzzing and aching, and thought about how long he'd been lying unconscious in the cell. It could have been minutes or hours, he had no way of knowing. He tilted his head and looked into the piercing glare from the ceiling light, wondering if it was day or night. In this windowless cell there was no way of telling.

The rattle of keys in the lock made him start and a stabbing pain shot through his body. The door swung open and in walked Murphy followed by the other two detectives.

'Well,' he snapped, 'ready to talk?'

'I've got nothing to say.'

Murphy threw the other two a sneering grin. 'A glutton for punishment. Right! Bring him down.'

They grabbed Bill under the arms and raised him violently to his feet. His jaw was set tight, as he fought against the rock-pounding agony of his pains. They dragged him out of the cell and along the corridor towards the shooting range door.

Murphy walked behind and commented nonstop on the fate that awaited him, 'Think you're tough, eh? We'll see about that. Maybe this time we'll give you a breather between beatings, save you passing out on us.

'We can keep going a lot longer than you can, Sutton. We can go home, get a good night's sleep, and come back fresh as a daisy and start over. Think about it, Sutton. Whatever happens, you're gonna talk. So it might as well be now.'

Inside the shooting range, Bill was again made to strip before they handcuffed him, and shoved him back on to the table, like a carcass on a butcher's slab. Murphy was first to start pounding him with the hose. This time the pain was so unbearable that he screamed out. Murphy ignored it and continued whipping him like a possessed, demented torturer. A crusading, self-righteous zealot hell-bent on extracting a confession.

Bill could feel himself sliding into unconsciousness again.

But, just as he was about to surrender to the blackout, the beating ceased leaving his body aching with such excruciating pain that uncontrollable tears ran down his cheeks.

'Okay,' Murphy said. 'I think he's had enough for now. Let's take a breather. I could do with a smoke.'

They went out and left him lying on the table. He didn't dare move. Every muscle, nerve and sinew in his body was agonizingly raw. And soon his tormentors would return to continue the assault. How much more could he stand? Maybe they were right. It was just a question of time. He would eventually sign that confession. There was only so much a man could take.

He lay motionless, the air ringing painfully in his ears and every nerve in his body raw and bleeding. It seemed as though he was drifting in eternity and no longer belonged in the mortal world.

He heard the door of the shooting range squeak open and their footsteps approaching the table. He kept his eyes tight-shut as though he could make the monsters vanish. The pain was so bad now he was unable to differentiate between reality and the nightmare world into which he had sunk.

He heard the detective called Matt speak, a throaty, lustful request, a voice used when demanding a girl to strip. 'Let me have ten minutes with the son of a bitch.'

A scuffling sound, followed by a sudden air-whistling sound, then unbelievable pain. Bill screamed, the high-pitched cry of a wounded animal. More and more pain. More than he could possibly bear. The agony increased as his screaming scraped his throat raw like sandpaper.

Then...

A heavy giant of a man, the ogre of his childhood nightmare visits, hacked at his head with an axe. The ogre kept hacking away at his head while Bill tried to fight him off. He raised his hands to protect himself, the axe slashed at his arms, severing them at the elbows. He was helpless to protect himself as the axe continued slicing and hacking into his head. He screamed, but couldn't hear himself. His mouth was open, silently screaming...

He knew he was back in his cell. He was lying on his back on the bed staring at the light on the ceiling. He closed his eyes again and lay without moving for what seemed like hours. He was incapable of movement. He knew he had to do something in order to survive, but what? He had no way of knowing how long he'd been here or when his torturers would return. And he knew they were going to continue beating him until they got their confession.

With tremendous effort, he managed to raise himself into a sitting position. The pain no longer mattered. He was feverish with the urge to survive. He grabbed his clothes and struggled into them, crying out each time the material rubbed against the bruises on his body. As he shoved his shirt into his trousers, his index fingernail caught on a corner of his pants' fly. The jagged edge of the nail was the least of his worries, but it gave him an idea. If only he had the guts to do it.

He finished dressing and sat on the edge of the bed, contemplating what it was he had to do in order to survive. It involved more excruciating pain. It was a drastic plan, but he had no choice.

He opened his mouth, took a deep breath, and began clawing away at the roof of his mouth with his jagged fingernail. The pain shot up through his head, like broken glass cutting into his brain. He tried to shut his mind to the pain and continued working away at his mouth with the nail.

It seemed to take forever, the pain going on and on like a discordant note. Blood spurted into his mouth, warm and metallic tasting. He had burst a blood vessel. He leapt to his feet, staggered across the cell and rapped loudly on the door.

'Help me!' he yelled. 'Help me!'

He kept up a barrage of banging on the door. He saw an eye peering through the Judas hole, so he let the blood trickle from his mouth. The cell door swung open and a uniformed cop, holding a nightstick ready to subdue him if necessary, stared at him impassively.

Bill clutched his stomach and spat and coughed blood. 'Help me!' he cried. 'I've a stomach hemorrhage. I need a doctor.'

'Stay put,' the cop told him and slammed and relocked the door.

Bill waited, sitting on the edge of the bed, hoping the burst blood vessel in his mouth wouldn't heal rapidly. At least, there was plenty of blood on his shirt front now to convince a medic that he had a stomach hemorrhage.

After what seemed like an eternity, a key turned in the lock and the guard re-entered with a tall, thin man dressed in a light brown cotton suit. He was carrying a Gladstone bag and had the air of a man who had seen and done everything and nothing could rattle his composure.

'Lie back,' he told Bill, 'and undo your shirt.'

Bill sunk back gingerly on to the hard bed and fumbled at his shirt buttons. The doctor's inscrutable face looked down at the bruising but his expression gave nothing away. He pressed his hands against Bill's abdomen and pushed down hard. Bill winced and gasped.

'Okay, here's what I want you to do. Think you can give me a sample?' the medic asked.

He reached into his bag, retrieved a small bottle and thrust it towards his patient. Dazed, Bill struggled to sit up and took the bottle. His eyes must have registered incomprehension, because the medic spoke to him as though he was a small child.

'Think you can pee into that bottle?'

'I'll try,' Bill muttered

While he unscrewed the bottle, the medic went outside with the guard. He could hear them outside talking in an undertone, and caught snatches of what the medic was telling the guard... 'He's had enough...unless they want to face charges of police brutality...suggest he's left to recover...do some serious damage.'

The effort of trying to urinate caused a great pain to shoot through Bill's stomach. Finally, he managed to squeeze out a miniscule amount into the jar. He was horrified to see its bloody color.

'Jesus Christ!' he exclaimed loudly.

The medic returned and took the jar from him. The cop peered over the medic's shoulder as he raised the jar to the light to examine its contents.

'Hmm,' the medic observed calmly, as though treating a patient for nothing worse than a head cold, 'seems the kidney's damaged.' He turned and addressed the cop. 'This man needs to take things easy from now on. You hear what I'm saying?'

'Yes, doc,' the cop replied, hesitantly. 'I'll - I'll let them know what you said.'

'You do that,' the medic insisted. He screwed the top back on the jar and left it lying on a table by the bed. Then, as though his visit had been extremely inconvenient and he now had more important things to attend to, he sighed deeply before exiting hurriedly, shaking his head as he went.

The cop flashed Bill a contemptuous look before following the medic out. Bill collapsed back on to the bed. He lay still for a long while. The beating had exhausted him and pretty soon he was fast asleep. It was a dreamless sleep.

When he awoke, he discovered a sandwich on a metal plate and a jug of water and metal cup had been placed on the table by the bed. His blood-soaked mouth had a metallic taste to it and there was a large and irritating piece of skin hanging from the roof of his mouth.

He poured himself some water and drank. He could feel the water mixing with the blood and sliding down his throat like oil, making him feel nauseous. He looked at the sandwich, decided he couldn't face it, and lay back again on the bed.

He spent what seemed endless hours slowly recovering from his wounds. His thoughts were mainly concentrated on his house in Queens and he wondered how Louise was coping with the knowledge that her husband had deceived her. He had brought her nothing but hurt from which she might never recover.

The remorse plagued him. And he was filled with shame whenever images of his beautiful baby daughter came into his head. He imagined her grown older and going to school; being questioned by other children. 'What does *your* daddy do?'

As his punishing thoughts became more and more indulgent, his feelings of guilt became a distraction from the pain of his beatings. And, as the time stretched interminably, boredom eventually got to him. He felt forgotten. And he had no way of knowing whether it was day or night, the unrelenting artificial light burned endlessly, shutting out time.

Every so often, different cops brought him food and replenished his water. He tried asking them how long he'd been there, but got only non-committal replies. Then, after what he estimated to be at least two or three days, two cops entered his cell.

'Okay, Sutton,' one of them demanded. 'On your feet. Time for a line-up.'

There were five others, and Bill was third in the line. A detective in his mid-forties, handsome with steel grey hair slicked back, conducted proceedings. First, he brought in the guard from the Jamaica Avenue bank.

'Have a good look at number one,' the detective told him.

The man stared at the first planted suspect, shook his head, and moved on to number two.

'What about number two?' the detective prompted.

'Nope,' said the guard, and moved so that he stood before Bill.

'How about number three?'

Bill avoided looking directly into the guard's eyes who stared at him for a long time.

'Well?' the detective demanded.

The guard chuckled. 'You kidding? This here's a skinny

young guy. Guy who robbed our bank was a lot older and fatter.'

Bill could have hugged him, but smothered his feelings. The guard moved on and looked at the other three phony suspects.

'Nope,' he said to each in turn.

Unable to disguise the disappointment in his voice, the detective said, 'Okay. Bring in the next one.'

One by one, they brought in all the staff from the Jamaica Avenue bank, the Bronx Savings Bank and the Rosenthal jewelry store. None of them could identify Bill as the robber who had held them up and it began to look as though he was off the hook.

He could sense the detective's deep frustration, the suppressed anger in his voice, as each witness said that he was either too young or too thin to have been the robber. Bill congratulated himself on his technique of wearing stage make-up for each job.

Finally, they brought in the black porter from the jewelry store. Bill saw the man staring at him before going through the routine of looking at the first two men. When he stood in front of Bill, he stared long and hard,and his eyes seemed to bore into his soul.

Eventually he spoke with the deep conviction of a man who knows when he's right.

'This is the man who robbed our store,' he said.

CHAPTER 7

JULY, 1931

Jim Vitale was shown into Bill's cell. He shook hands with his client and sat on a rickety chair opposite Bill's bed, and placed a large Gladstone bag on the floor next to him. He wondered why his lawyer needed a bag of this size seeing as on previous visits he had opened it to reveal nothing more than a few papers.

As soon as the guard had gone, Bill asked him about Jack's trial.

'Not good,' the lawyer said. 'Guilty.'

Bill sighed impatiently. 'I know that. He pleaded guilty. It was a foregone conclusion. What was his sentence?'

Vitale shrugged, as though apologizing for something out of his control. 'Sentence has been deferred until after your trial. But I wouldn't worry about it. That's usual when there are two defendants accused of the same crime.

'And Jack Bassett stood no chance. Not with Woody Silverman defending him. Stick with me and your plea of not guilty and you'll be okay, kid.'

Bill felt slightly reassured by his lawyer's words. He knew Vitale to be a shrewd operator who had defended some pretty crooked clients in his time, and had managed to get them not guilty verdicts on some technicality or loophole in the law.

He had once been a magistrate but had been struck off after he was compromised by a newspaper photograph showing

113

him at a dinner held in his honor and attended by almost every powerful mobster in the city. Although he was barred from the bench, he was still permitted to practice law.

He was an affable, outgoing man in his early forties who liked to dress smartly, and sported a neat, thin moustache, black as his hair, with faint traces of grey. His hair was neatly parted at one side and gleamed with an expensive lotion that smelled faintly of liquor.

He grinned mischievously at Bill. 'I expect you're wondering why I carry this huge Gladstone with me, since it only contains a few notes.'

'That had crossed my mind,' Bill replied.

Vitale looked round behind him, to make certain they were not observed. 'Take off your shirt,' he told Bill. 'Quickly!'

The lawyer bent over, unclipped the catch on his bag and took out the sort of flash camera used by news photographers. Bill stood up, dropped his shirt on to the bed, while Vitale quickly took a photograph of his bruised body, before stuffing the camera back into his bag.

'This'll give the jury something to think about,' the lawyer grinned. 'Coupled with the medical evidence of your damaged kidneys...'

'You mean that if Jack's confession was obtained by police brutality...' Bill asked.

Vitale interrupted him. 'Exactly! There's only one piece of evidence the DA can use against you.'

Bill frowned deeply. 'Being picked out of that ID parade.'

'I wouldn't worry about it. Out of all the employees at the banks and jewelry store, only one of them identified you. And he was a colored man. By the time I'm through with him on the stand, he won't seem a very creditable witness.'

'I hope you're right,' Bill muttered.

Later that day, the guard unlocked the cell door. 'On your feet, Sutton,' he said. 'You've got visitors.'

He rose too quickly and he felt sharp needles of pain from deep inside his body. As he followed the guard along the corridor, the twinges reminded him of how merciless the cops had been in working him over. A dull pain like a heavy stone in his lower back worried him, especially as he was still passing blood in his urine.

'Know who my visitors are?' Bill enquired as he hobbled along.

The guard ignored the question, didn't even acknowledge it, or maybe he was pretending he hadn't heard. Bill wondered if it might be Louise and his heart pumped faster. He desperately wanted to see her again, but at the same time he was scared of the depths of his guilt, knowing how difficult it was going to be to face the wife he'd hurt so deeply.

He was shown into a room that looked as though it hadn't been cleaned in years and had no character whatsoever. It was anonymous and impersonal, a room that might have been overlooked. It was hard to guess what its function was. There was only one small wooden table in the centre, but no chairs. Blocking out most of the light, a man stood looking out through a small grimy window overlooking a drab courtyard of pipes and fire escapes. As though it had been rehearsed, he turned round as Bill entered.

'Thank you, Tom,' he said to the guard with a studied familiarity and a faintly dismissive manner. The guard shut the door as he left.

Bill studied the man carefully. He was heavily built, blond-haired, with an honest and open face, maybe mid-thirties or older, it was hard to tell. He had a scrubbed and healthy country appearance and seemed to Bill that he could have been a small-town sales representative or realtor, though he doubted it.

'My name's Jackson. Mr. Charles Jackson,' the man said, donning a salesman's smile as he came towards Bill, holding out his hand.

Bill shook it, surprised to experience such a limp handshake from this powerfully built, outgoing guy.

'I expect you're wondering who I am.'

Bill nodded dumbly and blinked. Recent events had left him feeling dazed, disoriented like he was a scrap of litter drifting uselessly down a rain-flooded gutter, unable to make decisions. It was a numbing sensation and most of the time his thoughts flitted about, never forming complete ideas. But, on this occasion, Bill was alert enough to realize that, if it was a question, it was rhetorical and didn't necessarily require an answer. He merely grunted, permitting the man to continue with his explanation.

'I'm a Pinkerton's agent,' Mr. Charles Jackson said expansively as though he expected the whole world to swoon at his feet.

'A private cop, 'Bill acknowledged. 'So what do you want with me?'

'Our clients are the insurers of Rosenthal & Co. You know how it works, Mr. Sutton. The jewelry store stands to lose nothing. But the insurance company...'

The Pinkerton's detective gave a whistle to signify that his clients were about to lose a substantial sum.

'So what has this to do with me?' Bill enquired.

'I've spoken with the DA and this is the deal. The insurance company would like to recover its money. Frankly, they're more interested in that than seeing you go to jail. Now, I want to get that jewelry back for my clients and we can do that if we can nab the fence you used. We can trace that jewelry if you tell us who he was. And I, Charles Jackson, and the DA will give you a written guarantee that you'll be allowed to plead third degree robbery with a sentence of no more than five years.'

His offer was completed by a small coda of a crooked smile and two upward palm gestures.

The offer rattled through Bill's head like the Coney Island subway. Crossing a man like Dutch Schultz was more dangerous than playing in a nest of rattlesnakes. Besides, even if the fence was not someone as powerful or dangerous as the Dutchman, he was not an informer. It was against his code of decency. Since he had put himself on the wrong side of the law, he had to abide by the rules. And the unwritten rules clearly stated: Thou shalt not inform on a fellow criminal.

'You're wasting your time,' he told the detective.

The Pinkerton's man's face flushed with anger, his apple cheeks aflame. 'I've got plenty of time to waste,' he snapped. 'You haven't. You'll go down for thirty years unless you go along with us.'

Bill began in a quiet, reasonable tone, 'But I'm pleading not guilty to this charge. You see there's not much evidence against me, and...'

The private detective stepped closer to Bill and poked a finger in his chest. Bill winced.

'I don't care about that, Sutton. You're as guilty as hell and you're going down for it. So how about it? Play ball with us and you'll have an easy five years. How old are you. Thirty? Thirty-one? You'll be an old man by the time you get out. Jesus! What a thought. An old guy having missed out on most of the best years of his life.'

An image of himself as an elderly man burst into Bill's head and he wanted to scream, to tell this asshole to stop. It was useless. There was no way he was going to turn informer, even if it meant going to prison for the rest of his natural life. So why was he tormenting him in this way?

Bill could see the anger in the detective's eyes and he knew that it was because now the Pinkerton's man would have to go back to his bosses or clients and tell them his mission had been unsuccessful. Bill almost felt sorry for him.

'Look,' he said, 'if I could help you, I would. But, like I said, you're wasting your time. I'm sorry.'

He turned away from him and looked out of the window. Not much of a view, but at least it was a view. He would savor it while he could.

Angrily, the detective flung open the door. 'Okay,' he told

the guard posted outside. 'We're through in here. This guy's a loser.'

The Pinkerton agent proved prophetic. Just over a week later, following the trial, the newspapers screamed 'GUILTY' in banner headlines. The tabloids christened Bill 'WILLIE THE ACTOR'. Every New York paper ran the story, and even the broadsheets gave the news prominence above the collapse of the German banks.

From the moment Bill stepped into the courtroom, things went badly. In his opening address to the jury, the DA talked about the suspect's plea of not guilty and the fact that there was no confession.

When it came time for Bill's lawyer to produce the photographic evidence of the bruising, it was rejected as inadmissible evidence. And there was worse to come. When the black porter took the stand, Jim Vitale did his best to discredit him but came out of it badly burned.

It looked to the jury as though the lawyer's tirade against the black porter was racist and, even though every jury member was white, it nevertheless made them feel uncomfortable and they sided with the porter who gave his evidence in an unshakably clear and stoic manner.

He described all the details about Bill that he remembered, observant details that no amount of make-up and disguise could hide. Bill had known throughout the trial that he was going to lose.

The Pinkerton agent's words echoed in his head. And he couldn't stop thinking about Louise. Had she visited him, it might have brought him the little bit of luck he so desperately needed.

While he waited in his cell for the trial to begin, his heart went out to her and he longed to see her once more, if only to beg her forgiveness. But, perhaps because she was too grief stricken, she didn't visit or send any message.

When he came into the courtroom on that first day, his eyes darted around searchingly, hoping to find her sitting amongst the crowd. He needed her goodness to sustain him, to help him to think positively. But, in spite of her love for him, and in spite of her decency and kindness, she remained significantly absent throughout the trial.

Jack Bassett was brought back into court for the sentencing. He looked wretched, and Bill could see that he seemed to be squirming inside from feelings of guilt and betrayal. He avoided catching Bill's eye. As they waited for the judge to come back into the courtroom, Bill tried to get Jack to look his way so that he could show him there were no hard feelings.

Even though Jack had behaved stupidly over the women, it was Kitty who was really to blame. And, even though Kitty had betrayed them, Bill tried to hate her but found he couldn't. He could see it from her angle. Jack had treated her so badly she had reacted with bitterness and hate.

If anything, he felt sorry for her; because now she would have her entire life to reflect that she was responsible for sending two men to prison for a very long time, one of them being the husband she had loved so much. No, he didn't blame Kitty. He had no one but himself to blame. He was the one who had brought others shame and disgrace.

Judge Cornelius Collins returned to the courtroom. Nervously, Bill tried again to catch Jack's eye again, almost to reassure him. After all, they were in this together. Partners in crime. But Jack's eyes still remained fixed in the distance, like a caged tiger.

The judge cleared his throat noisily before speaking. 'I find it hard to understand this crime. On one of the world's busiest streets, these two men, Sutton and Bassett, calmly took their time and carried out a robbery while thousands of people passed the door outside without noticing anything was wrong.

'Their victims were not only the insurance company who will have lost hundreds of thousands of dollars, but the staff at the jewelry store, who were terrified of the loaded guns these two carried. The porter made a positive identification of Sutton and Bassett named him in his confession.

'What I find hard to believe is that these two men spent a considerable amount of time at the store, robbing it, while behaving as though they were at a tea party. It was not the Wild West, but a family-owned store on Broadway, and these sorts of robberies must not be allowed to continue. I therefore sentence you both to thirty years.'

There was a kerfuffle in the courtroom as reporters dashed out, eager to phone their copy to their newsdesks.

'I'm sorry, Sutton,' Vitale said. 'Of course, we'll appeal.'

Before being taken down, Jack turned towards Bill and looked him straight in the eye. He didn't say anything but Bill could read his mind. It was an apology, a desperate plea for forgiveness. Bill gave him a feeble, half-hearted grin. Not much of a consolation for someone facing a thirty-year stretch, but it was all he could manage.

They sent Jack Bassett to Dannemora Penitentiary and Willie the Actor went back to Sing Sing.

CHAPTER 8

AUGUST, 1931

Through the wire mesh that separated them, Bill gazed with longing at Louise. 'I'm sorry,' he mumbled over and over like a mantra. It was all he could think of saying and he began to wonder if he was losing his mind.

Louise gave him a sympathetic smile though tears glistened in her eyes, sparkling like the diamonds that had brought him so much trouble, brought him to this prospect of thirty years of hell. Never again would he make love to Louise; and never, like other normal fathers, would he see his daughter growing up. Eventually, like a clockwork toy winding down, he ended his apologies with a feeble, 'I wish I could turn back time.'

'So do I,' Louise whispered. 'But that's not possible.'

Bill shook his head feebly. He had longed for this visit but was now finding it awkward. He was no longer a part of her world and had become a stranger. The division between them was widening and he knew he was helpless to keep her from drifting away from him for good. Pretty soon, he would be dead to her. She would be a widow, grieving for a while, and then he would become a distant memory.

'I'm glad you came,' he managed after an uncomfortable hiatus. 'I wish you could have brought Jenny.'

She shook her head. 'Not a good idea, Bill.'

'I know, but...if only I could have seen her once more. It might have kept me going. Given me hope.'

'As long as she's a child...' Louise began awkwardly, then blushed and avoided looking at him.

'You're right,' he managed, knowing what she was about to say. 'She mustn't know about me. Not while she's of school age. Other children can sometimes be very cruel.'

Louise looked up and smiled at him. 'I'm glad you understand. Maybe when she's a lot older, I'll tell her about you. Maybe I'll tell her what a devoted and loving father you would have made. I know you're not a bad man, Bill. I just wish I could understand what made you do it.'

'I wish I could understand that myself,' he said, shrugging helplessly.

Louise sighed. 'I know I should have visited you before, but I couldn't stop crying. All night and every day. I just couldn't come to the court like that. I didn't want the newspapers to see me in such a state. I had Jenny to think about.'

Bill smiled knowing that, however soft and gentle Louise was, she was also a tower of strength and he was comforted by the thought that his daughter would have a mother to be proud of.

She returned his smile for a moment and then dropped her head. When she looked up again, her eyes were sharp and focused. 'I'm sorry,' she whispered.

He leaned forward so that his head was almost touching the partition. 'What do you have to be sorry for?'

'Thirty years is a long time, Bill.'

'There's my appeal,' he said. And even as he said it, he realized how weak it sounded. How much hope was there?

'I can't face thirty years of visiting you in this way. I'm sorry.'

Like a stone falling into a deep well, he heard the distant splash as his hopes for any future vanished.

'You mean you won't be coming back,' he said, unable to keep the tremor out of his voice.

'I'm sorry. I can't.'

'For Jenny's sake,' he prompted.

'Yes, for Jenny's sake,' she replied.

Two weeks after Louise's visit, Bill lay on his back in his cell. In his raised hand he held a photograph of Jenny and he stared at it for ages, his arm growing tired, so that every so often he would drop it back on to the bed and drift into a reverie about his wife and daughter, imagining the perfect life that might have been.

Following her visit, Louise wrote to him enclosing the snapshot of Jenny, snug in her baby bonnet, staring at the camera intently. In her letter, Louise gave Bill snippets of domestic and social news as though his crimes had never been committed and he was now a distant relative with a need to be updated on family matters.

She said she was now living with her mother and Bill was comforted by the thought that his daughter had a devoted grandmother as well as a loving mother to look after her.

However soothing these thoughts of Jenny's upbringing were, the thoughts inevitably turned sour as he was forced to dwell on his own predicament and the wheel turned full circle as he was brought to the point of deep depression. He was reminded that this small cell would be his home for the next thirty years. And he knew that, if he had been given a sentence of ten or even fifteen years, he might have been prepared to do his time as a model prisoner.

But there was no way he could face a never-ending thirty-year stretch. He would be over sixty by the time the gates opened for him. Up until that time, this lousy little cell would be his entire world. No, there was no way he was going to remain here as a guest of Uncle Sam.

In the two years since he had been at Sing Sing, there had been major changes in security. A new thirty-five foot high concrete wall had been built around the prison and he was incarcerated in a new cell block that was considered to be escape-proof. Four locked steel doors lay between his cell and the yard outside. He realized the outlook was bleak unless his appeal to the Appellate Division was successful. If not, he needed a contingency plan. He brightened considerably once he put his mind to working out a way of escaping from this hellhole.

CHAPTER 9

NOVEMBER, 1932

During their exercise break in the yard, Johnny Eagan, wearing a large padded glove, casually tossed a ball in the air, and walked over to where Bill stood leaning against the wall by the dining hall. Eagan was tall and lean, blond-haired and blue-eyed and, apart from a crooked nose broken in a boxing tournament, was considered to be quite good-looking.

He once had a reputation as a good all-round sportsman, but became something of an 'also ran', due to his fondness for liquor. As soon as he opened his mouth to speak, Bill detected the harsh-sweet smell of liquor on his breath.

'Okay,' Eagan said. 'Let's play a little handball.'

He handed Bill a glove and they both walked along the wall to where a handball court was marked out. Although he was wary of forming an alliance with a guy who had a reputation as a drinker, if ever he was to escape from Sing Sing, Bill knew he had to have Eagan's assistance. Eagan was the prison repairman and had access to most places in the penitentiary. And, like Bill, he was serving a long stretch for robbery and had little to lose by attempting an escape.

'Careful!' Eagan cautioned as Bill slid on the glove. 'You don't want to cut yourself.'

Inside the middle finger of the mitt, he felt the hacksaw blade jabbing into his palm. He closed his fingers around it, glanced over his shoulder to make sure no guards or other inmates were watching and, keeping the glove close to his stomach, he slid the blade out and into his shirt.

It lay cool against his skin, lodged between the waistband of his pants. He slipped the glove back on, as Eagan began knocking the ball against the building. With barely a glance in his partner's direction, Bill spoke the way most cons did, hardly moving his lips and out the side of his mouth.

'You told me you were off the sauce, Johnny,' he said, returning Eagan's serve. 'Two years you said.'

Bill knew that certain jailers were prepared to sell hard liquor to prisoners with connections on the outside and willing to make a payment. There were also some prisoners talented enough to build small stills in which to ferment raw spirits. Inside the pen alcohol was readily available for the right price. And if Eagan had now slipped back off the wagon, it was worrying.

Deliberately missing Bill's return, Eagan stooped to pick up the ball and mumbled, 'It was only a small drop, Bill. Nothing to get excited about. Can't a man have a drink on his birthday?'

Bill stared at the wall as he replied, 'Happy birthday, Johnny. Try to stay sober for the rest of the week.'

'Will do.'

They began playing handball again, holding a conversation without looking at each other. From a distance, guards would barely see their lips moving.

'Thanks for the blade,' Bill said. 'Getting over the wall's going to be the biggest headache. It's more than thirty-foot...'

Eagan interrupted him, 'I've located a couple of ladders in the cellar below the dining hall. We can lash them together.'

'I estimate we should be through those bars in about four days,' Bill said. 'We go on the night of the fifth.'

'What about the car?'

'It's all arranged. Patterson was released yesterday and he's got a guy on the outside willing to arrange it. It's going to cost, so we'll need to do a bank once we get out.'

'How about those doors, Bill? Think you can pick your way through the locks?'

'I had a very good tutor,' Bill replied, Doc Tate slipping briefly into his thoughts. 'One of the best in the business. He taught me everything he knew.'

Five nights later, just before midnight, a guard making his routine inspection shone his flashlight into Bill's cell. Bill feigned sleep as he felt it shining like bright sunlight through his closed lids. As soon as he heard the sound of keys and the door clanging shut as the guard left the landing, he rose hurriedly and rearranged the blankets so they formed an outline of his sleeping form.

He was already dressed. He drew his hacksaw blade out from under the pillow and slid it into the already sawn-through bar section of the cell door. There was one small section to go. He worked quietly, so that no other convicts would hear, and was through the small section of steel in less than a minute. He grabbed the bar and pulled it away.

He had fourteen minutes left before the guard returned. They routinely did their rounds every fifteen minutes. Bill had timed it over the last three months and they never varied their routine. Had they made random checks, then he and Eagan would have stood little chance of escape. It was because of this loophole, and because this cell block was considered escape-proof, that gave them at least a slim chance of escape. If only he could pick his way through at least three locks on the steel gates. But first he had to get Eagan.

He breathed in and squeezed his way through the narrow gap between the bars of his cell door. A small sliver of jagged steel scraped against his stomach and caught the cloth of his shirt. There was a moment when he was halfway through when he felt he couldn't move either way, trapped and helpless, and he experienced the whimpering panic of a trapped animal.

He breathed in again and, with one final effort, he was through. He shoved the section of steel bar back into place before walking stealthily towards Eagan's cell, keeping well away from the others in the tier, in case any other convicts heard him.

Although slimmer than himself, his accomplice was struggling to squeeze through. Bill grabbed him round the shoulders and tugged. He heard him gasp as he stepped out into the corridor.

Silently they made for the first steel door at the centre of the tier. Bill got to work with the lock pick. The clicking of the tumblers sounded intrusive and he prayed the noise didn't wake the other convicts. A sudden cough from one of the cells startled them and Bill was sweating now as he concentrated on turning the lock's tumblers.

Click. Less than thirty seconds and it opens. He has passed his old mentor's test with flying colors.

Bill felt Eagan breathing sharply, shallow and tremulous, as he pushed open the door. They hurried through, carefully closing it behind them, and walked quickly to the next steel door leading to the dining room.

Right away, he got to work with the slender pick. This lock proved to be harder than the first. He listened intently for the tumblers and, like a dentist jabbing at a stubborn tooth, he prodded and poked, but nothing was happening. As the minutes ticked by, the fear and impatience mounting in his partner increased his own body heat and the sweat dripped from under his arms. He could smell his own fear, an odor of rotting garbage, like the lousy prison food.

Eagan counted every second in his head. 'Five minutes,' he whispered. Bill ignored him and devoted all his attention to the lock, concentrating on the tumblers, shutting out all other sounds.

Finally, the lock clicked loudly in Bill's ear. He pushed open the door, feeling the relief surging through him as they entered the dining hall. Eagan led the way across the hall to a door at the far end. This was an ordinary door with a commonplace lock and he had this one unlocked in less than thirty seconds.

They knew they had to work extremely quickly because they had no sure way of knowing how long it was until the guard returned to do his rounds. They could only estimate the time they had taken and Bill thought they probably had six or seven minutes left.

They rushed down the metal staircase and entered the cavernous cellar. Stacked along a workbench were two ladders. Eagan had previously appropriated some copper wire and they hurriedly bound the two ladders together. Taking an end each of the ladders, they made their way back to the dining hall. There was just one more major steel door get through and then they would be out in the yard.

Bill knelt down and delicately inserted the pick into the lock with the sensitivity of a considerate lover. He knew he didn't have much time left. A minute or two at the most before the guards returned to do their rounds. He tried to concentrate, ignoring the rivulets of sweat pouring effusively from his armpits, backside, shoulders and forehead, and immediately drying cold as fear took hold.

'Jesus Christ!' he heard Eagan exclaim, as the terror of being stuck in the dining hall confronted him. They knew that, if they were caught, they faced a year - maybe longer - in the isolation block. A small pressure and the tumbler moved fractionally. One final delicate twist and it clicked into place.

'We made it,' Bill whispered.

Eagan patted him on the shoulder and walked quickly to the back end of the ladders. They lifted the ladders and Bill pushed open the heavy steel door. It was a dark night, no moonlight, and they knew if they ran under the shadow of the walls they might be in with a chance.

They had only one open yard to cross before reaching the high wall but they needed an element of luck now. The area was given scant attention because the prison authorities and guards considered the new high wall to be impregnable and the new cell block to be escape proof. Yet, it only needed one guard in the watchtower to see something moving down below, for the searchlight to pick them out, and they would be lucky if they didn't die in a hail of Tommy-gun bullets.

They came to the corner of the building. Bill looked up at the watchtower. It was too dark to see anything very much. He thought he saw the outline of a guard and waited a brief moment. It was so dark, he hadn't a clue whether the guard had his back to the yard or was facing it. If he couldn't tell, he reasoned, it might work in their favor. The dark could give them the cover they needed.

'Okay,' he said. 'Let's go.'

They ran the twenty yards or so across the yard, expecting a searchlight to pick them out at any moment, followed by a screaming siren. But all remained silent and dark, as they raised the ladder against the wall. Eagan scrambled up first followed closely behind by Bill. The ladder ended four-feet from the top of the wall and they both pulled themselves up.

Now they faced the worst part of their escape: the long drop from the wall. They both knew they might suffer a serious sprain or break an ankle. What the hell! Bones would heal in months and what was that compared with a lifetime of rotting away in a small cell.

Eagan hung for a moment from his hands, then pushed himself outwards from the wall. Bill did the same. The ground rushed up to meet him. As he landed, he bent at the knees. He felt his body jar as if his spine was being wrenched in two. He rolled over on to his side and lay still for a moment. He wiggled his ankles. One of them pained him, but it didn't seem too severe; there didn't seem to be a break or a sprain. Eagan was already on his feet as he struggled to stand up.

'How are the ankles, Johnny?'

'Bit painful, but no serious damage.'

'Right let's find that Buick,' Bill said.

They found it parked on a hill that ran from Ossining towards the penitentiary. The door was open and the key was in the ignition. Their contact had done the right thing: a parked car never arouses suspicions, as long as no one is behind the wheel.

Bill jumped into the driver's seat and turned the ignition key. The engine spluttered and died. Despite the pitch black, from the corner of his eye he sensed Eagan's anxious expression and heard him coughing nervously. He turned the key again and this time the engine roared into life, as he pressed the accelerator. Bill grinned at Eagan.

'Right,' he said. 'Let's head for New York City.'

The address they'd been given was on the Upper West Side. It was an unobtrusive and somewhat dingy basement apartment, but at least it was somewhere safe to hide out until the dust settled.

Bill tried the door and it opened. A smell of damp hung in the air like a wet towel and a sharp odor of decay greeted them. With a sense of despair, Bill fumbled for a light switch in the darkness, his hand running along the uneven, crumbling plaster walls. He found it and clicked it on, but nothing happened. Gradually his eyes adjusted to the darkness of the dingy hallway and he saw a razor-thin beam of light glowing from under a door at the far end of the hall.

'Come on,' he whispered. 'Let's see if we've got a welcoming committee.'

The dust tickled Eagan's nostrils and he sneezed violently as Bill pushed the door open.

'Bless you!' John Doyle said from where he sat, sprawled in a decaying armchair, a glass of bourbon in his hand. As they entered, Bill noticed the hungry look that came into his partner's eyes when he spotted the bourbon bottle at Doyle's feet.

Doyle rose and shook both their hands. He was an angular-looking man, as if his features had been sculpted. His nose was sharp and he had sea-green eyes and receding salt-and-pepper hair. As he smiled, his mouth glittered with several gold teeth. He was lean and trim, like a dancer, and wore a tuxedo with a carnation in the buttonhole.

'You made it bang on time,' he said.

'We cut across the state and came down the east side,' Bill said.

'Smart move,' Doyle agreed. 'Though I expect they're still searching the woods around Sing Sing.'

Bill gave him an impish grin. 'We were probably halfway across the state before they noticed we'd gone.'

Doyle nodded, shrugged apologetically, and gestured at the surroundings. 'Best I could do. Still, I guess it's only temporary.'

Eagan figured he ought to contribute to the conversation. 'Thanks for providing the car. Without it, we'd never have made it.'

Doyle smiled thinly at him. It lacked warmth and Bill observed that Doyle's green eyes were cold as marble and he knew the friendly, outgoing chap in the tuxedo was as phony as bootlegged Scotch whiskey. He sensed that Doyle was cast in the same mould as Dutch Schultz and there was a violent streak that lurked beneath the affable disguise, a nastiness that had grown over the years and left its indelible mark on the gangster's reptilian features.

'Ah yes, the Buick,' Doyle said slowly. 'Any idea how you might pay for it?'

'Don't worry,' Bill assured him. 'You'll get your money.'

Doyle sniffed loudly and his mouth took on a pinched look, as if he doubted Bill's word. 'That's ten grand for the car, five grand for this fleapit, and three hundred percent interest on your pocket money.'

He fumbled in his breast pocket and removed his pocket book. He rifled through a wad of money then handed it to Bill.

'That's two grand. That'll be another five you owe.'

Eagan gave a low whistle. 'That's twenty grand for a car and apartment...' he said. 'Rich pickings!'

Doyle looked sharply at him. 'You have a problem with that?'

Eagan's face colored. 'Hell, no! N-no,' he stammered. 'I was just saying…'

'Okay,' Doyle snapped, suddenly brisk and businesslike. 'I won't keep you gentlemen. There's no rush to deliver, but I'll give you, say, three months. You should be able to pull something off during that time.'

'Don't worry, Mr. Doyle,' Bill said. 'You'll get your money.'

Doyle turned at the door, his face expressionless. 'Oh, I'll get my money all right. I always do.'

They waited until they heard the main door slam. Eagan, who realized he had been holding his breath, exhaled loudly. 'Jesus Christ!' he exclaimed. 'What a dump.'

Bill cast his eyes around the room. Wallpaper was green in places where the damp had turned to mildew and the threadbare carpet was pitted with burns and cigarette butts. The room was pathetically furnished with junk, everything broken and dilapidated. The only warmth came from a small, one-bar electric fire that gave off a tiny glow and little heat.

Bill breathed in the dank air and nodded thoughtfully.

'Don't worry, Johnny,' he said, 'we'll soon knock off a bank and then we'll be back on the East Side again. In clover.'

Johnny grinned and looked down at the bottle of bourbon. 'Things are looking up already.'

Bill bent over quickly and grabbed the bottle. It was only a quarter full, and that amount shouldn't seriously affect a drinker like Eagan, but he wasn't taking any chances.

'No liquor before work, Johnny. You promised.'

A childlike whine entered Eagan's tone. 'Aw, Bill. Just a little celebration. Whaddaya say?'

Bill opened the door of the kitchenette, his knuckles white as he clutched the bottle tightly, in case Eagan tried to grab it. 'I say this goes down into the sewers where it belongs. Once we've done a job, Johnny, you can hop off to Mexico and get drunk on the proceeds. Drink until it comes out of your ears for all I care. But not before we do a job.'

Eagan looked contrite, like a young boy. 'You got me all wrong, Bill. You got me all wrong. I promise.'

Bill smiled grimly, as he went into the kitchenette, and poured the remains of the bourbon into the filthy kitchen sink. 'I hope so, Johnny. I hope so.'

CHAPTER 10

DECEMBER, 1932

He checked his watch. It was almost 6.45. It would take him at least another hour to break into the safe and the security guard was due to arrive at eight. It was arranged that Eagan would have the car waiting outside in fifteen minutes' time, and he needed to tell him to go away and come back at 7.45. He didn't want him parked outside the bank for over an hour where he might arouse the suspicions of a passing cop.

A small Brooklyn bank, Bill had picked it because of its location. It was on the corner of an alley on the opposite side to the Keith Theatre. If a cop did happen to ask Eagan why he was loitering outside, they had a story ready that he was waiting to pick up an electrician after having worked an all-nighter at the theatre.

He knew he'd be cutting it fine, allowing only fifteen minutes before the arrival of the security guard. The reason he was behind was because of ceiling bars which he hadn't anticipated. He realized it was dumb of him. He should have guessed that the bank would reinforce their ceiling.

The bank was below a small shopping mall on the second floor and, at closing time on the previous evening, he concealed himself in the gents' toilet. He had broken into a clothing store and had dug up the floor to get to the bank below. That was when he discovered the ceiling was reinforced and it took him an hour to saw through them.

Once he dropped into the bank, he disabled the alarm and sawed through the bars of the side window facing the theatre's stage door entrance. So far, so good. Now he was an hour behind and he needed to warn Eagan.

Making certain the stage door was shut, he raised the bank window and dropped into the alley. He walked briskly to the main street and looked for Eagan's car. He was driving a six-year-old Model T Ford because not only had it been cheap to purchase it was also quite commonplace. In fact there were several Model Ts parked along the street. But not Eagan's. He should have been there by now.

Bill checked his watch again. It was 6.48. He'd risk loitering for another couple of minutes, but no longer. He needed Eagan. Without him, there was no way of escaping with the money. A helpless, impotent feeling caused him to shake inside and he became angered by Eagan's absence. All along he had doubts about his accomplice's reliability and now he was being proved right.

On the other hand, supposing Johnny had run into some sort of trouble? After all, his picture had been in the papers. He was a wanted man on the run. Maybe he'd been spotted and apprehended. Or perhaps it was nothing more than a simple explanation, like the car not starting. As he stood on the sidewalk, blowing hot air into his leather gloves and shivering from the early morning cold, he felt depressed.

Bill felt another surge of anger. A voice nagged away in his brain, telling him how unreliable Johnny was. He reminded himself that, had it not been for Johnny Eagan, he wouldn't now be a free man. Positive and negative thoughts bounced back and forth as he stood on the edge of the sidewalk, craning his neck hopefully, praying that Eagan was delayed due to some minor reason.

As he waited and tried to confront the disappointment biting into him, he began to despair. He'd been so close to getting a good haul from this small bank. They could have paid off Doyle and maybe still had plenty to tide them over for a while.

In the distance, about five hundred yards along the street, he saw a blue uniform darting in and out of the shadows. A cop! There was a lightness in his gait and he was swinging his nightstick jauntily. Probably ending his nightshift, he guessed, on his way back to the station.

He was coming towards Bill, getting closer and closer. Pretty soon he'd arouse the cop's suspicions. He glanced at his watch once more. It was 6.55. Eagan was a good ten minutes late and it didn't look as if he was going to show. Bill turned and headed for the nearest subway, his anger against Johnny rising and falling. Where was he?

Back at the apartment, Bill stood in the shadows outside for a long while watching the building, just in case his partner had been apprehended, worked over and told the police everything. After ten minutes - a long ten minutes that had him shivering from the cold - everything seemed to be normal. There was nothing to arouse his suspicions. The street was waking up. People were setting off for work, their reluctance for the daily grind showing in their demeanors.

He decided to risk it. He began crossing the street and a warning bell rang as a man on a bicycle raced towards him, a canvas lunch bag strapped across his chest. The normality of the street reassured him and he gave the cyclist a friendly wave as he walked towards the apartment.

As soon as he entered, he heard a rumbling noise coming from the living room and right away he knew what had happened. He knew he'd been right not to trust Eagan. He opened the door, just to make certain and, sure enough, there was his partner, fully clothed on the sofa, snoring loudly, an empty rum bottle held against his breast like a comfort blanket.

'So long, Johnny,' he muttered. He went into the bedroom, grabbed his small suitcase, shoved the few clothes he owned into it and left the building. He had already split Doyle's

$2,000 with Johnny, and now he had only $700 left, but he reasoned, if he acted prudently, it was enough to last until he could pull off a few small burglaries to pay Doyle what he owed. Then he would see about planning a major bank robbery. But for now, he needed to get himself a decent apartment and tell Johnny Eagan that he was dissolving their partnership.

He knew that when Johnny came round and realized what had happened, he'd be full of abject apologies. He would have that alcoholic's optimism, the unrealistic expectations of being forgiven, truly believing it was a temporary fall from grace and, in future, things would be different. Well to hell with that!

Bill was not taking any more risks. Eagan was dangerous on two counts. Not only did the booze make him unreliable, but there was also the female company he kept. He was having an affair with Frank Costello's mistress. Costello was one of the deadliest of New York's gangsters whose associates included Meyer Lansky, Charlie Luciano and Bugsy Siegel. Johnny was playing with fire and this made Bill even more determined to sever their relationship. He didn't owe him a thing. After all, without his lock-picking expertise, Johnny would still be serving time. They were even.

Bill knew Johnny had a date to meet Costello's girl at a speakeasy that evening. After he'd found himself a room in the Bronx, passing himself off as a traveling salesman, he set off for the Garment District of Manhattan, intent on finding Johnny and giving him the bad news.

It was a terrible evening. Heavy rain lashed against the sidewalks as if New York was in a monsoon season, but the stinging coldness that came with the rain scotched any thoughts of tropical rainstorms. Bill knew it was useless to use an umbrella as he passed people battling with theirs turned inside out against the harsh wind, spokes mangled beyond repair. By the time he reached the speakeasy, he was soaked through to his underwear and rain cascaded off the brim of his hat and ran down his back. He shivered intensely as he entered.

The speakeasy was hardly swinging. It was more like a funeral parlor. The music was turned low and the atmosphere was somber. A bartender absently flicked the pages of a tabloid and barely looked up as Bill entered. The only customers present were Johnny and Frank Costello's girl.

If the rain had deterred most of this speakeasy's customers, he reflected grimly, it hadn't stopped Johnny whose face was flushed from alcohol and his eyes were glassy. They were so wrapped up in each other they didn't notice him and the girl giggled as Johnny leaned close to her and said something suggestive.

As Bill stood over their table, Johnny looked up. It took a moment for him to register who it was before he cracked a smile.

'Bill,' he said, oozing well-oiled charm. 'How you doing?'

'You forgotten something, Johnny?'

A momentary expression of incomprehension flashed across Eagan's face, then a sudden realization. 'Jesus, Bill! I forgot. It went clean out of my head.'

'That's because *you* were out of your head, Johnny.'

'I swear to you, Bill, it'll never happen again.'

'You're right,' Bill replied. 'It won't happen again. You and I are through, Johnny.'

'Hey! Now wait a minute...' Eagan protested. 'You can't do that. What about Doyle? We need to do a job to pay Doyle.'

'You should have thought of that last night before you went out and got loaded.'

'It was a m-mistake,' Eagan stammered. 'A fucking mistake.'

Eagan's head dropped forwards as though a wire holding it up had been cut and he stared miserably into his drink. Bill noticed Frank Costello's girl was studying him with great interest. Maybe it was because he had the upper hand. She was the usual gold-digging good-time girl, attracted to men like

Costello and Eagan. Trophies for her bedroom shelf. She gave Bill her sexiest smile, shrugging off the loser and favoring the winner. Bill ignored her.

'No hard feelings, Johnny,' he said. 'I wish you luck.'

Eagan slurped some liquor noisily, and it gave him the impetus he needed. He rose and shook a finger at Bill. 'You can't do this. Not after what I've done for you. I got you out of Sing Sing, remember?'

'Keep your voice down,' Bill hissed.

'If it wasn't for me,' Eagan ranted, 'you'd still be sitting in a fucking five-by-nine.'

Bill glanced nervously at the bartender who was now paying them particular attention. He knew there was only one way to get Eagan to shut up.

'Okay, Johnny,' he said. 'We'll talk about this later. In private. When you haven't had a drink.'

Bill turned abruptly and walked towards the door. He could feel the bartender's eyes boring into him as he left the speakeasy. He heard Eagan calling after him, 'Okay! We'll talk later, Bill. We'll sort something out.'

Bill had no intention of talking to Johnny Eagan ever again. He would work on his own for a while, do some burglaries like he and Doc used to do back in the early twenties, which would provide him with enough money to pay off Doyle. Technically speaking, he realized Eagan owed Doyle half. But he didn't think his ex-partner would ever conquer his addiction. And rather than work with a liability like Eagan, he would sooner pay Doyle the full amount himself.

Outside the speakeasy, rain was falling like a tap had been turned full on. Although he was soaked through, Bill couldn't stand the way the rain filled the brim of his hat, then trickled over and poured down his face and neck.

In the vain hope that it might ease off in a little while, he took shelter in the doorway of a barber's shop. There was a closed sign on the door and the shop was in darkness. He stood there shivering, wondering what his next move should be. Run to the nearest subway and head back to his room? He was trying to avoid the subway as much as possible.

His picture had been blasted over the front pages of all the tabloids and he didn't want to sit opposite anyone who could stare at him for any length of time wondering where they might have seen that face before.

As he stared at the driving rain, the bleakness of the night emphasized his feelings of loneliness. There was an aching emptiness inside him. He longed to see Louise and his baby daughter. He thought about how close they were. He was in the same city as them, less than twenty minutes on the subway, yet they might as well have been on the other side of the world. He couldn't hope to see them. He knew the cops would keep them under surveillance, just in case he decided to show up.

A car pulled up outside the speakeasy. From the shadows of the shop, Bill watched a man wearing a trench coat step out of the back of the car, while the driver stayed put, keeping the motor running. He was carrying a Tommy-gun, held down by his side. As he stepped inside the speakeasy, he raised the gun to waist level.

Bill felt helpless. He was unarmed and there was no way he could warn anyone without endangering his own life. He felt numb with the shock of what he knew was about to happen.

A brief moment passed until the sound he was expecting shattered the peace: a deadly staccato, the stuttering of the sub-machinegun as it spat out its lethal spray of bullets. Bill's body trembled and shook, and he knew this had nothing to do with the cold.

The man in the trench coat ran out, leapt into the car, and barely had the door shut before the driver gunned the engine and the car took off like a thunderbolt.

Oblivious now to the rain, Bill stepped out into the street, and made his way back to the speakeasy. As he swung open the door, the music from the radio was playing low and distant, like an eerie requiem, which accentuated the bar's solemn silence.

He approached Eagan's table and was filled with horror at what he saw. Blood formed great puddles on the floor like bright paint seeping slowly from a can. He looked away. There was nothing he could do. There was no sense in dwelling on the horror of the murder scene.

As he started to walk away, glancing quickly over the bar, he saw the bartender lying face down in a puddle of blood, senselessly gunned down simply because he was in the wrong place at the wrong time.

Bill got outside quickly. He wanted to put as much distance as he could between himself and the speakeasy. As he splashed through the heavy rain, he stopped several times to collect himself, bending over like he had cramps in his stomach.

He was trying to suppress an instinct to vomit. He induced saliva into his mouth and swallowed, eventually overcoming the need to be sick, and struggled on through the rain, his wet clothes clinging to his body.

He thought about his ex-partner, whose partnerships had been terminated twice in as many minutes. Eagan had been stupid having an affair with a mobster's girl. But had he deserved to die over it? And what of the girl? She was just a kid. Murdered, simply because of one man's damaged ego.

CHAPTER 11

MAY 1933

*A large bonfire lit a square in front of Berlin University
last night. The flames were not fed by logs or kerosene.
Books were burned - books the Nazis have decided are
'un-German'. And in Munich yesterday, thousands of
schoolchildren watched as books described as Marxist were
burned. "As you watch the fire burn these un-German
books," the children were told, "let it also burn into your
hearts: a love of the Fatherland."*

Bill sighed as he closed the paper. He loved books. More than
anything else it was what had kept him sane during his prison
stretches, and the thoughts of burning books - any kinds of
books - filled him with dismay.

He dropped the paper on to the floor and lay back on the
sofa, his feet up on the armrest, and drew heavily on a
cigarette. He coughed and his chest hurt from the dryness of
it. A metal ashtray lay on the floor, brimming with cigarette
butts, spent matches and ash.

Usually meticulous and tidy, Bill had recently been careless
about his domestic standards. His heart was sinking rapidly
and he couldn't seem to do anything to block the fall into deep
depression and apathy. He was desperately lonely. He longed
to pick up the phone and call Louise, but knew it would be
foolish. The police probably had the phone tapped.

Feeling the heat from the tip of the cigarette burning his

fingers, he sat up quickly and ground it into the ashtray. He stared into space for several minutes. He needed to drag himself out of this rut. He knew he couldn't just sit around the apartment for the rest of the day. During the last two months he'd barely been out, except to pick up groceries and newspapers, and had spent most of his time reading or listening to the radio.

His apartment was on the third floor on East 97th, a district that tipped over into El Barrio, but at the same time was comfortably close to the more opulent streets below East 96th. It was a small but comfortable apartment and he'd been lucky in renting it, as few questions were asked once the landlord saw the color of his money.

He'd lived here for more than three months now and had rented it on the proceeds of three burglaries that had netted him $3,000 dollars, once he'd paid Doyle what he owed. He now had only $2,000 dollars left, a substantial enough sum, but it wouldn't last indefinitely and he needed to reconnoiter a few banks and start making plans. He'd need some accomplices and he knew that most of the joints where the criminal fraternity hung out was where he was most vulnerable and risked being caught.

He looked over at the window. A beam of sunlight streamed in, throwing a bright pool of warm yellow on to the drab carpet. After months of depressing rain and drizzle, sunshine was the tonic he needed and he snapped out of his ennui and made up his mind that he was going to go out somewhere. Anywhere.

He felt the need to walk in the long-awaited warm weather. But he had become so sedentary in recent months that, when he rose from the sofa, his body ached from the effort. He went over to a wall mirror and studied his reflection, smoothing his newly-grown moustache with an index finger. The face that stared back at him was nothing like the police photograph on the wanted posters and he seriously believed he could go to any police precinct and stand under one and nobody would recognize him.

He changed into a black, chalk-striped, double-breasted suit, checked his appearance in the mirror again before grabbing his hat. But there was something on his mind, something that made him stop and stare at the copy of the *New York Times* that lay on the floor by the sofa. It was as if it was trying to tell him something. What was it? He looked at the date: 11th May, 1933. There was something about it that was...

It came to him in a flash and he smacked the heel of his palm on to his forehead. Of course, it was Jenny's birthday. His beautiful baby daughter was two years old today. How could he have forgotten such an important date? He should have sent her a gift. Or a card, at least.

He remonstrated with himself for forgetting and wondered how he could rectify the oversight. Western Union. That was it. He'd send her a telegram. He realized that it would be meaningless to a two-year-old, but he felt the need to send it anyway. Maybe in years to come, his lovely little girl might appreciate the telegram she'd received from her daddy on her birthday.

Bill intended taking a long walk in the sunshine, maybe through Central Park but, after he'd sent Jenny the birthday telegram, he felt desperately lonely. So much so that it seemed to hurt him physically, a pain that stretched across his chest. Or maybe that was the tobacco. Perhaps he was smoking too much. He made up his mind that he'd try to cut down. As soon as he'd made this resolution, he noticed a neon sign for Lucky Strike cigarettes, saying: *It's toasted.* Immediately, he wanted to light up but he resisted the urge.

He wore his loneliness in the way he slouched along, shoulders hunched, hands embedded deeply in his pants' pockets. He passed the Roseland Dancehall where any man could get dance with a dime-a-dance hostess, provided he had ten cents to spare. Although he hadn't been on a dance floor for many years, Bill considered himself a reasonably able dancer and he felt in need of some female company, even if it meant paying for the privilege.

He realized it was still quite early and things might not be in full swing yet. Inside the dancehall it was surprisingly busy, with dozens of men like him desperate for some female company. He reminded himself most were good honest men, maybe unemployed, waiting and hoping for Roosevelt's New Deal to have some significant effect. Not living off the fruits of armed robbery like him. These poor Honest Joes had to cherish each dance and make each ten cents count.

Onstage a band played "Stormy Weather", and a crooner sang smoothly into a closely held microphone...."since my gal and I ain't together, I'm weary all the time..."

The words echoed his feelings. He needed to put some action back into his life. The only times he felt truly alive were at high risk time when he was relieving a bank of its money or when he was in the arms of a beautiful woman.

He purchased two dollars' worth of tickets and looked around at the dancing couples. Right away, he spotted a truly attractive girl, maybe in her mid-twenties, her brunette hair bobbed and shiny, with a cute little button nose and full lips. She was dancing with a tall, lanky guy, who stared down at her and grinned, moving zombie-like, as if he'd never danced with a real girl before and couldn't believe his luck.

When the number petered out the man looked awkward and lost, and his smile faded as he backed away from her, nodding his thanks. Bill watched him carefully. He felt sorry for the guy, shy and out of money, using a dime to buy a fantasy that the attractive girl who danced with him would become his lover. Like most of the men at Roseland, hope was the one luxury he could afford.

As soon as the man had shuffled off, Bill went over to the girl,and handed her a ticket. 'Care to dance?'

'It's why I'm here,' she replied, slipping the ticket into a small purse strapped diagonally across one shoulder.

The band started playing a more up-tempo number and she slid a hand into his, while he slid his other hand around her waist. She smelled vaguely of roses and the linen of her dress felt cool to his touch, despite the heat in the dance hall.

They danced a foxtrot, weaving around the other couples on the crowded dance floor and only occasionally bumping against them. Every time they did, his partner giggled.

'How long is it since you danced?' she asked him.

'It's been a while,' he admitted. 'But at least I haven't stepped on your feet.'

Her eyes flashed teasingly as she looked into his. 'Don't count your chickens.'

Her attractiveness and easy manner were so disarming that he lost concentration and stepped on her toes. 'See what I mean?'

'Sorry,' he mumbled, and he felt a slight pressure on his hand as she squeezed it reassuringly. From then on he concentrated on the foxtrot, avoided looking into her eyes, and managed to dance with reasonable agility. As soon as the dance ended, he took another ticket from his pocket and offered it to her.

'My name's Bill.'

'Jean… Jean Courtney.'

The next number was "Love Letters in The Sand", and he was relieved that it was slower. As they shuffled around the dance floor, he gazed into her eyes, making it obvious that he found her attractive.

'So, Jean, where are you from?'

'Pennsylvania.'

'And what brings you to New York City?'

'I want to pursue an acting career.'

You and hundreds of other girls, Bill thought. It must have shown on his face.

'Is there something wrong with that?' she asked.

He felt guilty. 'Of course not. I think that's a great career to have.'

'Then why did you frown?'

'I wasn't aware that I did.'

'It was only a tiny frown, but a frown all the same.'

Her eyes twinkled as she spoke, and he was conscious he was being teased.

'Please accept my apologies for the frown. I'll try not to let it happen again.'

'It's your dance. You paid for it. You can frown all you want.'

He laughed.

'And what do you do for a living, Bill?'

'I sell insurance.'

'You work for a particular company?'

'Freelance.'

She ran the jacket lapel of his expensive suit through finger and thumb. 'You must be pretty good at it.'

'I get by.'

'These are hard times. You don't look as though you suffer much hardship.'

'Well,' he muttered, averting his gaze from hers, 'I work hard, I guess.'

They danced in silence for a while. As the band came to the end of the number, Bill asked, 'Fancy some dinner sometime?'

She seemed both amused and flattered by the offer. 'Let me think about that.'

Bill, his confidence growing, smiled at her. 'Meanwhile, can I buy you a soda?'

He could see her deliberating, assessing his interest in her, and he thought she was about to acquiesce when they were interrupted by a man in a striped blazer. He looked hale and hearty, an out-of-towner putting on a show of enjoying himself.

'Great band,' he announced. 'Mind if I ask the little

lady for a dance?'

'Sure. Go ahead,' Bill replied, trying not to sound too miffed.

The man handed over his ticket. 'May I have the next dance, Miss?'

The band struck up "I Got Rhythm", and Bill watched Jean and her partner for a while. The man was a much better dancer than him and Bill felt disappointed. If it was a case of prowess on the dance floor, he hadn't been much of a catch.

He decided he needed more practice and asked another girl to dance. This time he concentrated hard on dancing, paying little attention to his partner, and his co-ordination and rhythm seemed to improve. He had three more dances after that, each time with different girls, so that he could adapt to a variety of styles and movement. Then he decided he'd ask Jean for another dance.

He cast his eyes round, focusing on all the hostesses in turn. He couldn't seem to single her out at all. Then he spotted her at a corner of the dance hall talking to a man with dark, slicked-backed hair. There was something familiar about him.

Bill stared for some time and watched while the man smiled and charmed Jean, waving his hands about, telling his usual lies, no doubt. Weaving between dancing couples, Bill hurried over to rescue her. As he arrived, the man was taking out a pencil and small notepad and was about to get her telephone number or address. Bill tapped him on the shoulder.

'Hello, Frankie.'

The man turned to look at Bill. 'Who are you?'

Any congeniality put on for Jean's benefit vanished.

'This here's my cousin Jean, Frankie,' Bill said. Then turning to Jean, he told her, 'This is Frankie Marshall. Frankie acquires women to work in one of his, shall we say, houses of ill-repute.'

Jean's mouth fell open. 'He told me he was a theatre producer.'

Bill laughed humorlessly. 'It's his usual opening gambit.

The only thing Frankie produces is women for clients.'

The pimp regarded Bill with loathing and squinted as he tried to place him. 'If I knew who you were, I'd tell you to mind your own business.'

Unruffled, Bill told him, 'I worked for the Dutchman a few years back. I remember you provided girls for him. These were some of the classier types. Not your usual three-dollar hookers. And don't tell me to mind my own business, Frankie. Jean's my cousin. So it *is* my business.'

Perhaps it was the mention of working for Dutch Schultz that did it, but the pimp shrugged hugely. 'Okay. No offence, pal. No offence.'

He patted Bill on the shoulder, as if they were the best of friends, and vanished into the throng milling about waiting for the next dance.

Jean stared at Bill for a long time before speaking and he could tell there were dozens of thoughts flitting through her mind.

'Thanks for rescuing me,' she said. 'That man, I take it, was a pimp.'

Bill nodded. 'One of the lowest of maggots in this big apple.'

'And what about you, Bill?'

He raised his eyebrows quizzically, and waited for the inevitable question. 'How is it you seemed to know him so well? Did you sell him some life insurance?'

Bill grinned at her. 'It's a long story,' he said. 'Why don't I tell you about it over dinner?'

CHAPTER 12

JUNE, 1933

Jean lay with her head on Bill's shoulder and gently kissed his skin, her fingers idly twirling the hairs on his chest. She could sense his deep contentment from his breathing which was like a gentle breeze, calm and cooling in what promised to be another scorching day.

'Bill,' she whispered, 'that was terrific, honey. It gets better and better.'

'It was wonderful,' he acknowledged. 'Out of this world. Although words seem feeble to describe the way I feel when I make love to you.'

She giggled playfully. 'Some people have a way with words, Shakespeare, for instance. He wrote "increase of appetite grew by what it fed on." What exactly did he mean by that?'

'That was Hamlet describing the way his mother loved his father.'

'She must have loved him deeply.'

'Actually, she betrayed him a month later.'

She felt Bill's body stiffen as he stopped breathing evenly. She sat up and leant across him, staring deep into his eyes.

'That'll never happen to us,' she said. 'I promise you, Bill. I love you too much. You know I worry about you, every time you go out on the street.'

'I know you do,' he said.

And it was true. She liked to accompany him wherever he went. She knew if she was with him he was less likely to be apprehended because they looked like any normal couple going out together and he stood less chance of being spotted by a vigilant policeman.

She smiled wistfully and stroked the back of her hand across his cheek. 'You don't regret telling me.'

'Of course not. I trust you, Jean.'

He had told her about his escape from Sing Sing before she moved in with him. He needed someone he could trust. He knew he was taking a risk but, as he had no intention of making his life complicated by being unfaithful to her, he had no reason to worry about her loyalty. And she had already guessed that he worked on the wrong side of the law. Her suspicions had been aroused when he'd rescued her from the pimp during their first meeting.

They trusted each other. And they had a great deal in common. She came from Harrisburg, Pennsylvania. Her father was a supervisor in a cigarette factory and, like Bill, she hadn't got on particularly well with her parents. She had two younger brothers and, being male, they were considered to be much more important in the pecking order.

She did well in English and literature at high school and she was expected to work in an office as a secretary where she would no doubt meet some eligible young man, then settle down and have a family. But her love of literature and plays had given her a taste for something different, something important and life-enhancing, and she became ambitious and dreamed of fame and fortune in New York City. Her parents disapproved and she arrived in New York without their blessing.

Not long after her escape from Harrisburg, she found herself working as a dime-a-dance hostess at Roseland, hoping, like many other attractive girls, to hit the big time. But after attending a few auditions over the following six months, fame and fortune seemed as elusive as they had been back in Harrisburg.

Then, on that first dinner date with Bill, she discovered his love of books and a shared love of Charles Dickens, in particular, and right away they hit it off and Jean's optimism returned.

Although he'd been honest in telling Jean about the bank robberies and his escape from Sing Sing, he still couldn't bring himself to be entirely open with her. He neglected to tell her about his marriage to Louise and about his baby daughter. He didn't feel particularly guilty about this as it was more a sin of omission than a downright lie. Life was complicated enough as it was and it wasn't as if he was able to make contact with Louise. Their life together was over.

He glanced at the bedside clock. It was late in the morning and he had an important meeting at noon. Sensing his sudden restlessness, Jean said, 'What time are you meeting this man?'

'I'm meeting Eddie in an hour. So I'd better get a move on.'

'I worry about you going out on your own.'

'I'll be fine.'

Bill pecked her on the cheek, climbed out of bed and went to the bathroom. As he began to lather his cheeks and gazed at his reflection, he knew he'd have to be really unlucky to get caught by someone identifying him. Sure, the added precaution of going everywhere with Jean offered him extra protection, but he could hardly bring her in on his meetings with Eddie, that would have made her an accessory to their next bank job.

He'd been lucky bumping into Eddie Wilson after all those years. Eddie was one hundred percent trustworthy. It was with Eddie he'd done the job on the safe with oxy-acetylene back in 1924, the job that got them both sent down for a five stretch. On his release, Eddie dabbled in small-time crime and hadn't been caught for so much as a parking ticket since then.

They were planning to hit a bank on the Lower East Side, but this time Bill wanted a third man, someone to pull up in a delivery vehicle of some sort outside the bank just before it opened, so that they could make a quick getaway, then switch vehicles in a quiet part of Brooklyn.

Eddie told him he knew a driver who was reliable. His name was Joe Pelango. Again Bill had misgivings about working with an Italian. Loads of Manhattan cops were Irish and, if Joe Pelango was picked up, Bill could imagine them saying, 'Okay, let's work the guinea over.'

The Irish were brutal where Italians were concerned.

But he needed a driver and, although he had Eddie's word that Pelango was reliable, he felt he ought to check the Italian out for himself.

Looking every inch the successful businessman, Bill caught a cab to Wall Street. He was heading for the Staten Island ferry and he was taking no chances. Just in case the cabby recognized him, he got out across the street from the New York Stock Exchange, paid the fare, walked briskly down Broad Street and vanished into the busy lunchtime crowds in Exchange Place, before walking briskly towards the ferry.

It was a blazing hot day and he was perspiring profusely by the time he reached the boat. As soon as he boarded, he leant over the rail at the stern and watched the seagulls gliding and swooping over the Statue of Liberty.

As it chugged across the water, the sea breeze was refreshingly cool and he began to feel relaxed. He didn't have a care in the world, even though the meeting was to assess their getaway driver and make final preparations for a bank robbery that would have all the papers screaming that it was another Willie the Actor job. For he planned on using the same method, this time wearing a police uniform.

Eddie Wilson's apartment on the island was on the top floor of a four-storey red brick building. It was a considerable walk from the ferry terminal and, by the time Bill reached Eddie's front door, he had to lean over to catch his breath and recover before ringing the doorbell. But, before he could push it, he heard some female voices and the door swung open. A girl about to leave started when she saw Bill.

'Sorry,' he offered. 'I didn't mean to startle you. I was just recovering from the walk and the four flights. I've come to see Eddie.'

She was a stunning redhead - probably no more than twenty, Bill guessed. Her fingernails were bright red talons that matched her lipstick. She wore expensive jewelry and flashed Bill a perfect set of teeth.

'You must be Bill,' she said. 'Eddie's told me all about you. I'm Lydia Romano, Eddie's girlfriend.'

Before Bill could reply, another young woman appeared in the doorway. She also had red hair but it was a less startling auburn color and she was more of a natural beauty.

'And this is my sister, Nina.'

Bill nodded. 'Pleased to meet you both.'

'Bill! Good to see you. Come in,' Eddie's voice boomed. He stood framed in the doorway, grinning like a Cheshire cat. He was in his thirties but still retained a boyish eagerness about him. He was clean-shaven and had sandy hair, with a longish fringe that fell over one eye, and he had an annoying habit of intermittently brushing it to one side.

'See you later, girls,' he called after the sisters. 'Don't spend too much money.'

His girlfriend waved a goodbye without turning round. He clapped Bill on the shoulder and brought him inside the apartment and into the living room.

'Let me introduce you to Joe Pelango,' Wilson said. 'Joe, this is Bill Sutton.'

The Italian was slouched in an easy chair and he acknowledged Bill with a laidback military salute.

Bill nodded. 'Good to meet you, Joe.'

He tried to take in Pelango at a glance. He was at least five or six years younger than Bill. Dark and Mediterranean-looking, olive-skinned, with high cheekbones and warm brown eyes, but his demeanor suggested the studied nonchalance of a tough guy. Bill was immediately on his guard.

'Yeah, and you,' Pelango said, after the two men finished sizing each other up. 'I been hearing from Eddie what a great plan you got for doin' this bank in the Financial District.'

Bill expected a slight Italian accent but there was no trace. It was nasal Bronx.

'We need a driver who can manage to be outside the bank exactly at the appointed time, but not a second before.' Bill said.

Pelango shrugged. 'That's no problem. I used to be a cabby.'

'And get us away from the bank with a minimum of fuss. In other words, positive driving but no daredevil stunts.'

Pelango grinned. 'Unless the cops get on to us.'

Eddie laughed and brushed the hair away from his eyes. 'Joe's your man. He worked a whiskey run across the Canadian border and he ain't never been caught.'

Bill stared at Pelango. 'That must be a good living. And if you're good at it and have never been caught, why try something as risky as armed bank robbery?'

'Because they reckon Roosevelt's gonna change the law. No more prohibition; no more smuggling.'

'Talking of which, anyone fancy a beer?' Wilson offered.

He fetched cold beers from the kitchen and all three drank thirstily. Bill talked over the finer details of their plan, going over it many times, testing the young Italian to see if he became impatient with the repetition. But Pelango seemed quite easy-going and was able to recount the plan in detail, including the hold-up inside the bank which wasn't relevant to him. Bill saw that Pelango knew he was being vetted and that he was trying to make a good impression.

He finished discussing the robbery and Pelango glanced at his watch. 'If we're all through here, I said I'd visit my mother. It's her birthday today and we're having a family celebration later.'

'Sure. Go ahead,' Bill replied.

As he left, Pelango gave him another affected salute. Once he'd gone, Bill sighed deeply and shook his head.

'What's wrong?' Wilson asked.

'It's just his manner. Something about him. He acts like a movie hood.'

Wilson laughed. 'Yeah, I know what you mean. Regular little James Cagney. At least he's good to his mother!'

There was a long silence, both men mulling over the enormity of the undertaking and whether they were doing the right thing using Pelango.

Wilson broke it. 'Look, he's a good bright guy. He's just a kid and they like to put on a bit of an act.'

'What worries me is whether he can separate that act from reality when it comes to crunch time,' Bill said.

'Believe me, he comes with a great pedigree,' Wilson argued, stabbing a finger in the air for emphasis. 'I promise you, Bill, he's reliable. We've done a few jobs together - nothing major, admittedly - but he's good. I wouldn't hesitate in giving him a platinum reference.'

Bill pondered before deciding he'd give the kid the benefit of the doubt. After all, not once had he referred to Bill as Willie the Actor which would have impressed most young men trying to act like a hoodlum.

'Okay,' he agreed. 'We'll use him.'

Roosevelt had just signed the National Recovery Act, the fastest bill ever to get through congress, so the robbery hadn't made the front page of the *New York Times*. Bill found it at the top of the second page, folded the paper, and handed it across the table to Jean. He watched her carefully as she read.

He suggested that she go out and buy the paper while he fixed breakfast, because he knew she would find out about the robbery sooner or later.

"WILLIE THE ACTOR STRIKES AGAIN!"

"Yesterday an armed robbery took place at the Union Bank of America in the Financial District of Manhattan and thieves

got away with an estimated sum of more than $80,000. The robbery bore all the hallmarks of William Sutton, still at large following his escape from Sing Sing prison last November. Two men, disguised as uniformed policemen, bluffed their way into the bank an hour before opening time and held up staff at gunpoint, as they arrived for work. Eyewitnesses saw the two men escaping in a blue delivery van, which was later found abandoned in a side street near Prospect Park in Brooklyn."

Jean placed the paper on the table by her coffee cup. Bill's police photograph stared up at her from the paper, daring her to believe she was calmly sitting at breakfast with New York's most wanted man. Her breakfast of ham and eggs remained untouched.

'Well,' he said, 'so now you know.'

A tinny sound came from the radio, the volume turned very low, but it was still too much of a distraction. She got up and switched it off. Although she knew almost from the start of their relationship how Bill made his money, it still came as something of a shock that she shared her bed with a man who might be sleeping in a police cell the very next day.

At first, the prospect of living with a bank robber had excited her. She had seen it as a great adventure. But, now that she had grown to love him, she knew she faced the very real danger of losing him.

When she returned to the table, she looked him straight in the eye. He gave her a reassuring smile. She began slowly, 'I wondered why you shaved off your moustache two days ago.'

'I wanted to be a clean shaven cop. I'll re-grow it now.'

He saw her hands were clenched tightly and she seemed to be struggling to control her emotions.

'How d'you feel?' he asked gently.

'Nervous.'

'I guess that's only to be expected.'

'Or perhaps I should change that to downright scared.'

He reached across and squeezed her hand. 'Not of me, I hope.'

She shook her head. 'No. I love you, Bill. That's what scares me. I don't think I could bear it if...'

Tears overwhelmed her and she heaved and sobbed. He leapt up and rushed to her side, holding her close, her head cradled in his side.

'Jean, Jean, my baby,' he soothed. 'Nothing'll happen to me. I promise you. Everything's going to be okay.'

He waited while her body shuddered. He could feel the wetness of her sobs through his shirt. He gently stroked her hair knowing that, once the tears were out of her system, she would calm down. Eventually, in a small quivering voice, she asked him to get her a handkerchief. He went into the bedroom, came back with one of his own, and handed it to her. She sniffed, then blew loudly into the linen, and wiped her eyes.

'It was the shock,' she explained. 'I'll be all right.'

'I'll lie low for a while, then we'll go to Philadelphia,' he said. 'I've been out of Sing Sing since last November and I'm still free. And the police photographs are nothing like me. There's nothing to worry about.'

She dabbed at her eyes with the handkerchief before looking up at him. 'Why Philadelphia?' she asked.

He paused. He had to tell her, but he didn't know how she would take it.

'One more job,' he said.

She frowned and her mouth half opened as if she couldn't quite comprehend what he was telling her.

'It's just one more bank before I retire,' he continued quickly. 'Eddie's already cased this one in Philadelphia and after that we can go away somewhere and start afresh. California, maybe. One last job, then we can take off to pastures new.'

CHAPTER 13

SEPTEMBER, 1933

He bought a copy of *The Philadelphia Inquirer* at the newsstand, strolled to a crowded bus stop and got on the end of the queue. Nonchalantly, he unfolded the paper and stared at the front page. This time they were the main story. A banner headline screamed across the top that a Philadelphia bank had been robbed of $160,000 by a New York gang and the police had quickly put two and two together and worked out that Willie the Actor was responsible.

He was now becoming more famous than Adolf Hitler whose policy of sterilizing people with hereditary diseases and disabilities in order to create a master race merited fewer column inches at the bottom of the page.

A bus came along and he eased himself away from the queue, walked to the corner of the next block and hailed a cab. He gave the cabby a phony address, just half a mile from Eddie Wilson's apartment, where he got out and walked the rest of the way. He wasn't particularly worried about being spotted.

While still in New York he had grown another moustache, which he had worn for the Philadelphia robbery, and padded his cheeks with cotton wool, coloring them to give himself a ruddy complexion and darkened his eyebrows. Immediately after the robbery, he had shaved the moustache and was now wearing spectacles with plain glass.

And his police photograph, which the newspapers were still using, was not a good likeness. It had been taken less than two years ago; he was thinner-faced then and much younger looking. Walking along, he felt comfortable, just one of the teeming populace. As long as he kept away from the places the bad guys hung out, such as racetracks and speakeasies, he felt safe.

He knocked on Eddie's door, their prearranged identifying knock, and Eddie opened it quickly and let him in. Joe Pelango was sitting in an easy chair, his legs dangling over the armrest. He gave Pelango a cursory nod and was surprised to find Nina Romano present sitting on a sofa, her shapely legs crossed, smoking a cigarette in a holder. Bill looked from her to Pelango and back again. He removed his glasses and tucked them in his breast pocket.

'Nina sweetheart,' Eddie said, 'fancy a little shopping expedition? Treat yourself, honey.'

She got up off the sofa, pressed her cigarette into the ashtray on a small occasional table and walked over to Eddie as he tugged a bundle of ten dollar bills from a wad. She moved close to him and kissed him full on the lips.

'How long's this expedition gonna take?' she said as he pressed the bills into her hand.

'Take a couple of hours,' Eddie told her and patted her on the backside as she left. With a grin, he turned to look at Bill who glared at him.

'What's wrong?'

'I thought you were going out with her sister.'

'I was.'

Bill felt the anger growing inside him. He'd never been a violent man, but he suddenly wanted to strike Eddie hard in the mouth, especially to wipe off that smug look on his face. Instead, he did what he always did and controlled himself.

'You're a fool, Eddie, a damned fool. As intelligent as a peanut. I told you what happened to Jack Bassett.'

Wilson looked serious and a trifle hurt. 'Relax, Bill. Lydia knows.'

'She knows?'

'Nina squared it with her sister. Everything's rosy.'

Bill frowned. 'You mean she didn't have any objections?'

Wilson shrugged. 'Well, maybe a little to begin with...'

Bill sighed and shook his head in disbelief. Wilson continued speaking hurriedly, 'But she's finally come to accept it. And Nina's seeing her at the end of the week. Everything'll be fine.'

'Lydia's coming to Philadelphia?'

Wilson shook his head. 'We're going to New York.'

'Are you kidding?' Bill thrust *The Philadelphia Inquirer* at Wilson. 'They know it's a Willie the Actor job, Eddie. They know we're from New York. You'd be better off lying low in Philly. They'll be expecting us to hightail it back to New York and they'll be on the lookout at all the ports of entry. Try going through the turnpikes and you could be in trouble.'

Wilson read the first paragraph of the robbery news and nodded in Pelango's direction. 'Joe's already worked that one out. We'll head upstate then come down from the north.'

'It's still risky.'

'At least we know the territory in New York,' Pelango said. 'We're strangers here. We feel...what's the word I'm looking for?'

'Vulnerable?' Bill offered.

'Yeah. If you say so.'

'Okay,' Bill reluctantly agreed. 'Let's agree to differ. But I'm staying here for a while.'

'Suit yourself.' Wilson grinned hugely and rubbed his hands gleefully. 'Now - it's pay day. And if I'm not much mistaken, $160,000 divided by three gives us each a handsome $53,000 plus. Not bad for a morning's work.'

Wilson's buoyant mood was infectious and Bill grinned back.

'Joe,' Wilson asked, 'would you be so good as to fetch the

loot? We've got some counting to do.'

Jean bought a good supply of food, and they stayed in their apartment the rest of the week. She was getting restless and worried. It was being cooped up that did it. Was this what it was going to be like for the rest of their lives, constantly looking over their shoulders? She felt the need to travel, go somewhere hot and sunny where she could feel they'd escaped. On Friday it rained and she stood at the window and watched the scene in the street below, grey and miserable, pedestrians and traffic limping slowly by. Bill, who was reading a Thomas Hardy novel, heard her sigh. 'What's wrong?'

'Oh, nothing.'

'Are you getting bored?'

'It's not boredom. I'm worried. If we stay indoors constantly, we might arouse someone's suspicions; that odd couple who never go out. People might start asking questions.'

'I'm happy to risk a walk if it'll make you feel better.'

She rushed instantly to the side of his easy chair, knelt on the floor and leaned affectionately against his leg. She looked up at him with a pleading expression and he could guess what she was going to say. 'When we were in New York, just after the Union bank robbery, you said you were thinking of retiring after this Philadelphia job. You said we might go to California. Let's go now, before it's too late.'

Bill hesitated. 'Er …yeah. We will go, but not just yet.'

'But why not?' she begged. 'What's to stop us?'

'I've got some business to take care of in New York first.'

'What sort of business?'

'I left someone with $10,000 to look after. I'll need to collect it.'

It was true he had left this amount of money in New York, only he hadn't given it to anyone to look after. Three weeks after the Union bank job, he returned to Prospect Park and buried the money behind the rhododendron bush. When he thought about it, it was an admission of defeat, burying it as insurance in case he was caught. He knew that if they caught him next time, they would throw away the key. *And there was no way he was ever going to serve out his time.*

But now Jean was urging him to go to the west coast, he thought of returning to Prospect Park to collect the money. This would give them $63,000 to start afresh.

Jean stared sadly into the distance. 'I have a terrible feeling about New York.'

He brushed her hair with the back of his hand. 'It'll be fine. I promise you.'

North of New York, Joe Pelango is driving through Washington Heights. Eddie Wilson sits in the passenger seat and Nina is in the back. The nearer to the centre of Manhattan they get, the more elated they become. Pelango tells them about his grandparents who came from Salerno in Southern Italy, and how he plans to use some of the money to take a trip to Italy, to see the land of his forefathers.

He is so busy dreaming and talking of this long vacation, he doesn't notice the black sedan that has been following them for about a mile. They stop at an intersection and the black sedan accelerates, pulls out on their left and screeches to a halt is it draws level with them. It all happens in an instant. None of them has much time to register the three men with guns clambering out of their car.

Eddie Wilson is the first to react as he tries to open his door. He has his hand on the handle as the bullet bursts through the window, narrowly misses Pelango, and enters his head at an angle. Pelango, frozen with fear, starts to raise his hands in surrender as another shot is fired. It is intended for Pelango but misses and blasts into the back of the car where it hits Nina Ramona's wedding ring finger. She doesn't feel much pain at first until she sees the blood and the gap where her finger should have been. She begins screaming hysterically.

Pelango starts yelling, 'Don't shoot. I'm not armed. Don't shoot.'

Eddie Wilson is taken to hospital, where it's discovered he will live, but will be blind for the rest of his life. The bullet has severed his optical nerve. Nina Ramona is also taken to hospital for treatment. Joe Pelango is taken into police custody where he is charged with armed robbery. He denies taking part in any robberies and says he was only hired by Eddie Wilson to drive him into town. Two Irish detectives and a uniformed sergeant take him down to the cells to question him. They also take a rubber hose with them.

On Saturday morning, while Jean cleared away the breakfast things, Bill read a news item on the front page of *The Philadelphia Inquirer* about Nazis in Germany sending hundreds of Jews to concentration camps such as Dachau. Thoughts of incarceration make him brood about escape and migration to a place of safety.

Life on the west coast would be relatively secure. He could forge a new identity for himself and start a small business and, for the first time in his life, he could go straight. The idea appealed. Suddenly he longed to kiss goodbye to Willie the Actor, the most wanted bank robber in the USA.

'Jean, don't bother with the washing up,' he said, as she was about to disappear into the kitchen with the breakfast plates. 'We're getting out of here.'

Her face lit up. She came back to the table and put the plates down.

'Where are we going?' she asked, the expression in her eyes pleading for the words she wanted to hear.

'We're going west.'

She hugged him. He felt the moistness in her eyes against his cheek. She looked at him with tears of happiness and he glowed with a new sense of purpose. At least he had a dream. He could make someone happy and be content with the more modest pleasures in life. But it was also time for action, for making plans, and for covering his back.

'When we leave this apartment,' he explained, 'they'll eventually put two and two together and find out it was none other than Willie the Actor who rented it. So here's what we do: we'll drive say a half-mile away from the station and leave the car in a side street. Then we'll catch a train somewhere, say Detroit or Chicago. They'll be on the lookout for New York State or Pennsylvania license plates, so we'll buy a car with Illinois plates. Then we'll head out west. See all those places we've only read about.'

She kissed him and squeezed him tight. 'Oh, Bill! I'm so excited. I can't wait.'

'You don't have to,' he said. 'We're going right away. Just an overnight bag each. To begin with we'll travel light.'

She beamed at him, her face radiant with excitement. She spun round and headed for the bedroom. 'I'll go and pack,' she said. Then she stopped at the door and turned to face him. 'What about your $10,000 in New York?'

Bill shrugged. 'In a year's time you'll probably want to come back to Pennsylvania to see your folks. The trail will have gone cold by then. We can come back east and I'll get my money then.'

She flashed him a grateful smile and vanished into the bedroom. He heard her humming a popular tune. He stood up and folded the paper, relieved that a decision had been made…

A sudden roar, an ear-shattering noise almost caused his heart to stop, splinters of wood blew from the door across the room. He hit the floor. It was the only thing he could do to protect himself. Staccato gunfire terrified him as bullets sprayed through the door and hit the furniture.

The door was kicked open and three cops wielding Tommy-guns charged in. Bill found himself staring down their deadly barrels, praying that none of the cops was too trigger-happy.

'Willie Sutton, you're under arrest,' one of the cops yelled triumphantly. 'What have you got to say for yourself?'

'You only had to ring the doorbell and I'd have let you in,' he replied sardonically.

The cop kicked him as hard as he could in the chin. From the bedroom doorway, Jean screamed.

CHAPTER 14

MARCH, 1935

He stood in front of Warden Herbert 'Hard-boiled' Smith's desk, looking suitably respectful, his hands behind his back. Warden Smith was a heavy-set man, with bushy, grey eyebrows and a large forehead. He had cold steel-grey eyes, which bore unnervingly into every convict, most of whom responded with suitably obsequious behavior. He was a man who commanded fear and respect and usually got it.

Compared to the warden, Bill was lean, as if he exercised regularly. But, in actual fact, nothing could have been further from the truth. Bill had been in solitary confinement for eighteen months. After his trial in 1933, a further twenty-five to fifty years was added to his original sentence, to be served at the harsh Eastern State Penitentiary with eighteen months in the isolation block to kick off with.

He was now thirty-four years old, so it meant he would not be due for release until somewhere towards the end of the century. If he lived that long. Somehow he doubted it. The prospect was grim so there was nothing to lose by attempting an escape as far as he could see.

'Well, Sutton, since I've been running things at Eastern State Penitentiary,' the warden began, 'no one - not a single convict, you understand - has ever escaped. I have an unblemished record and I intend to keep it that way.'

The warden's eyes cut through Bill's brain like a blade through butter. He knew damned well what he was thinking.

'You're here to serve your sentence,' he added, 'and I'll be keeping a close eye on you now you're no longer in the isolation block. You're being transferred to the seventh gallery. As you've been in isolation for the last eighteen months, you are probably unaware of its reputation. It's escape-proof, Sutton, so don't even think about it. Is that clear?'

'Yes, sir.' Bill made it sound as if he meant it. But the warden was eyeing him shrewdly, knowing full well he couldn't be trusted.

'I know you'll be scheming and plotting, Sutton, but I want you to know that I'll be ahead of your every move. Well?'

His eyebrows shot up expectantly, waiting for Bill's response.

'I think,' Bill said carefully, 'that I've resigned myself to my fate, sir.'

'I wish I could believe that, Sutton. And it wasn't fate that put you in here. It was choice. You chose to rob those banks. Now you must pay the price. Have you anything to say for yourself, Sutton?'

He thought about it. 'Yes, I'd like to thank you, sir.'

Smith glowered at him, wondering if he was trying to be funny.

'All the time I was in solitary,' Bill continued, 'you allowed me all the books I wanted to read. It's what kept me sane.'

The warden's expression softened. 'If you want to read or study to improve yourself, that's fine by me. But you won't be allowed to work in any machine shop, or do carpentry, or use any tools, Sutton. Not while you're in my prison. Is that understood?'

'Yes, sir.'

The warden nodded at a warder, who stood at a right angle to Bill. 'Okay, take him to his cell.'

Bill could feel the strength of the warden's eyes on his back, as he turned and walked towards the door.

Before the end of the month, Bill received a letter from Louise. She had finally given up on him.

"Dear Bill,

Since reading about your escape and your other robberies, I find it hard to continue to even hope we might have a future life together. You are a loving man and I will cherish thoughts of our brief life together both before and after Jenny was born. However, our time apart has been and will be longer, and under those circumstances I would like to ask you for a divorce. I have met someone else and we would like to get married. He's a lovely man and he knows all about the situation. I do hope you understand, Bill. I will pray for you, and hope you find some peace someday.

Love,

Louise"

Of course he'd agree to a divorce. He'd brought her nothing but misery and pain. But the thoughts of the divorce left him feeling lost and helpless, like a motherless child.

CHAPTER 15

OCTOBER, 1935

There was an overpowering and familiar stench in the dining hall: a mixture of sweat, potato starch and grease. As Bill shuffled along in the dinner queue he felt that, instead of a lifetime behind bars, he'd really been condemned to walk that treadmill of relentless boredom for eternity. A sinner's fear of limbo had been an early conditioning process.

He held out his tray as a mushy pile of waterlogged mashed potatoes was slopped on to a plate followed by grayish-brown unrecognizable meat and inky-bright green peas. The plate came down on to his tray with a clatter.

'Bon appetit!' the convict serving sneered. Bill gave him a weak smile and shuffled further along, where he was handed rubbery rice pudding in a tin dish. He picked up a bread roll and a tin mug of water and went to see if he could find a seat near his friend Jerry O'Hagan. Danny Savino tried to grab his attention as he passed between the rows of convicts on benches. Bill pretended not to see him and found somewhere further along to sit.

Three months after his release from the isolation block, Bill's reputation as a bookworm resulted in him being allowed to work in the prison library. It wasn't much of a library, just a small room with a dozen bookshelves, filled mostly with books that had seen better days, but he was grateful for this oasis of familiarity; books were his friends in this hostile environment.

On his first day, he was approached by Danny Savino who didn't strike Bill as much of a reader. He knew that Savino had another four of a ten-year sentence left to serve and was keen to make a good impression with the parole board to get it reduced. Bill's suspicions were aroused when the convict asked him if he could recommend any book to read while glancing furtively over his shoulder.

Lowering his voice, he offered his services to help Bill escape. Bill said adamantly that he wasn't planning on escaping and was reluctantly prepared for a long stay. The convict whispered that if he changed his mind, he could count on his help. Bill suspected he was being tested by the warden and the prison authorities.

Over several months, he was approached by numerous other cons with offers of help and each time he declined knowing that it would get back to 'Hard-boiled' Smith. He hoped it would convince the warden that he was resigned to serving his sentence. But when he thought of the punishing sentence stretching interminably across the century, he became more determined than ever to escape. Apart from the times when he lost himself in the reassuring oblivion of an involving book, his thoughts were almost entirely consumed in plotting.

Like other convicts, he always mashed the meat and gravy into his potatoes making them less starchy and watery, then chewed and swallowed hurriedly trying not to taste what he was eating.

Halfway through one meal, he stopped eating and looked around the dining hall, trying to spot Jerry.

He spotted him three tables away, his bald head bobbing as he ate. He tried to catch his eye, but Jerry was obviously concentrating on getting over the odious task of eating as quickly as possible so that he could return to his cell and escape back into his world of painting. As a model prisoner, Jerry O'Hagan was allowed to indulge his artistic skills.

Bill watched as Jerry finished his meal, returned his tray to the hatch, and quickly left the dining hall. Bill hurriedly finished his own dinner and went to look for him. When he got to Jerry's cell, his friend had wasted no time in getting started on his latest painting, a memory of a landscape of trees and rolling grassy hills, of freedom. He was stood behind a medium-sized canvas on an easel, cleaning a long, thin paintbrush.

'Hello, Jerry, hope I'm not disturbing you. Mind if I come in for a minute?'

'Sure, Bill, as long as you don't mind if I carry on painting. I can talk at the same time.'

He finished cleaning the brush, dipped it lightly into a light blue color on his palette and applied it delicately to the canvas. The easel took up much of the room in the small cell so Bill squeezed himself between its back legs and sat on the edge of Jerry's bed. Fascinated, he watched his middle-aged friend for a while whose tongue protruded in childlike concentration between his lips. Both men were comfortable with the silence until Jerry broke it. 'What's on your mind?'

Although Jerry O'Hagan was serving life for first-degree murder, he didn't appear to be a violent man. Far from it. He was a thoughtful and gentle soul and Bill sympathized with him when he related his tragic history.

Jerry once ran his own small business, mending clocks and watches. He was deeply in love with his young wife and wanted to start a family. One lunchtime, an important customer asked him to deliver a watch. It wasn't usually part of the service but he saw it as an opportunity to surprise his young wife, and he readily agreed to deliver the watch and miss out on lunch.

He arrived home to hear noises coming from the bedroom and he knew at once something evil was happening. It took possession of his soul. Instantly, he was no longer a rational, loving human being.

Something was about to destroy him. The noises coming from the bedroom penetrated him like sharp instruments of torture. By now, he was out of control and ran crazily to the bedroom. He wanted it to end, the painful sound of all that pleasure. When he saw them together, he went berserk, picked up a crowbar and bludgeoned his wife and her lover to death.

Things might have been different if the crowbar hadn't been where it lay on top of the chest of drawers in the bedroom. There would have been a fight, vicious and violent, no doubt, but not an extremely bloody murder, with two corpses bleeding profusely like a busy day at the abattoir. But the crowbar was convenient, lying there in the bedroom, as though it was meant for this incident.

Fate.

A few nights prior to the murder, one of the wooden shutters on their bedroom windows became jammed, and Jerry used the crowbar to force it back into its groove. At his trial, the District Attorney said he found the crowbar story difficult to believe. He insisted there was a time difference between the accused finding the lovers in bed, then rushing downstairs, going out to his workshop, fetching the crowbar and returning to the house to kill them.

It was, insisted the DA, a premeditated act. And, as Jerry had a poor lawyer who did little to defend him, he was sentenced to die in the electric chair. Later, after a meeting with his parents, he agreed to appeal and found a better lawyer who got his sentence commuted to life.

Bill felt sorry for Jerry who had lived an honest, unblemished life up until the incident that was to destroy him.

Now he was about to ask for help, knowing his friend was unlikely to refuse, and he was worried about involving him in case something went wrong. The only escape for Jerry now was his art and, if he lost this privilege, it would surely kill him. But when Bill thought about his own sentence, stretching to infinity, he knew he had no choice but to ask the favor.

'Jerry,' he began. 'I'd like your help.'

Jerry stopped painting and peered over the canvas. 'I don't see how I can help you to escape.'

'How did you know I was planning to escape?'

Jerry smiled a secret smile and resumed painting. 'You managed to escape once, you're a great lock artist - it doesn't take much to work that one out.'

Bill sighed and frowned. 'Yeah, and the warden can work that one out too.'

'But the warden's got to look after hundreds of convicts, not just think about one man,' Jerry reasoned. 'So what is it you want me to do?'

'Before I tell you, let me ask you something. Why don't you come with me?'

Without taking his eyes off the painting, Jerry shook his head slowly. 'You know better than to ask, Bill. I killed two human beings. I'm here because I deserve to be here.'

'You can't keep torturing yourself about it. You've got to let it rest.'

'I can't, Bill. There's not a day goes by I don't think about it. I'm here for life.'

'As long as you're sure.'

'Oh, I'm sure. Now what is it you want me to do?'

'I want the odd bit of paint - certain colors - a tiny bit at a time. And I know artists sometimes use plaster of Paris for making models and things. I need you to give me small amounts - say, over a year.'

'Okay,' Jerry agreed. 'I'll do it.'

'Thanks. I really appreciate it.'

Jerry threw a glance at Bill. 'It's what friends are for.'

Bill smiled back at him as he got up from the bed. 'Thanks, Jerry, you're a good friend. I'll leave you in peace now to get on with your painting.'

As he was leaving the cell, Bill turned back. 'Don't you want to know what the stuff is for?'

Jerry grinned. 'I think it best I don't know. Total ignorance is safer. For us both.'

'Yeah, you're right. Thanks, Jerry. See you later.'

'Oh, I'll still be here.'

Bill walked thoughtfully along the corridor, past the other cells, towards his own. Not only was he going to need Jerry's help but others' as well. But who could he trust? He needed some new friends, men with access to some tools; prisoners who were allowed to work in the printing, woodworking and maintenance shops. He could exclude anyone who approached him, planning a breakout. It would be certain to be a trap laid by the warden. He needed to be very selective in his choice of conspirators. Then there was the cost. The prison currency was tobacco, so he would have to give up smoking.

'Sutton! I was looking for you.'

It was Skelton, a weasel-faced guy, and Bill was always wary of him.

'Something wrong?' Bill asked cautiously.

Skelton grinned. 'I heard you worked for the Dutchman.'

Bill nodded.

Skelton's grin widened, as he relished his tale. 'Schultz ain't with us no more. Gone to that speakeasy in the sky.'

Skelton paused dramatically, savoring the effect.

'What happened?'

'Shot at the Palace Chop House in Newark. He was still alive when the cops got there. They took him to hospital. He died almost a day after the hit. So they took him to the morgue and laid him out on the cold slab. So long, fucker!'

Skelton laughed, slapped Bill on the arm and walked off.

He thought about Dutch Schultz, tried to picture the scene in vivid detail. The Dutchman's bullet-riddled body slumped over a restaurant table, blood seeping from his wounds like Johnny Eagan at that speakeasy. And Doc Tate, knifed in a senseless brawl. The endless list of the people he'd worked with, all met with a violent end. And poor old Eddie Wilson. He'd heard Eddie was in Sing Sing, and was blind.

A blind prisoner! Jesus! It didn't bear thinking about. The jinx. It had to be the jinx. Everyone he touched, even his women friends, and his beautiful daughter, he'd brought them nothing but bad luck.

CHAPTER 16

OCTOBER 1937

Two years. Two whole years almost to the day and now he was ready. The wind was billowing outside and he could hear the rain lashing against the prison walls. It was a perfect night for an escape as visibility would be almost down to zero.

With Jerry's help, he had made a lifelike plaster mask of his face. It had taken him over a year to perfect this dummy, laboriously fashioning the hair on the dummy's head from strands he had taken from the mop he used to clean out his cell, taking a little at a time. From some of the other inmates, he managed to get a grappling hook and hacksaw and, over the two years, he had collected bits of cord and rope which he braided into a twenty-foot long rope, light but of adequate strength.

At precisely 11.30, the guard shone his flashlight into the cell, while Bill feigned sleep. He gave the guard a few minutes to clear, then carefully got out of bed and knelt on the floor. Just beneath his bed, he removed the wooden floorboard and dug down into the rotten concrete beneath. In this secret hole, he had hidden his props.

He placed the dummy head on the pillow and plumped up the blankets to make it look like his sleeping form. He got his rope and grappling hook and hacksaw from the hole, replaced the floorboard and climbed on to the table beneath his cell window.

He had already sawn through two bars on his cell window and had filled the crevices with soap that he had painted over.

Now, the blade of the hacksaw slid easily into one of the bar's crevices and he sawed through the rest of it in less than a minute. Once he had the other bar dislodged, he grabbed his rope and grappling hook and threw them on to the ledge outside. He grabbed the ledge with both hands and pulled himself up. His hands were cold and wet and he feared he might slip back into the cell. He tightened his grip on the wall outside, took a deep breath, then pulled himself through the narrow gap as a blast of wind and rain stung his face.

He was soaked through, but at least he was outside, huddled on the narrow window ledge. He estimated it was around 11.50. Now, all he had to do was wait until the whistle blew at midnight to signal a change of shift for the guards. He worked out that guards coming on to the new shift would be less attentive in their first few minutes on duty. They would arrive at the watchtowers cold and wet and they would probably spend their first few minutes getting warm and dry. That was when he planned to drop into the yard below, cross the courtyard and throw the grappling hook to catch the rim of the guttering on top of the wall.

As he cringed, shivering in the shadows, he felt good inside. He felt lucky. Everything was going according to plan. He'd been ready for this break, praying for bad weather, and it had come along in answer to his prayers sooner than he expected.

For the last two years, he had worked hard learning Spanish, shorthand and typing. He figured once he was on the outside, he'd head for the Puerto Rican colony in Brooklyn, where they read only the Spanish language papers, which rarely reported the New York crime news.

The rain ran down the back of his neck and he was reminded of the rough night when Johnny Eagan was machine-gunned to death. He shook the thought from his head and concentrated on listening for the whistle to signal the change of shift. He reckoned another five minutes had past. If he could get clean over that wall and, if the sleeping dummy fooled the guards on their nightly rounds, he wouldn't be missed until the morning.

The wind raged and roared as he strained to hear the whistle. Any minute now he'd be over that wall. But if the whistle blew, Bill didn't hear it. Suddenly, the siren began its mournful wailing and searchlights swung and arced their beams across the yard below as men shouted and screamed followed by shots. What the hell was going on? Whatever it was, Bill knew he had to get back into his cell and cover the traces of his attempted escape.

He squeezed quickly back through the window and dropped on to the table. He slid the bars back into place, hid the grappling hook, rope and dummy back in their hiding place beneath the bed and climbed hurriedly into bed.

He lay shivering in the dark, his clothes saturated and clinging to his body, as he listened to noise going on all around him. The entire prison was suddenly alive with activity and chaos as orders were shouted and heavy boots pounded along corridors. He heard the chink of keys and feet marching towards his cell. A flashlight shone on to his face and he blinked as if a deep sleep had been disturbed.

'What the hell's going on out there?' he asked the guard.

'Two fucking idiots tried to go over the wall,' was the gruff reply.

Bill cursed his luck. How could he have known two others would have the same idea and pick the same night? And why did those two idiots get the timing wrong? They should have waited until after midnight, then they might have all got clean away.

He almost wept with frustration, and knew he wouldn't get much sleep that night. Whenever anyone tried to make a break for it, security was routinely tightened up and he was aware that this usually resulted in a search.

Bill stood before the warden, a guard on either side of him. He felt like he'd been chewed up and regurgitated and there was an unreal buzzing in his ears. There were dark bags under his eyes and his face was drawn. He knew he'd be back in solitary now, but it wasn't that that bothered him. It was the sheer disappointment of the frustrated escape attempt. He'd been so close to pulling it off.

The plaster head, the rope and grappling hook, and the hacksaw lay accusingly on a corner of the warden's expansive desk. The warden didn't look up but continued studying a report that lay before him. It was, Bill knew, an effect the warden liked to use, a trick to keep his anger in check in case he lost control. It was how he maintained a healthy respect. Eventually, the warden sniffed loudly, and pushed the paper to one side. When he looked at Bill, his eyes were like two burning embers. The anger was still raging inside him, but under control. 'I'll only ask you this once. Where did you get the stuff to make the dummy?'

'Jerry O'Hagan,' Bill replied.

For a moment the warden looked nonplussed. He hadn't figured Sutton for an informer. 'You telling me O'Hagan helped you?'

Bill shook his head emphatically. He had already worked this out with Jerry so as not to get his friend in trouble if the plan went sour.

'I lied to him,' Bill said. 'I asked him for some paints and plaster of Paris to make sculptures. Said I was interested in art.'

The warden's eyes narrowed. 'You expect me to believe that?'

Bill looked him in the eyes. 'It's true. I'm a friend of Jerry. I wouldn't do anything to get him into trouble.'

'He get you the grappling hook and hacksaw?'

'No, sir. Just the artistic stuff. Like I said, Jerry had no idea...'

'Never mind that,' the warden snapped. 'I want to know who gave you the other items.'

Bill stood up straight, hands behind his back, and stared into the distance.

'You'll make it easier on yourself if you give me their names.'

Bill continued staring ahead, making it quite clear that he had no intention of informing on them.

The warden sighed impatiently. 'I'm not going to waste any more time with you, Sutton. Two years in the isolation block and loss of privileges. Okay! This meeting is over. Get him out of my sight.'

CHAPTER 17

JUNE, 1940

Over the clatter of his typewriter, he heard Dr. Schwarz sighing deeply and he knew the psychiatrist was troubled. He stopped and looked across his desk at the doctor who was shaking his head slowly in disbelief. Schwarz, in his mid-thirties, handsome and broad-shouldered with friendly brown eyes and a clear complexion, was an avuncular man with an easy bedside manner.

'You had no choice,' Bill said, referring to a prisoner that that had been certified by the doctor as insane and sent to Fairview State Hospital where he would spend the rest of his days in the company of some of the most dangerous lunatics.

'It always depresses me though,' the psychiatrist said.

'One stroke of my pen and off they go to that...that...' He pursed his lips as he searched for an apt description of the asylum.

'Like I said,' Bill cut in, 'you had no choice. He was schizophrenic and they were dangerous multiple personalities controlling him. I know it's not a decision you made lightly.'

Schwarz smiled at him. 'And what about you, Bill? You've never felt stir-crazy violent rages, have you?'

'I might have done if it hadn't been for books. They kept me sane.'

During Bill's two-year stay in the isolation block, the

warden had allowed him as many books as he cared to read and also a typewriter to continue his touch-typing lessons. Bill appreciated that Warden Smith was a reasonably fair man and he managed to survive the solitary years by escaping into the world of fiction. And, because he still nurtured the dream of one day escaping to the outside world, he continued to improve his Spanish. Then, after his term was served, the warden gave him the job of assisting Dr. Schwarz.

'I think it's more than that,' the psychiatrist added. 'I don't think violence is in you.'

'Maybe not,' Bill agreed, thoughtfully. 'But I still rejected the accepted rules in society and became a parasite. Why was that?'

The psychiatrist stared openly at Bill, deliberately remaining silent, knowing that his assistant was capable of providing his own analysis. Dr. Schwarz had never known a prisoner like Bill Sutton. His intelligence was remarkable and, since coming to work for him, he'd taken a keen interest in psychoanalysis and had read up on Freud, Jung and any other books on psychology and psychiatry he had managed to get his hands on.

'I guess,' Bill began tentatively, 'my existence never had purpose. I needed a challenge. I think maybe I was insecure and I needed money to give me a false feeling of security. But that still doesn't explain why I robbed those banks. I've read so many books in your office and none of them could give me an answer. Now I've spent thirteen years of my adult life behind bars, I wonder what would happen if, just supposing, I was released. You think, doctor, I could adjust and become a normal member of society and go straight?'

Bill saw the cloud of doubt in the doctor's expression as he thought about this.

'Only you can answer that,' he said. 'I'm sorry, but I can't tell you yes, you could become an honest member of society. That's your decision, Bill, and you know it.'

Bill looked down at the typewriter keyboard. It hadn't been a satisfactory answer; not the one he wanted to hear.

He guessed the doctor didn't think he could change and, for the first time, he felt irritated by Schwarz's opinion. He respected the doctor, but now, more than ever, he felt the urge to escape and put it to the test. Maybe if he managed to live in the free world, he could go straight, hold down a decent job. Then, one day let Dr. Schwarz know he was wrong. Was this a fantasy? Could he find a way to get out of Eastern State Penitentiary?

The doctor was staring intently at him and Bill felt as if he could read his mind.

'You think a country can go insane?' Bill asked.

Dr. Schwarz waited for him to elaborate.

'I always dreamt that one day I might go to Europe, but now the swastika's flying in nearly every civilized country. Even Paris. Romantic city like that. It's madness. You think the whole of Germany could be certified?'

Bill realized he'd been babbling and Dr Schwarz was eyeing him knowingly. He seemed slightly amused, like a father having caught his son out in a minor misdemeanor.

'Bill, don't think about escaping,' he said. 'Not unless you *want* to go back into solitary.'

Bill could feel himself blushing. 'You're wrong about me,' he mumbled, unconvincingly.

'But I've noticed some depression lately.'

Bill shrugged. 'I had bad news. I don't think I told you.'

The psychiatrist remained silent, waiting for Bill to elaborate.

'I wrote to my father. Months ago. Someone must have opened the letter. It came back with my father's name crossed out on the envelope, and someone had substituted it with the word "Deceased".'

Bill stared at the typewriter keys. There was a long, awkward silence. From the corridor outside came the sound of marching boots and the jangle of keys.

'How did you feel about that?' Dr Schwarz asked.

Bill shrugged again. 'I'd better get on with this report,' he said and continued typing furiously.

CHAPTER 18

OCTOBER, 1940

Over and over, information gathered across seven long years rippled through his brain. There wasn't much he didn't know about the prison, the materials that had been used in its construction, how wide the walls were, how deep the foundations, where the sewers were located, and thousands of other details, much of which would prove to be invaluable for planning an escape.

He'd always known the information was readily available, almost for the asking, as if the prison authorities wanted the cons to know how futile an escape attempt would be. He also thought this was a weakness, a flaw, because, armed with information, there was always a loophole in any system and he thought he'd found it.

At times he wondered if he was crazy and if his plan would work. Digging a tunnel beneath the ground until they were on the outside seemed impossible, far-fetched, but the more he thought about it, the more the idea took him over, so that it became an obsession. There were certain cells only thirty feet from the outside wall, but these cells were inspected regularly.

He'd have to choose one of the end cells, furthest from the outside wall, that needed a tunnel of at least ninety feet and wouldn't arouse any suspicion, as, face it, he was thinking of a near-impossible undertaking. One man he knew in one of these cells on the ground floor was an expert forger by the name of Clarence Kliney, an affable man he'd been sounding out for some time now. And Kliney was known to be a model prisoner, never in any trouble, so he wouldn't draw attention to himself as a potential escapee.

He felt the time was ripe to approach Kliney with his proposition, and went to visit him during a yard-out period. Going out into the yard wasn't mandatory and convicts could choose to remain in their cells during the recreation period or even congregate in the corridors outside.

'Bill! Come in, come in,' Kliney said enthusiastically when Bill approached.

Kliney ran a hand through his ginger hair and gestured to a chair. Bill sat down and looked up at him, wondering if he could trust him. He was a warm guy and looked like a stern but approachable schoolteacher. His friendly manner seemed genuine but, as Bill well knew from his own frauds, all it takes to earn some credibility is a little acting skill. However, he had a gut instinct about Kliney and decided to go with it, to risk it.

'Ever thought about getting out of here?'

'Never stop thinking about it, but will I make it in my lifetime? Or do I go out in a wooden box?'

'I think it's time we took the matter into our own hands.'

A glint came into Kliney's eyes and Bill saw hope in the man's soul take wing. He knew he'd found his first recruit.

'I want out,' Kliney said. It was a no-frills statement, bald but sincere.

'It's going to be tricky,' Bill warned.

'I don't care about that. Anything's worth the risk to get out of here.'

'I don't get it. You're a model prisoner. No previous attempts. Why risk it now?'

Kliney pursed his lips and gave it some thought. 'Just had enough, I guess. And if I could remain free for just a year - just one glorious year, that's all I ask - and be at liberty to walk into a restaurant and order what I like, or watch kids playing in the park, go to the movies when I like...I think the trade would be equitable.'

Bill smiled with understanding and the pact was made. They both knew it was a bond and neither would go back on their word. It was like a marriage - for better or worse.

'So what have you got in mind?' Kliney asked.

Down to business. Bill tapped the wall of the cell behind him. 'This wall is five-feet thick, but I reckon once we've gotten through five or six inches, it'll get easier. I suspect we'll find soft, crumbling concrete that shouldn't be too difficult to penetrate.'

Kliney's eyes grew bulbous, like a man parodying astonishment.

'Let me get this straight, you plan to dig your way through to the yard outside? Then what?'

'No,' said Bill. 'Dig directly down - I reckon about thirty feet. I know the prison wall goes down twenty-five feet below ground. And it's fourteen feet thick at the base, made of stone not concrete, so we'll have to burrow under it.'

'How far from here to the wall?'

'Ninety feet.'

Kliney gave a long low whistle of amazement.

'Well,' Bill smiled weakly, 'you think it's harebrained?'

Kliney chuckled. 'I think it's so audacious it could work.'

'It's an enormous undertaking, Clarence.'

Kliney nodded thoughtfully before speaking. 'What about the hole in the wall? How we gonna cover it up?'

'I've given it a great deal of thought. We need to make a plasterboard frame to cover the hole. You've got pictures on the wall. You can add to the collection. We remove the pictures, start digging, cover the hole, and stick the pictures back over it - I don't think any guard would give it a second look. It'll always look familiar and normal.'

'And what do we do with all the plaster and earth?'

'Stick it in our pockets, carry it away from the cell and flush it down the toilets. The biggest problem will be the recruitment of labor. We'll need another five or six men at

191

least. That'll be the hardest part, finding the guys we can trust.'

'And I'm no engineer,' Kliney mused, a small frown furrowing his brow, 'but to build a tunnel, doesn't it take shoring up? I mean, like in a mine. We'll need timber.'

'There's a guy I've been sounding out in the woodworking shop, guy by the name of Freddy Tenuto. I'm certain he can be trusted, because...'

'I know him,' Kliney interrupted. 'He's doing time for murder. I'd be wary of using a hotheaded guy like that.'

'Relax, Clarence,' Bill said. 'We're limited in our choices. And none of us is here because we're model citizens.'

'I suppose,' Kliney conceded. 'And it can't have been first degree murder, because otherwise they'd have sent him up the river to Sing Sing and fried him for sure.'

Kliney talking tough-guy was out of character and an amused smile played at the corners of Bill's mouth. That's what a stretch in the pen does for you, he thought. Learn the lingo and blend in with the rest of the inmates.

Kliney caught Bill's amused expression. 'What's so funny?' he asked.

CHAPTER 19

APRIL, 1942

It took six months for the tunnel to reach the outside wall. Six months of back-breaking work, digging, scraping and crawling. Lack of oxygen in the tunnel meant that two men worked for a half-hour, after which they reached a point of total exhaustion, when another two took over. After nine weeks' work on the tunnel, the diggers reached the main sewer, and any earth removed was deposited into the putrid water. Things speeded up considerably after this.

Prior to the building of the tunnel, Bill had recruited eight men. It took six months of careful vetting to avoid picking informers. Six months of calculating the odds on an expression, the shifty look of a stoolpigeon, the guy who would shop his own mother, someone smarmy and amoral. Pick the wrong guy and the whole scheme was blown.

But he was smart enough to realize that his first instinct was usually the most accurate and, once having adopted this method, he thoroughly checked out his man, dropped hints about escaping, and eventually managed to recruit his team. Not a single convict proved to be false. Each man worked in the various shops and managed to steal the tools that were needed for the job.

Bill was working a shift with Peter Van Sant, a dour man, dark like his moods, who could never adjust to life in prison. The magnitude of his hatred of the regime that kept him behind bars often reached boiling point, like a volcano about to erupt, and in yard-out periods he'd often pace like a jungle cat, staring at the guards and machine guns malevolently, and convicts who observed him knew it was only a question of time before he flipped.

But once he began working on the tunnel, his demeanor changed. The small chink he could see, the glimmer of freedom, renewed his life-force. He proved to be one of the most reliable and hard working prisoners on Bill's team.

It was cold and damp in the tunnel and they worked in their underwear, but both men were sweating with the effort of their digging. Bill put down his shovel and wiped the sweat from his eyes with his arm.

'Another fourteen feet,' Bill grimaced, 'and we should be on the outside.'

Van Sant grunted, conserving his energy. None of the men wasted effort on speech since they knew every half-hour's energy was taking them ever closer to freedom. To a man, they fantasized at night, seeing themselves vanishing into the heartland of America, driving west to escape to faraway places in the sunshine where no one would ever find them.

Van Sant knew his half-hour was nearly over. He raised his pick and summoned up one final effort and cracked into stone and solid earth. A fountain of water spurted into the tunnel, a powerful spray of freezing water flooding the tunnel.

'Fuck!' Van Sant yelled. 'We've hit an underground spring.'

In seconds they were drenched in freezing water. Bill's mind was surprisingly clear. He felt no fear. He was almost resigned to his fate as the cold water engulfed them, rising upwards, and threatening to reach the roof and cut off their air supply, it struck him that he was returning to how it all began. Bill felt his life unwinding, running back to the beginning and he was ready to give up.

'Turn round!' Van Sant shouted. 'Grab my arm. Take a deep breath – now! We can make it back to the cell!'

Bill struggled to turn in the confined space, thrust his head at the roof of the ceiling, took a deep breath and pushed himself back along the tunnel with Van Sant's help.

They reached "Kliney's Hole", as the drop into the tunnel had become suggestively known, and Van Sant pushed Bill ahead of him up the hole. At the top, Bill gave the lightest of taps on a plasterboard cover. Kliney, who was sitting with his ear close on the other side, caught the eye of a lookout keeping watch outside the cell and jerked his thumb at the wall. The convict nodded that it was all clear and Kliney removed the pictures and the board. He pulled Bill and Van Sant into the room, and saw from Bill's expression that something was seriously wrong, 'What's happened?'

'Tunnel's flooded,' Bill said, simply.

'Jesus!' he exclaimed. 'Six months work down the pan.'

Bill and Van Sant grabbed their clothes from under Kliney's bed blanket, and hurriedly dressed. They used toilet paper to wipe the mud from their faces and hands and shoved the sheets into their pockets.

Outside the cell, the lookout clicked his fingers twice, a signal that a guard was making his way along the row of cells. Bill was under the most suspicion for escape attempts. He smoothed his hair down and hurriedly left Kliney's cell, cursing their bad luck, as he made his way back to his own. Just another month - weeks even - and they'd have made it through to the outside.

For the next week Bill went outside during the recreation period. If the tunnel spring was a powerful one, he was worried the water might seep up to ground level. And if the yard became swamped, then it was inevitable that it would be inspected. It hadn't rained for some time so it would be bound to look suspicious if a pool of water suddenly appeared in the yard. But, when after a week, the ground remained dry; Bill decided to return to the tunnel to investigate.

'Well?' Kliney demanded, when he surfaced from the hole.

Bill grinned. 'There's two feet of water so we have a

clearance of two feet. It'll be hard digging in water. Much slower. But we're almost there. I think we can do it.'

Kliney's face lit up. 'Praise be the Lord!' he intoned.

CHAPTER 20

JUNE, 1942

After breakfast they were always sent back to their cells; but six weeks to the day when Van Sant's pick had hit the underground stream, Bill's eight hand-picked convicts, Kliney and himself, finished their breakfast, left the dining hall in relays, and made straight for Kliney's cell. Once inside, they hurriedly took down the pictures from his wall, removed the plasterboard cover, and crawled into the hole. They dropped into the cold water below. Bill was the last inside.

The nine men splashing their way to freedom in front of him sounded frantic, like so many crazed rats. He could hear them panting and wheezing as they crawled along the hundred and twenty feet to the end. Van Sant was at the head. He crawled up the hole and began frantically digging and clawing at the final two feet of earth. Soil and concrete showered down on him and the others behind. They closed their eyes or covered them, and spat out dust and dirt.

Then, through the darkness, they felt the power of the light as it reached down into the hole. They were through. Through to the outside world.

Now it was each man for himself. Van Sant lost no time in clambering out and the other convicts quickly emerged behind him into the street. Rows of cars parked by the sidewalk offered a bit of cover from the stores and offices opposite the prison, but ten men scattering crazily in all directions would be bound to claim some attention.

As soon as Bill clambered from the hole, he took a brief moment to get his whereabouts, confused as to which direction to take. He didn't want to follow the other escaping convicts. Now was the time to go it alone. He'd stand more chance that way. He'd try to make it to the Puerto Rican district of Brooklyn and, with his knowledge of Spanish, he could hopefully blend in.

Following the prison wall away from the main entrance, he pounded along the sidewalk. He decided that he'd slow down at the next corner, cross the road and disappear down the first side street.

He turned left and almost ran into two cops. It took them a few seconds to react. One recovered a beat quicker than his colleague and reached for his gun.

'Put your hands up or I'll shoot,' he yelled.

'Go ahead and shoot!' Bill yelled.

He turned and ran across the street. He heard the blast of the gun and the bullets ricocheting off cars parked on the opposite side of the street. Any moment now he'd be hit, he thought. But he didn't care. He was desperate.

As he dodged across the street, the cop emptied every bullet in his gun at him. Miraculously, each one missed him.

By now the second policeman had withdrawn his gun and aimed. The first shot missed Bill's head by less than an inch and the bullet smacked into the windscreen of a Chevrolet.

He thought he could make it now. He got between the Chevy and another car, jumped on to the sidewalk, but missed his footing. The pain screamed across his nervous system, as his ankle twisted into the gutter, and he came crashing down on the side of his face. He heard the pounding of the cops' boots, as he tried to get up. Too late. They grabbed his arms and he heard the rattle of cuffs above the wailing of three cop cars cruising the district.

Back in captivity after less than one minute of freedom.

Later, he discovered most of the others were caught in less

than five minutes, with the exception of Tenuto and Van Sant, who made it to New York, but were back in custody a few months later.

CHAPTER 21

JANUARY, 1943

Day fifteen: Feeling light-headed. Not so bad now. Day thirteen was the worst. The stomach cramps. Doubled over in pain. Excruciating pain. But now the light-headedness had an almost mystical feel about it. Floating. Gently floating on a sea of nothingness. Everything white. Even the sound. The occasional drift of colors. Red and pink, like a sunset. Sometimes blue. But no more pain. Just emptiness. And acceptance of death, if that's what it took.

A key turned in the lock. Laid out on his bed, Bill opened his eyes. A guard stood aside and Warden Smith loomed into view. He coughed before speaking, the precursor of a long speech, and Bill smiled up at him. As weak as he was, he hadn't a care in the world.

'Well, Sutton, all the others have caved in. I've seen hunger strikes before and they never work. Most of the others in the isolation block didn't get past day ten. Another one managed it as far as day thirteen, but then the pain got to him. It seems you're the only one stubborn enough to keep this up.

'I know that once it goes this far it becomes easier to go the whole way. I don't mind telling you, I don't want that stain on my record. But let me tell you this, Sutton, you wouldn't be the first. Men kill themselves when they're inside. Always have, always will. Guys flip. They hang themselves. Goes on all the time.

'But this is senseless. You're an intelligent man. You've read a lot of books. Dr. Schwarz tells me you're a smart man. So what's eating you? Let's hear it - if you're capable. What's your beef?'

It took Bill a while to understand what he was being asked. His lips were dry as leather, wrinkled and tight. Inwardly he felt he was somewhere else - another person. His instinct told him the warden was here to negotiate. He tried to sort out what he wanted to say, but his communication skills had slowed right down. Then, from somewhere deep within the pit of his stomach, he managed to summon up the strength to address the warden.

'When we were caught attempting to escape, Warden, we had to stand trial again. I had another fifteen to twenty years added to all the other sentences. Most of us accept this philosophically, and I feel I speak for most of us. But two years' isolation seems excessive on top of the added twenty years.'

Smith shook his head impatiently. 'You knew the rules, Sutton. Before you planned this escape, you knew what would happen if you were caught.'

'Yes, and I accept that my sentence would be increased. But isolation as well. Murderers get off lighter than that. You can only execute a man once.'

Bill waited for the warden's reaction. It was hard to tell what he was thinking, though his stare was penetrating.

'I've already spoken to the State Department of Correction,' he said, 'and I've reached a solution that seems...well, the only solution. I'm having all of you transferred to other institutions. You, Sutton, will be going to Holmesburg County Prison in Philadelphia. You'll be starting your sentence there with a clean slate. Now perhaps you might like to end your fast.'

It was a compromise and Bill accepted it with a small nod of acquiescence. Eastern State Penitentiary had beaten him after ten long years. But at least he wasn't returning to 'solitary', which was a living death. All those wasted years he had spent with no one but himself for company, always longing for night to come, waiting for an end to the mind-numbing day. And then there were the nights, the endless, sleepless nights, knowing that his waking day would be exactly the same as the previous one.

The only thing that had kept him from going mad was his escape into the world of literature. And, like a fictional character in a book, he held on to his sanity by dreaming of a successful escape.

'Get this man some food,' the warden instructed the guard. Then he turned briskly and left the cell.

Bill closed his eyes and let his mind wander, imagining the insipid thin prison gruel would be the most exquisite cuisine in the world.

CHAPTER 22

FEBRUARY, 1947

One minute to midnight, tense and silent, Bill and four other convicts crouched on the other side of the cell block door. They heard the guards' approaching footsteps and the rasping sound as the key slid into the lock. There was a metallic click and the door started to swing open. Two of the convicts hurled their combined weight against it. The two guards were taken completely by surprise and crashed to the floor. When they looked up, Van Sant was aiming a .38 caliber gun at them.

Bill had worried about Van Sant having the gun, knowing how much he despised the prison regime. But it was Van Sant's contact who had smuggled the weapon in, concealed among vegetables in a delivery truck. Not that it made much difference now who had the gun, he thought, as two of the other convicts relieved the guards of their weapons. They were five desperate men who would chance anything in their bid for freedom, although each of them was aware that any killing could send them to the electric chair.

Bill grabbed the keys from one of the guards and the other convicts forced them to walk ahead with their arms raised. Quietly, they padded along the cell block until they reached H-Block, which adjoined the engine room, where they knew there were some ladders.

Bill unlocked the adjoining doors and they entered the

engine room. A guard came forward to meet the guards with their hands in the air. His perplexed expression changed to one of alarm and his hand automatically reached for his gun. Van Sant appeared from behind the two disarmed guards and aimed his gun at him.

'Get your hands in the air,' he said, 'or you're a dead man.'

The guard sensed the men's desperation, and his hands shot up as though jerked by a puppeteer. He glowered at Bill as Bill unclipped his gun from his holster, but didn't dare move. He knew these cons had nothing to lose now.

Van Sant kept his gun trained on the guards while Bill and three other convicts found ladders and lashed them together.

'Don't try anything,' he warned them. 'I'm on a short fuse.'

Once the ladders were securely fastened together, they forced the guards to remove their coats and hats. One of the convicts, Dave Akins, grinned as he stuck the hat on his head and slipped into the guard's jacket. Akins, an affable man in his fifties, always got on well with the guards. He had a great deal of charm and they often laughed at his jokes. Now they stared at him with revulsion, as if dressing in their uniform was their final indignity.

Two of the other convicts slipped into guards' jackets, before tying the guards' hands behind their backs with various lengths of rope produced from their pants' pockets.

They forced them to the floor on their stomachs, and Bill unlocked the door to the yard outside. Now for the hardest part: crossing the yard with the ladder.

They had chosen this night because of the severe weather conditions. That morning, after a spell of freezing temperatures, the skies became leaden and dark and, by mid-afternoon, there was a heavy snowfall that didn't look like abating for some time. That's when they nervously agreed that it just had to be tonight.

It was now just after midnight when the guards on the machine gun towers would be starting their shifts. Snow was swirling and gusting, everything a mass of white, and the watchtowers were barely distinguishable from other shapes and shadows. Each convict held a section of ladder as they ran through the snowdrift towards the wall.

As they raised the ladder against the wall, there was a staccato crackle and a spitting sound as a hail of bullets hit the wall close by. They'd been spotted by a guard in one of the towers. Dave Akins ran several yards towards the tower and, for an instant, the other convicts thought he must either be crazy or trying to surrender.

'Stop! Stop!' Akins yelled. 'We're guards. Can't you see we're guards, you sons o' bitches? Get away from that gun. Move away from that gun. Now!'

The guard, confused and scared, and blinded by the furiously swirling snow, moved away from the gun to consult with a colleague. The convicts wasted no time in shinning up the ladder to the top of the wall and leapt into a soft pile of snow on the other side. They ran three blocks to where it was prearranged that a car would be waiting. Panic! Either there was some mistake or their contact on the outside had failed them.

'It has to be the right place,' Akins said, huddled over against the blinding snow. 'We were told by the timber yard. This is it. Brewer's Wood and Timber. No car!'

'Fucking cocksucker!' yelled Van Sant. 'If I ever get hold of him...'

The prison siren began wailing. By now the guards knew they had an escape on their hands.

Pretty soon the district would be crawling with cops. The convicts began running, trying to cover as much ground as possible between them and the prison. They ran along the suburban streets, houses pale and ghostly. In the white silence, all they could hear was their own breathing and the urgent crunching of their feet in the snow.

Then they heard the faint clink of bottles. They sprinted around a bend in the road to find a milk wagon, its motor idling, parked in the middle of the street: a milkman who began his deliveries really early.

They ran towards the wagon, now their only hope of escape. The milkman was delivering to a nearby house and didn't hear them as they bundled into the wagon on the passenger side. They sat squeezed tightly together, breathless from their sprint in the snow, and waited for his return. They heard him coughing as he neared the wagon. Crunch of heavy boots in snow. The wagon door squeaked as the milkman pulled it open to find himself staring down the barrel of Van Sant's .38, inches away from his nose. Four other pairs of eyes stared at him from the darkness of his wagon.

'Drive us to Philadelphia,' Van Sant ordered.

The milkman climbed into the cab, threw the engine into gear and drove off carefully towards the city centre. Each of the convicts grabbed a bottle of milk from the back and enjoyed its taste for the first time in years.

'The company will take that out of my pay,' the milkman complained.

'We can't have that,' Bill said, and gave him ten of the fifty dollars that had been smuggled in to him a few months ago.

They threaded their way towards the city centre. Police cars, sirens blaring, tore past in the opposite direction towards the prison. The snow was still falling heavily and visibility was poor, but the milkman was a cautious driver and was clearly not going to take any risks. As they arrived near the city centre, it struck Bill that six people crammed tightly into a milk wagon would arouse suspicion if spotted by any other drivers. He ordered the milkman to stop the wagon.

'Right,' he said. 'This is where we leave you.'

The milkman tried to speak, but what came out was a croaking sound which petered out. Then they heard him swallow loudly.

'It's okay,' Bill reassured him. 'We're not going to kill you.'

Then he remembered his old psychological trick when he'd been robbing banks.

'Go back to Holmesburg and continue delivering your milk.

But if you go to the cops, there'll be some time in the future when one of our men'll come looking for you. Understood?'

The milkman nodded silently, too shocked and frightened to speak.

'Right! Let's go,' Bill told the others.

They clambered out of the wagon and watched it U-turn and head back towards Holmesburg. They quickly walked several blocks towards the centre of Philadelphia, looking for a car to steal.

They had walked only three blocks when all hell broke loose. One moment there was silence, except for the sound of snow under their boots, the next a police siren wailed nearby and they saw its lights flashing as it headed towards them.

Immediately, they scattered like a flock of frightened birds. Bill dashed between two houses and clambered over a wooden fence into the yard at the back of one of them. Looking back over the fence, he saw the cop car screeching to a halt outside the house and the milkman's wagon pulled up behind. His threat hadn't worked.

Bill ran across the yard and leapt at a fence. It rattled nosily as he pulled himself over. A cop spotted him. There was a loud blast and a bullet hit the fence near his hand as he dropped on to the other side and landed in a drift of snow. He ran close alongside the wall of a house towards another street as lights came on in upstairs rooms. He imagined the frightened but curious residents plucking up the courage to peer from behind their curtains.

As he reached the street, he thought he recognized it from the time he'd spent in Philadelphia over a decade ago. It looked like Frankfort Avenue. He ran as hard as he could in the soft snow. Ahead, siren screaming, the cop car came hurtling round a corner, skidded in the snow, straightened itself and hurtled towards him. Bill's mind raced. Evidently, the cops hadn't followed him on foot. When they saw him heading for a parallel street, they must have got straight back in their car to give chase.

He raced between another two houses and discovered he was in a cul-de-sac. At the end of it was a high brick wall, partially covered by a huge snowdrift, possibly four feet high. He attempted to go over the wall, but instead, he dived into the side of the snowdrift and crawled along the ground close to the wall.

He lay in his frozen tomb and waited for the cops to approach. He heard the sound of their boots come to a halt just feet away from where he lay. They clicked on their flashlights and shone them up the wall.

'We've lost him,' one of them said. 'He must've gone over the wall. Let's go after the others.'

The police car siren started its urgent screaming again. As soon as Bill heard it fading into the distance, he crawled from out of his hiding place, and shook off the snow. He was shivering. He couldn't ever remember feeling this cold. He hurried along Frankfort Avenue. He knew that the entire police force would converge on the area within minutes and he needed to find somewhere to hide. It was too dangerous being out on the streets.

He walked another two blocks and came across a used-car lot with at least fifty cars for sale. He wound his way through the cars towards the back of the lot, found a large sedan, climbed into the back and lay huddled on the floor.

He was wet and shivering. The shivering became more violent, but at least this was a way of keeping his body from succumbing to sleep which could be dangerous in this weather. If he went to sleep in this temperature, he might never wake up.

Every so often, he heard a police car wailing past. He tried to work out a plan. As soon as morning came, there would be hundreds of people about, heading for work. Perhaps he could get lost in the crowd. Who was he trying to kid? He was wearing standard prison clothing: a thin khaki windcheater, black prison trousers, and a baseball cap. He'd been in the prison baseball team and he'd decided to wear the cap during their breakout to keep some body heat from escaping. But wearing a baseball cap in a severe February snowstorm would look odd. He decided there was nothing he could do about it and would just have to chance it. What other choice did he have?

While he cowered, shivering in the dark, his thoughts roamed. He thought of Louise and Jenny. And some of the guys he'd worked with: men like Doc Tate who was convinced Bill was jinxed. Maybe he was right. He brought everybody bad luck. Then he thought of his time with Jean, his final lover. After his capture in Philadelphia, they had tried to implicate her, made out she knew he was a criminal. She denied it, and so did he, and she never went to trial.

After his trial, she didn't return to New York but beat it back home to Harrisburg instead. He wondered what became of her and her thwarted ambitions. Probably settled down with some fine young lawyer. Young lawyer? Jean would be almost forty by now. If she *had* settled down to marriage and motherhood, it would have been some time ago. It was over fourteen years since they'd met at Roseland. Time had dragged by since then. He wondered if Jean or Louise ever thought about him. Somehow he doubted it. They had to get on with their lives. Move on and stop thinking about him. A forgotten man. Forty-six years old and twenty of them spent behind bars. What a waste.

Yet here he was, after battling to stay sane over the last fourteen years, finally free. For the time being.

Eventually, the miserable grey dawn arrived. He guessed it must be almost seven o'clock, as crowds of people shuffled along the sidewalk through the snow. More and more people, all going in the one direction, so he guessed they were heading for a train or bus station.

He couldn't risk the early arrival of someone who worked at the car lot, so he opened the door to let himself out. He pushed hard against a large mound of snow that had accumulated overnight. A blast of cold air clutched his body like an icy hand. The snow was still falling, getting thicker and thicker.

He spotted a large skip at the back of the car lot, brimming over with junk, threadbare tires and rusting automobile parts. He got rid of the gun he'd taken from the guard, covered it with an oily rag, and pushed it as far as he could into the rest of the trash. He threaded his way through the cars and joined the crowd of people walking along the sidewalk.

After two blocks, he reached a bus station. There was a bus leaving for West Philadelphia and he jumped on. Eastern State Penitentiary was in West Philadelphia, he noted with some irony.

As the bus took off, any worries he had about being recognized proved groundless. Frozen early-morning risers were huddled and cocooned in their own separate spaces, glad to be out of the snowstorm for a while. No one gave him a second glance. He sank down in a window seat and basked in the warmth, almost wishing the journey would last longer than it did.

When he alighted, not far from the penitentiary, he was comforted by the arbitrary choice of this particular route. He didn't think the cops would be looking for escaped convicts stupid enough to head in the direction of their old prison. But he still had to be extremely cautious and he kept away from anywhere public. He didn't know if his face would be in the papers yet, but it would be certain to be in the noon editions.

He found a small clothing store that was just opening up, disposed of his baseball cap in a garbage can, and went inside. The proprietor was busy putting items of clothing on to a rack and gave Bill a cursory glance as he entered.

'Morning,' he said.

'What a day,' Bill acknowledged. He selected a working man's dark blue donkey jacket from a rack, grabbed a cloth cap from a pile in a basket, and took them over to the counter to pay. The proprietor hurried over and frowned as he took the two fives from Bill.

'Don't I know you?'

Bill's heart stopped. Should he make a break for it? The man was staring at him, waiting for him to speak. The silence stretched taut, like an elastic band about to snap. Then the man seemed to relax, glad that he'd reached a solution.

'You ever hang out at Barney's pool hall?'

Relieved, Bill gave the man a caught-out grin, as if he'd stumbled on his guilty secret. 'Cannot tell a lie,' he said.

'Been there a couple of times,' the man continued, feeling quite chatty, now he'd made his early sale. 'Never been much good at the game myself, so I stopped going. You want these in a bag?'

'Sure,' Bill said, knowing it would look suspicious if he said he'd wear them immediately. 'I only live round the corner.'

The proprietor bagged Bill's purchases and handed him his change. 'Mind how you go,' he said.

Bill thanked him and left. He wheeled round a corner into a side street, took the coat from the bag, and slipped it on over his windcheater. Then he tugged the hat on and headed back to the main street. Now he looked like any other guy down on his luck and looking for work.

He mingled with the crowds along the main street for a few hours. Although he was hungry and thirsty, he couldn't risk going into a diner. More than anything, he wanted a steaming cup of coffee. So much so, he could 'smell' it in his mind.

At noon, he bought a paper. On the front page, large pictures of him and Van Sant stared out. The others had been recaptured. Van Sant and he were the only two still at liberty. And the state police, as well as the Philadelphia police, were looking for them. Bill decided his only hope was to try to make it to New York.

He caught a bus to Roosevelt Parkway which was the main route to New York. Snow was hurling down and he was soon drenched in white which worked in his favor as everyone else looked the same. He stood at the edge of the highway and jerked his thumb at trucks and cars as they went past, but no one stopped. He couldn't feel his toes and he stamped his feet up to keep the circulation going.

After an hour, he was just beginning to despair when a battered old coupe crawled to a stop. The driver hadn't pulled over too close to the sidewalk, in case his car got stuck, and Bill hurried out into the road. A truck overtaking the car widely honked a horn angrily. Bill swung open the door. 'Thanks. I sure could use a lift.'

The driver was a mild-mannered elderly man, his skin wrinkled like parchment.

'And on a day like today, I could use some company,' he replied. 'I'm headed for Princeton.'

'Princeton'll be fine.'

Bill settled back into his seat and noticed a noon edition of a newspaper in the back, his picture staring up from the front page. He wondered if the driver had seen it yet. He must have done. Headlines sell newspapers so he would probably have glanced at the front page as he bought it.

'Where you headed?' the driver asked.

'Boston,' Bill lied. 'I've been unemployed for a while now. I'm a plumber. And I've got a cousin in Boston who can fix me up with a job.'

The man chuckled. 'Good time for plumbers, I'd have thought. All them frozen pipes.'

Bill laughed along with him. 'Yeah. Maybe I'll do okay in Boston.'

'From Philadelphia?'

'Originally from Newark. Moved to Philly 'bout ten years ago. What about you?'

'Philadelphia born and bred. On my way to Princeton to visit my granddaughter. Got scared of this weather. What with that and the escaped convicts.'

Bill stiffened. He knew he had to sound indifferent, almost like he wasn't that interested in the story.

'I haven't read the papers,' he said. 'What happened?'

The man spoke excitedly, 'Group of prisoners escaped from Holmesberg Prison. Tied the warders up, took their guns and escaped over the wall. Then they held a milkman up at gunpoint and forced him to drive them into Philly. Armed and dangerous they were.'

'Were?' Bill questioned.

'They captured them. They're back inside now so we're quite safe.'

Bill guessed the driver had read the story hurriedly and hadn't picked up on all the details.

'That's a relief. I'm glad they caught them.'

'So am I. I wouldn't want to meet one of those guys on a dark night.'

Bill smiled wryly to himself. Although he'd carried guns, he'd never ever fired one. As for the other convicts who'd escaped, not one of them wanted to risk the ultimate sentence in the chair at Sing Sing.

The driver was a cheerful man and continued to talk excitedly about the escape, and Bill threw in the odd comment as though he knew nothing about prisons and their inmates. The snow continued to fall and the car's wipers brushed it to the edges of the windscreen where it lay thickly so that the view through the windscreen was restricted.

At an intersection, a light turned red and there was a traffic booth on the side of the highway with a cop sitting inside. As the car stopped, he got up out of the booth and walked over to their car. He peered inside through the windscreen, looked at Bill, then at the driver.

This is it, Bill thought. The end of the road. Back inside with another fifteen to twenty added to the original sentences. He'd need to live as long as Methuselah if he was ever going to be paroled.

The light turned green and the cop waved them on. Bill tried not to show his relief.

They reached Princeton in the late afternoon and the driver slowed to a halt. 'Well,' he said, 'we've arrived. I turn left here to the campus. If you head straight on, you'll be going north. Good luck with the frozen pipes.'

Bill laughed politely, thanked him, and got out of the car. He waved and watched as the car turned the corner, regretting the loss of shelter and warmth. He trudged steadily through the centre of Princeton, heading towards the New York highway.

The streets were deserted and treacherously icy. He slipped several times and was soon wet through. By the time he reached the highway on the outskirts of the town, it was almost dark. New York was only fifty miles away, but it might as well have been on the opposite side of the world.

Pretty soon the cold feeling in his body changed to a deadly numbness and he became worried about freezing to death. He left the highway and cut across some fields to try to find some sort of shelter. The snow was knee-deep and he found it difficult to walk. By now it was pitch black and he was starting to panic. After all he'd been through, was this how it would end? A useless parasite, frozen to death in some lousy field.

His eyes strained in the darkness. Up ahead, something black contrasted with the whiteness of the snow. It looked like a building. He moved quicker, shivering and panting with the effort. The shape turned out to be a derelict barn, its door hanging off and its one window broken.

He went inside. It was pitch black and empty. At least it offered some sort of shelter. He knew, if he was to survive this night, he had to keep moving. He jumped up and down on the spot and smacked his arms against himself. He desperately wanted to sleep, he could feel the tiredness washing over him, his brain telling him to lie down and take it easy.

Reaching out for the side of the barn, he steadied himself then slid to the ground. He closed his eyes and the relief was unimaginable. A soothing phrase drifted into his mind: To sleep, perchance to dream. Where had he heard it before? It was...it was on Broadway. Yes, that was it. He and Jenny had been to see *Hamlet*. A tragic death. Death! The word screamed at him from the deeper recesses of his soul.

He opened his eyes and held on to a groove on the wall of the barn. With an enormous effort, he pulled himself to his feet and began slapping his sides and moving round in circles. Move! Move! He had to keep moving. Keep his circulation going. But he was exhausted. This was his second night without sleep.

The night dragged on forever. More than once he decided he'd had enough and was tempted to settle for much needed sleep. But as soon as he huddled on the floor for a brief respite, a warning screaming voice inside his head made him get up again. Then he'd have to start painful movements to keep from freezing and to keep himself awake. It was a nightmare, this never ending night of cold exercise. Slowly, the pitch blackness outside became a charcoal grey. The dawn light revealed it had stopped snowing and a weak amber sun glinted through the clouds.

As soon as it was light, he left the barn and trudged across the field towards the highway. While he couldn't really feel much warmth from the weak morning sun, at least he knew he wouldn't freeze to death now. And the effort of clambering through the snowdrifts helped to keep frostbite at bay. As soon as he reached the highway, he began to feel more optimistic. If he could survive a night like that, he could surely overcome any more hard knocks.

He'd been trying to hitch a ride for only five minutes when an old rusty Packard chugged past and then stopped. Bill ran forward and swung open the creaking door. The driver was wearing oil-stained dungarees.

'Where you headed for?'

'New York.'

'Hop in. I could use some company.'

'Good luck with the job search,' the mechanic said. 'I hope you get fixed up real soon.'

He stood on the Bronx sidewalk and thanked him with

genuine warmth, gave him a half-salute, and slammed the door shut. He watched as the Packard coughed and spluttered, its gears grinding noisily, as it pulled away from the sidewalk.

Bill awarded himself a small, self-confident grin. He was back on form. He'd been lucky. The driver accepted his story about being down on his luck and seeking work. The approach to New York terrified Bill. He knew they'd be watching all the tunnels and bridges. The driver had chosen to enter across the George Washington Bridge, and Bill saw the toll booth looming ahead. He had no choice but to stay calm and bluff it out. The driver drew level with the booth and handed over his fifty cents. The cop barely looked up. Just two working stiffs on an early shift. It had been that simple.

He walked towards the nearest subway, bought a newspaper, and caught the first train heading for Brooklyn. He hated sitting on subways, where commuters randomly examine the faces of their fellow passengers.

He ducked behind his paper. The headline news was about Russian spies getting information on the atom bomb. The story of Bill's escape came a close second. He learnt the FBI were helping the police and were keeping tabs on all his old haunts, and anyone he had ever known was being kept under surveillance. Bill marveled at the stupidity of the police spokesman who had given the press this information. Now he was warned. Contact no one he knew.

He got off at Borough Hall station and mingled among the crowds in Fulton Street. He was desperate for something to eat so he found a crowded restaurant, went in and ordered steak, fries, mushrooms, fried tomatoes and coffee. It was the first meal he'd enjoyed since 1933. He had about thirty dollars left now which wouldn't last very long. He needed to get himself a job, something that provided him with accommodation. He decided to apply for a job as some sort of hospital orderly in a nursing home. They didn't pay much, but at least board and lodging was provided.

First, he needed to sleep. He paid for his meal and went into the men's room. There were three cubicles, and they were all vacant. It wasn't ideal, but snatching some sleep in one of them seemed to be his best bet. Recovery time.

As he sat on the toilet seat and leaned back against the cistern of one of the cubicles, his eyelids started to close. They were jerked awake again as someone banged into the cubicle next to his. Unable to fall sleep immediately, he couldn't help but listen to the undignified noises of some guy's bodily functions. Soon, the toilet flushed and the relieved man left as Bill's heavy eyelids closed again and he drifted into a deep sleep.

Louise stands in Times Square. Bright lights, but no people. Apart from Louise, Times Square is deserted. A taxi screeches to a halt close by and Dutch Schultz gets out. He puts an arm around her and escorts her into a restaurant. Bill sees himself panicking. He knows what is about to happen but is unable to do anything about it. He knows he is dreaming. He sees himself curled up against the cistern of the toilet. He also sees the Dutchman, sitting at a table opposite Louise.

Two waiters arrive to take their order, both carrying tea towels over their arms. The towels are whipped aside and are replaced by Colt 45s. The waiters shoot the Dutchman in the head and blood spurts everywhere, drenching the restaurant, like a color wash in a painting. Louise is terrified, screaming and screaming, and from somewhere a baby cries out for its mother.

He was still tired, exhausted, as if he were drugged. A strange buzzing sound echoed through his brain, and nothing about him seemed real. For a moment, he was completely disoriented, clueless as to where he was.

Gradually it came back to him: the escape from Philadelphia, the snowstorm and his arrival in New York, and the most wonderful meal he'd ever eaten. His eyes wandered around the cubicle until he was able to focus on his situation. But, as he didn't have a watch, he had no idea how long he'd been asleep. He needed to get out of here as soon as possible, just in case he'd outstayed his welcome.

As he weaved his way through the still busy restaurant, he was relieved to see that nobody paid him the slightest attention. Not a single waiter glanced at him. The way to remain anonymous in this teeming city, he realized, was to relax and not behave suspiciously, looking over his shoulder with fear. Melt into the crowd like he belonged there.

Outside, it was still freezing cold. He turned up the collar of his jacket and, with shoulders hunched, walked along the street looking for an employment agency. A clock in a jewelry store window informed him that he'd been asleep for less than an hour. But his cat-nap seemed to have done the trick. He felt able to cope and think clearly now.

He found an employment agency only three blocks away from the restaurant and went inside. A clerk with lank brown hair sat at a paper-strewn desk and stifled a yawn. She barely looked up as he entered. Her hand, nail varnish cracked and chipped on her fingers, gestured insolently to a chair in front of her desk.

'Take a seat.'

He sat and waited while she finished reading a document. He watched her enjoying the little power she possessed before finally pushing the paper to one side and staring at him.

'Well,' she said, 'what can I do for you?'

'I'm looking for a job.'

A quick appraisal, as she took in his dowdy appearance. She sniffed almost belligerently and said, 'Do you have references?'

Bill shook his head. 'I've been unemployed for some time now. That's why I've come to New York looking for work.'

'When did you last have a job?'

'About three years ago. In Detroit. I worked as a hospital porter. I've often done that sort of work, looking after elderly sick people. I know how to care for them.'

She brightened, and became more animated. Bill watched with some amusement, as a flurry of efficiency propelled her into reaching for an application form from a desk drawer. Perhaps it was because he'd chosen a job at the bottom end of the market. She could easily find that type of employment and she had the employment agency commission to consider.

She handed him the form and a pen and he filled it in, giving his name as Edward Lynch. As she accepted the completed form, he saw the faint glimmer of a smile, teasing the edges of her mouth. It wasn't much but it was the best she could manage.

'There is always a demand for hospital orderlies,' she said. 'I'll ring around. I might be able to fix you up. Come back in an hour.'

He thanked her, went outside to the bitter street again, and walked aimlessly around for an hour, stopping only to purchase a cheap watch at a small shopping mall.

When he returned to the employment agency, the clerk looked up and the same hint of a smile was still struggling to surface.

'You're in luck,' she said. 'The Farm Colony on Staten Island needs an orderly. Eighty dollars a month - not much I know - but you get your board and lodging.'

She handed him an introductory card to give to his prospective employer. 'I hope it works out.'

'It sounds like just what I'm looking for,' Bill replied.

He had never spoken a truer word in his life. It was his last remaining chance to make something of his life. If he got the job, it would be his first properly paid honest employment since working in a munitions factory in 1917.

Thirty years. It had to be some sort of record.

CHAPTER 23

MARCH, 1947

There were one hundred and twenty rooms in Ward 16, sixty on either side, divided by a long narrow strip like a runway. They were cubicles rather than rooms, each with a bed, chair and clothes locker. Although staff referred to them as rooms, these cubicles were missing a fourth wall and had no doors.

It was Bill's job to keep sixty of these cubicles clean, as well as doing other menial fetching and carrying tasks for the 'guests' - as Bill called them. Having been institutionalized for twenty out of his forty-eight years, he refused to refer to them as inmates.

The ruler of Ward 16 was Mrs. Chadwick, a matriarchal domineering woman, whose standards of cleanliness and efficiency were gargantuan and efficient to the point of possessiveness, for this was her domain, her world, and nothing was allowed to sully its smooth running.

As he was mopping the floor in Room Number 18 late one Monday afternoon, while its occupant was in the recreation room watching TV, Bill felt the shadow of Mrs. Chadwick's presence falling across the bed.

He turned and caught her stern expression, but this was softened by the halo of light coming from the window of the cubicle opposite; her red hair and the sunlight gave her a classical splendor, as if she had stepped out of a renaissance painting. This contrasted with the vivid blue of her eyes which had an unnerving coldness about them, and her unblemished complexion was as starched as her pristine uniform. Bill felt humbled by this holy matriarch.

'Eddie!' she snapped. 'That mark!'

Bill looked down to where she was pointing. All he saw was a lovely clean floor.

'What mark?'

She sighed deeply, shook her head with profound frustration and grabbed the mop from him. 'If you want a job to be well done,' she moaned, 'there is nothing for it but to do it yourself.'

She began mopping furiously and, sure enough, Bill saw the object of her irritation, the vague horseshoe outline of a heel. The imprint vanished and, satisfied that she had expunged the culprit, she handed the mop back to Bill and gave him a thin, triumphant smile.

He was tempted to tell her that throughout most of his adult life he had had to keep his cell spotless, lest he incurred penalties far more severe than her disapproval. But, of course, he kept quiet. He needed this job. This was his sixth week. Thankfully, he had passed the two-week trial period and was now accepted as part of the permanent staff.

'I'm sorry,' he said when it dawned on him that she expected an explanation. 'I was working as hard as I could. I guess I just missed that bit. Must've been the sunlight.'

Nurse Chadwick stared at him like a bird of prey about to swoop. 'Don't make excuses,' she said. Her eyes softened and she added, 'You look tired, Eddie. Let me get you a glass of orange juice to keep up your strength.'

She swept off to get him the drink, and he watched her upright figure swishing along the aisle. In his first three weeks, he'd often been tempted to tell her exactly what she could do with her job; but just when he felt he'd reached the end of his tether, she did something as disarming as this thoughtful gesture. He knew her irritation was due to her own high standards of cleanliness and her dedication to her work, and he became even more determined to stick with the job. He thought about Dr Schwarz and how he'd like to prove to him that he really could adjust to a normal life.

He lay on his bed in the dormitory, reading *A Farewell to Arms*. Much as he enjoyed being left alone to read, he couldn't concentrate. All his fellow male employees who shared the dormitory with him were absent. He worried that some of them distrusted him, simply because he was not a drinker, and because he kept pretty much to himself.

They were nearly all itinerant workers, going from one hospital to another; and they were all heavy drinkers, if not alcoholics. Most of their wages went on booze. Sometimes they just disappeared, gone in a haze of alcohol; then, when they sobered up, they found another job. Often the hospital where a man worked would give him back his old job. And Farm Colony was no exception. The most recent employee to go on a bender was Jim Stringer. He stayed sober for some time, managed to save a bit of money, then went out for a few beers one night and returned a fortnight later from a binge that lasted until his money ran out.

'Eddie!'

Jim Stringer suddenly appeared in the doorway. He grinned as he raised a pint bottle of bourbon, like he was sharing a secret with Bill. He staggered over to his bed, and sat down heavily on the edge. Bill sighed and put his book to one side.

'You don't drink, do you?' Stringer said.

It was more statement than question, and Bill knew it was part accusation. Whereas he'd been seeking anonymity, trying to blend in and not stand out from the crowd, the opposite had happened. He was different because he was not a part of the drinking culture.

'I like a drink like the next man,' he said. 'I'm just trying to ease up.'

Stringer thrust the bottle under Bill's nose. 'Here, why not join me in a little drink?'

Bill was aware he was being tested. He accepted the bottle

and gulped a generous measure. It was foul. The worst drink he'd ever tasted. His throat burned and the heat lit up his stomach like a furnace.

'That packs a hellava good punch, Jim,' Bill managed as calmly as his burning larynx would allow.

He saw the shifty, suspicious look in Jim's eyes disappear.

'Whadda yah say we catch a movie some night?'

Bill nodded and smiled. 'Yeah, I'd like that.'

He was accepted. They were buddies.

Bill became devoted to his sixty 'guests' and spent a great deal of time getting to know them and listening to their life histories. Most had been rejected by their families and friends, and were in Farm Colony to await a visit from the person they most feared. Once this visitor called, it was Bill's job to put the departed guest into a box and wheel him to the morgue.

Bill liked most of these elderly men and, although he had witnessed death and violence in his time, it always saddened him when they died. He became personally involved with them and tried to bring what little comfort he could to them, in what little time they had left.

One evening, he was making his way towards Ward 16, intending to spend some time with poor arthritic old Mr Calman, a mission beyond the call of duty, when an excited whoop stopped him in his tracks. It was Ethel Langster, the nurse's aide. She was carrying a copy of the *Daily News*.

'Hello, Willie Sutton,' she exclaimed triumphantly.

It was what he had feared the most and it hit him like a battering ram. He hoped the shock didn't show on his face.

'Willie who?' he said nonchalantly. 'What are you talking about?'

She showed him the newspaper. A big jewelry store had been hit for $200,000 and they were pointing the finger at Willie the Actor. Bill took in the information at a glance and laughed lightly.

'That's a lot of money. If I were Willie Sutton, you think I'd be at Farm Colony on eighty a month?'

Ethel was staring closely at him. She took the paper back and studied the photograph. 'You must admit, you look very like him.'

'You're right. I do. But then I believe we all have a doppelganger somewhere.'

Ethel looked blank. 'A what?'

'Sorry. A double. Almost a twin.'

'Oh, I see what you mean.'

Bill decided his best bet was to pursue this line of reasoning. 'You must have mistaken someone for a close friend or relative before now. It's happened to me quite a few times. You see someone you think you know, you approach them, and it turns out to be a complete stranger.'

Her face lit up as she remembered an incident. 'Hey! I know what you mean. I remember one time, years ago, I thought I saw my boyfriend staring into the window of a delicatessen and I prodded him in the back. It was so embarrassing. The stranger was as surprised as I was. Only, he was nothing like my boyfriend. But, just from behind…'

'Some people do bear an uncanny resemblance to other people though.'

Ethel laughed. 'Like you and Willie Sutton.'

'He's an ordinary looking guy,' Bill said. 'I'll bet there are lots of men who look like that.'

'And, as you say, you'd hardly be working at Farm Colony if you'd robbed all those banks.'

Bill grinned at this foolish notion and said, 'I must get on.'

As he walked away, she called after him, 'I can't see a bank robber looking after the sick like you do. You're a good man, Eddie.'

He thought he'd convinced her, but the incident had shaken him, made him feel insecure. He hoped and prayed she didn't show the newspaper to anyone else and gossip about his uncanny resemblance to Willie the Actor.

CHAPTER 24

AUGUST, 1949

Now a trusted and respected employee of Farm Colony, Bill had been promoted to work in Ward 20, a women's ward. Apart from the slight pay increase, he was flattered to be given this responsibility. Working on a women's ward was a job that was allocated to only the most reliable and dependable of hospital porters.

It was in Ward 20 that he met Mary Corbett, an Irish nurse's aide. A short, cheerful woman, with green-grey eyes and dark brown hair, she had sailed for America in 1938, following her three brothers over. She had worked hard for ten years and managed to save enough money to buy a small, two-storey house not far from Farm Colony. Bill heard she was about to place an advertisement in a Staten Island newspaper to take in a boarder, so he dashed off at the end of his shift and caught up with her in the hospital grounds.

'I know you're probably in a hurry to get home,' he said, 'but I wonder if I could have a quick word, Mary.'

She gave him a broad smile. 'Yes, Eddie. What is it?'

Bill loved the lilt of her Cork accent, unchanged from the day she sailed for America.

'I heard you're going to advertise for a boarder.'

A small, puzzled frown wrinkled her brow and the top of her nose.

'The thing is,' he continued, a little breathlessly, 'I'd like to apply for the room, and it would save you having to advertise.'

'Why would you want to do that, seeing as Farm Colony provides you with free accommodation?'

'It's just that I've never felt comfortable in the dormitory. Most of the other employees are drinkers. And I'd like my own room. It would be worth it for that alone.'

She hesitated. 'I - I'll have to think about it, Eddie. It's just that I haven't made up my mind about letting a room just yet. It was just an idea.' She looked embarrassed. 'No, I'm sorry, that's not true. I have made up my mind to take in a boarder; it's just that I'd like to think about your proposal. I'd like a little time. I hope you understand.'

He smiled at her. She was the most honest and sincere person he had ever met, and she was obviously incapable of telling even the smallest of white lies, he reckoned.

'Of course,' he said, 'I can't blame you for wanting to sleep on it.'

'Thanks, Eddie, I'm glad you understand. I'll see you tomorrow.'

'I'll be here,' he said, cheerfully.

He watched her walking towards the hospital gates and gave her a wave when she looked back. As he strolled towards the dormitory, he thought about the luxury and safety of having a room of his own, sharing a house with someone who didn't have a suspicious mind. For sometime now, living in the dormitory had become his worst enemy.

When he was working, cleaning the ward, he felt secure. And talking to the patients, he was the perfect listener, hearing all their problems, and they never quizzed him about his past. But when he tried to relax after work, feelings of unease grew to tormenting proportions.

Whenever the other guys in the dormitory probed him about his past, he could see the suspicious looks that came into their eyes, even though he always stuck to the same bland story and tried to tell them as little as possible. They surely suspected he had something to hide, and maybe it was only a matter of time before one of them stumbled on the truth.

As Bill knew she would, Mary Corbett made enquiries about him from other members of staff at Farm Colony, and he felt confident they would vouch for him. She also had a word with some of the patients in Ward 20, and was particularly impressed by his gentle patience in comforting them and listening to their life histories.

Three days after his request to board at Mary Corbett's house, she approached him in the hospital grounds where he liked to walk during his lunch break. As soon as he saw her expression, the beatific way she smiled at him, he knew he'd been accepted.

'Well, Eddie,' she said, 'you come highly recommended by staff and patients. I'd be honored to have you as my boarder.'

He returned her radiant smile. 'Thank you, Mary. I'm really grateful. A house, with a room of my own...'

'You really weren't happy at the dormitory, were you?'

'Glad to be out of it. I didn't fit in, seeing as I'm not a drinker.'

'Well, you may find my home a little on the small side...' Mary began.

'I'm sure it'll be fine,' Bill assured her. 'When can I move in?'

'How about Sunday? Early afternoon. I go to church in the morning.'

Bill grinned happily. 'Sunday it is.'

Mary's house was a red-brick building, comfortably furnished, with a living room and kitchen on the ground floor and two bedrooms and a bathroom upstairs. It was quite small but, after two years in a dormitory, it was like a palace to Bill. Each evening, as he returned after a hard day at the hospital, he enjoyed the luxury of relaxing in his own room, his own four walls, often leaving the door open. There was a small yard at the back of the house and, later on in the evening, when the sun had lost its fierceness, he enjoyed sitting outside, listening to Mary talking about her family and life back in the old country.

For the first time since his arrival at Farm Colony, he felt content and secure. Bill Sutton had been discarded. He was Eddie Lynch now, going straight, proving to himself that he could make something of his life.

During the last week in August, as the hot summer weather became more overbearing and humid, he began to feel restless. Although he still worked hard on the hospital ward, he began to feel the stirrings of discontent. With his prison education, the Spanish, and shorthand and typing he'd learned, he felt capable of so much more than menial work.

During a day off, and feeling particularly unsettled, he felt the lure of Manhattan pulling him like a magnet. He missed the sights, smells and sounds of Broadway, Fifth Avenue and Times Square. He decided he'd risk going over on the ferry and would give the subway a miss.

Manhattan at last and he began the long walk up Broadway.

It was too hot to continue on foot, so he bought a newspaper to duck behind, and caught the subway from Canal Street to 42nd Street. He went to see a matinee at a Broadway theatre and came out absently humming one of the tunes from the show.

He felt he was back where he belonged. He walked about aimlessly, drifting along with the crowds, staring at the shop window displays. Some expensive suits caught his eye at a gents' clothing store, and he spent some time wistfully gazing at them, as a part of him missed Bill Sutton, the snappy dresser.

'Hello, Bill,' a voice whispered close to his ear.

It struck the fear of God into him. He was afraid to turn round. He summoned the courage. It took him a while to recognize the overweight, grey-haired man in stained dungarees. The last time he'd seen Tommy Kling was more than ten years ago at Eastern State Penitentiary.

'Tommy!' Bill managed after a pause.

They shook hands warmly. They'd been firm friends at Eastern State, until Tommy was transferred to another institution. Bill felt a great deal of affection for Tommy. The ex-convict was like Doc Tate, a man he could trust implicitly. An honorable thief.

Tommy smiled and tilted his head towards the window display. 'Used to be quite a dresser myself. Not any more.'

Bill nodded at Tommy's working clothes. 'So what are you up to these days?'

'Work as a longshoreman on the West Side docks. What about yourself?'

'You mean you haven't read the papers?'

Tommy glanced over his shoulder and lowered his voice. 'Sure. I know you broke out of Holmesburg, Bill. What I mean is: how're you making out?'

'Surviving,' Bill said. 'Always looking over my shoulder. Mind if we take a walk, Tommy? I don't like to stay in one place for too long.'

As they walked towards West 44th, where Tommy had a room, he glanced at his watch.

'I know it's a bit early for dinner, Bill, but if you'd like to join me - I know this restaurant - the food is great. Cheap too. And if you ever want to get in touch, I always eat there, same time every day. An hour from now.'

'If you want to leave it for another hour,' Bill smiled. 'Don't change your habits on my account.'

Tommy chuckled. 'Stomach's already beginning to whine.'

Tommy's chosen restaurant was large, stuffy and noisy, and the customers seemed to be mainly working men, shoveling gargantuan portions of food into their mouths like hungry ogres.

Steam and cigarette smoke hung midway between the tables and the ceiling like a mist over a swamp, and the clatter of cutlery and the sound of raucous laughter echoed in the cavernous room like a distorted symphony. They found a table and Tommy picked up the menu. His eyes glinted hungrily, and Bill remembered their time at Eastern State Penitentiary. Tommy always had a childlike excitement in anticipation of eating. And, whenever the inmates criticized the food, he invariably protested that his tasted okay. Bill's heart sank as he imagined the culinary disaster facing him.

'They do a great stew here,' Tommy enthused. 'I can recommend that and the mashed potatoes.'

He spotted Bill's less than enthusiastic response. 'Or maybe you'd prefer something...'

'No, that sounds fine by me,' Bill said to placate his old friend.

As the waitress took their order, to be on the safe side Bill buried his nose in the menu. When she'd gone, Tommy took out a pack of Chesterfields and offered one to Bill. Bill accepted it and lit up. In prison he'd given up smoking to use the tobacco as currency instead. Now he was on the outside, he smoked occasionally. But if he needed to smoke when he was in Mary's house, he went out into the yard.

Tommy blew a cloud of smoke upwards, and fixed Bill with an amiable gaze. 'How much d'you need, Bill?'

'I don't need anything.'

'The offer's there. Need some cash, I can let you have a few hundred bucks.'

'Thanks, Tommy. I appreciate it, but I'm okay right now.'

The food arrived, steaming and strong smelling, piled high on the plate. Tommy's eyes lit up and he grabbed his fork. Bill stared at the plate with apprehension. Huge chunks of grey meat surrounded by a slurry of overcooked, watery mashed potatoes, and a portion of peas filled it. Warily, he tasted a mouthful of potatoes. A mulch of starch and salt. He tried the peas. Zero taste. This was prison food.

He looked across at Tommy, who was eating heartily. Prison chow had ruined his friend's taste buds but, if ever Tommy ended up back inside, at least the food wouldn't bother him.

CHAPTER 25

SEPTEMBER, 1949

Bill took two weeks' vacation, and during the first week he used the time to improve Mary Corbett's house. As well as painting the outside of the house, he waterproofed the cellar and put up shelves. At the weekend, he went into St. George and bought himself a secondhand typewriter.

At home, he sat listening to the radio, copying the programs in shorthand. Later, he typed them out as quickly as he could, testing his speed. When Mary came home from a Saturday shift, she was curious and wanted to know the reason for this seemingly pointless industry. He explained how he was trying to improve his shorthand and typing.

'Eddie,' she said, 'you seem to me to be much too clever to work as a hospital porter.'

'Well...' he began tentatively, wondering how she would take the news. 'For some time now I've been thinking of handing in my notice.'

At first she frowned, then she saw the mischievous glint in his eye and her face relaxed into a shy smile.

'Are you looking for a better job?'

He nodded and grinned. 'I'll quit at the end of October. But I'll start looking for a job right away.'

She gave a little whoop of delight. 'Oh, Eddie, I'm so pleased. I really am. I'm sure you'll have no difficulty in finding something decent. And I'm sure Farm Colony will give you excellent references. First thing Monday morning I'll ask the supervisor to provide you with references. Then you'll be able to make a start on Tuesday.'

Mary's excitement on his behalf was infectious, and optimism swelled inside him like an orchestral crescendo. For the first time in years his self-esteem had shot up.

People like Mary and the staff at Farm Colony believed in him, and he knew he couldn't let them down. To repay them for their belief in his dedication, he had no alternative but to adjust to a life of honest toil. Here was an opportunity to make something of his life. A clean slate, and this time he'd have legitimate references to show any prospective employer.

By Tuesday afternoon, after slogging round at least half a dozen employment agencies, his optimism gave way to a stunned disbelief. Every clerk at every employment agency expressed dismay when he told them his age. At forty-eight he was too old. Of course, he could have lied, but there didn't seem much point. He had to face it, he looked his age. Maybe even older.

For three days he applied for dozens of jobs at dozens of agencies. But it was the same story wherever he went. They didn't hold out much hope. Always a polite dismissal: 'We'll keep you on our list just in case something comes up.'

Towards the end of the week, the disappointment weighed like a stone in his stomach, and his neck ached from where he'd slept awkwardly the night before. Tired and thirsty, after a morning of further rejection, he found himself shambling along 47th Street in Sunnyside, Long Island. He passed the Manufacturers' Hanover Trust Company Bank and automatically reconnoitered the building, assessed the condition of the roof, weighed up the alarm system, calculated the risks involved.

He counted how many people went in and out, saw how busy it was, and walked inside. It was instinct, the way he could mentally photograph everything inside the bank and remember every detail. The temptation to hit this bank was so stimulating he began to feel like a different person. Whereas a few minutes ago he had suffered the shoulder-aching depression of a defeated man, now he experienced the challenging surge of power that came from knowing he could successfully rob this bank if he had to.

He still had his other options, and he owed it to Mary's faith in him to go straight. Shrugging off the temptation to steal, he left the Manufacturers' Hanover Trust Bank and headed for Prospect Park, Brooklyn.

He carried the jar of money in a brown paper shopping bag, on top of which was a loaf of pumpernickel and some cans of soup. As soon as he got home, he left the soup and pumpernickel on the work surface in the kitchen and went downstairs to the cellar. He took the mud and clay covered jar from the paper bag, wiped it clean, and tried to unscrew the lid. It wouldn't budge. He dashed upstairs and ran the jar under the hot tap for several minutes.

He had to hurry. Mary was due back any minute now.

He took a deep breath, braced himself and twisted the lid. The veins on his neck bulged with the strain and, just as he thought he might have to smash the jar, the lid rotated sharply. He rushed back to the cellar, unscrewed the top of the jar, turned it upside down and shook the money out. The bundles that plopped on to the workbench were stuck together and discolored.

Years of wet weather had somehow penetrated the jar and the banknotes were ruined. He pried apart some of the bills on the outside of a bundle. Many were useless, but the outer layers had protected the notes in the middle. With some care, attention and infinite patience, maybe he could salvage them.

Hearing footsteps in the hallway, he grabbed the banknotes and stuffed them at the back of the cupboard where all the painting and decorating materials were stored. Then he dashed upstairs. Mary was already at the kitchen sink, filling the kettle.

As he entered, she threw him a sympathetic smile over her shoulder. 'How did it go today?'

'Still the same old story. Man of my age. Hard to place. Of course, with my Farm Colony references they could find me employment in any New York hospital. But that's not what I want.'

'What are you going to do, Eddie?'

'I might go into business for myself. Open a small luncheonette or diner.'

'Wouldn't that be rather costly?'

'I've saved most of my wages. And I don't think I've ever mentioned it before, but I've got a relative in Buffalo who's well-heeled - quite wealthy in fact - he might loan me an interest-free sum.'

'That's wonderful news. Oh, Eddie! I'm so pleased for you,' Mary said, breathless with excitement.

He was touched by her enthusiasm and felt almost guilty about lying. But he had no choice. He was still a man on the run, constantly looking over his shoulder, scared of that look of recognition. A man who still owed the State a great deal of his time.

CHAPTER 26

NOVEMBER, 1949

THE MANUFACTURERS' HANOVER TRUST. THE MANUFACTURERS' HANOVER TRUST. It kept repeating itself like a litany. He couldn't get it out of his head. Like a neon sign in his brain. Or a catchy tune playing the same simple bars over and over.

Three times he'd been back to Sunnyside in October, thoroughly cased the bank building and had learned everything there was to know about it. If ever he'd seen a vulnerable bank before, this was it. The money was there for the taking.

It was bitterly cold, and the wind blew right through his layers of clothing and chilled his bones. He didn't dare stand opposite the bank for much longer in case he drew attention to himself. He walked on and couldn't resist looking back over his shoulder. The bank had become an obsession. At night he lay awake and, in his mind's eye, he could see the bank staff arriving. He knew them all by sight, could picture what they were wearing, knew all their routines and habits.

As he walked back towards the El, he thought about Mary, and how happy he was in her house. And the way he was respected at work. These things had to count for something. But he was starting to experience conflicting emotions now. He still worked hard, and still devoted much of his time to the 'guests' at Farm Colony, yet his esteem sank under the burden of this treadmill existence.

He resented this unskilled service, knowing he was capable of so much more. Only now it was too late. He was stuck with it. Either he could end his days in the routine drudgery of unskilled labor, or rob the Manufacturers' Hanover Trust and do what he should have done back in 1933 - head for California or Mexico and start a new life.

Now even his relationship with Mary was tenuous. The more he got to know her, the more he realized how one-sided it was. He could never be as open with her as she could with him. Whenever she asked him about his past, he had to lie, and this troubled him. He desperately wanted to lead a normal life. Her brothers, their wives and their children, whenever they visited her, were kind and pleasant to him, but he was always an outsider and, however much he conversed with them, it was always in general terms, for there was little he could reveal about himself.

Feeling despondent and a trifle confused about his purpose in life now, he caught the El and headed for Manhattan, where he was due to meet with Tommy Kling and another ex-con by the name of John Altieri who was looking to pull off a bank job.

As he waited for them in a bar on Columbus Avenue, he tried to read the daily paper but his attention span was diminished by the conflict raging inside him. He desperately wanted to stay on the straight and narrow path, but at the same time he could feel the bank in Sunnyside calling out to him like a siren.

Loud talk at the bar about a football game interrupted his thoughts and he knew they were talking about one of the main stories of the day, about the Army beating the Navy thirty-eight to nil in front of almost a quarter of a million people, including President Truman. This news, which was today's talk of the town, had escaped Bill's attention, as he struggled to come to terms with why he was meeting another crook.

Bill's distaste for alcohol forced him to eke out his beer by sipping it very slowly. He realized it could make him the focus of the bartender's interest, so he was relieved when Tommy and Altieri arrived. They joined him at his table and he ordered two more beers. Altieri got straight down to business, as soon as they'd been served,

'The joint we've cased is a big bank in Newark,' he said. 'It's a cinch, this one. A cinch.'

Bill had met him only once before and he was fascinated by the sibilance in Altieri's voice, which made him sound slightly effeminate. However, his looks were from the tough-guy school, dark and brooding, shifty eyes and a thin scar that ran from a corner of his mouth to his cheekbone.

'How many staff?' Bill asked.

Altieri hesitated before speaking. 'I know what you're driving at. It's okay. I've got some real good men on this job.'

'That wasn't the question, John. How many staff at this bank?'

Another slight hesitation. 'Seventeen.'

'I know what you're thinking, Bill,' Tommy Kling interjected. 'Lots of staff are hard to keep in order. That's why John plans on using at least five men on this job: John, you, me and two other guys.'

Altieri, who'd been staring intently at Bill, clicked his fingers. 'It's been bothering me since the first time we met. Now I know where I've seen you before. You're Willie the Actor.'

Bill didn't like what he was hearing. He didn't altogether trust Altieri, although Tommy assured him he was a regular guy.

Bill lowered his voice. 'Sure. And I've spent twenty years of my life behind bars. Not exactly a success. Why would you want to work with someone like me?'

Bill had already made his mind up that he wasn't going to work with Altieri, but he needed some sort of trade-off, in case the ex-con felt bitter about being turned down.

Before Altieri could reply, Bill added, 'Look, I've got this bank I've been casing, over in Sunnyside. Less than half the staff of your Newark Bank. Three men could take it easily. And Sunnyside's a prosperous area. How about it?'

Altieri glanced at Tommy for his opinion.

'Believe me,' Tommy said. 'Bill knows his stuff.'

'Why don't we go back to Tommy's room?' Bill suggested. 'I can take you through every detail of the Sunnyside bank. But one thing I want you to understand. I won't be in on the job.'

'Why would you go to all this trouble, casing the joint and everything, just to hand over details like this?'

'My face has been in all the papers. It's too well known. And they've distributed leaflets with my mug on it to all the theatre costumiers. "If this man tries to hire a costume from you...."'

Altieri's eyes narrowed suspiciously. 'So what's in it for you?'

'I've just changed my mind. I'm out of it. You can have the details free of charge. And you can go and check out the bank for yourself. You'll see I'm giving you good information.'

Altieri thought about it for a moment and drained his glass. 'Okay, let's go back to your place, Tommy, and iron out the details.'

As they walked towards West 44th, Bill began to feel proud of himself. He had looked temptation in the face then turned his back on it. It was like he'd been suffering from a disease most of his life, but he was fully recovered now.

He thought of Mary and how he wanted to measure up to her expectations. She wanted him to succeed, and just days ago he had quit his job at Farm Colony. Now he planned to put all his energy into the search for his own business. And he might just be able to scrape money together to make it work.

He had managed to restore seven thousand dollars of the Prospect Park money and, coupled with another six thousand he'd saved from his wages over the last two and a half years, it might be enough.

CHAPTER 27

DECEMBER, 1949

Two weeks before Christmas, he called at Tommy's restaurant at the usual time and found the longshoreman tucking into a massive steak and fries.

'Join me,' Tommy called. 'Come and have some grub.'

Bill was almost tempted. The meal looked tasty, but then he noticed how Tommy was chewing on the same piece of meat over and over again and decided against it. He ordered a coffee and doughnut instead. He leant across the table and spoke quietly to Tommy, though it wasn't strictly necessary with all the noise and babble in the restaurant, but he wasn't taking any chances.

'You thinking of teaming up with Altieri?'

'Why? What's the problem?'

'Let me give you a piece of advice. Don't do it, Tommy.'

'Why not?'

'The man has bad guy, hood, mobster, crook - you name it - written all over him. Soon as he shows up at Sunnyside, they'll call the cops.'

Tommy looked up from his plate and gave Bill a knowing look. 'Something tells me you'd like him to get caught.'

'What gives you that idea?'

'You're still on the run and planning to go straight. If Altieri was caught using the same *modus operandi* as Willie the Actor, it'd take the heat off you.'

Bill grinned at his friend. 'You ain't just a pretty face, Tommy. But if you think I'm setting Altieri up, then forget it. That bank's there for the taking. It's just that I don't think he's capable of it. My instinct tells me he's untrustworthy.'

Tommy chewed quietly for a while, then fixed Bill with a steady look.

'You were right to trust your first instinct, Bill. Know what I found out about Altieri? Tells people he was banged up for robbery. Turns out it was rape. Fifteen-year-old girl.'

An image flashed into Bill's mind of a young girl, a sweating Altieri, naked hairy buttocks, thrusting away on top of her. He stared at his coffee cup, lost in his thoughts of Jenny. Was she vulnerable, without a father to care for her and protect her? She was eighteen years old now, a young woman, and he'd missed her journey through childhood into the blossoming years of young adulthood.

'Maybe Altieri deserves to be set up,' Tommy mused.

'It'd only take one phone call.'

Bill drew his lips tightly together and shook his head. 'Much as I detest sex crimes, Tommy, I'm not an informer. It goes against my nature.'

'Same here.'

'Besides, I have another instinct about Altieri. I don't think anyone needs to set him up. I don't think he's up to it.'

Bill watched as Tommy dipped his last piece of steak in ketchup. 'And what about you, Tommy? You're all square with the law. You've served your time. What tempted you?'

Tommy shrugged. 'I guess I didn't have much of a life. So it was no great risk.'

Bill knew exactly what he meant. He could picture Tommy at Christmas, alone in his room, listening to the radio.

'And another thing,' Tommy added, 'I don't think my job's secure. They're laying men off all the time. I may be next.'

'So what are you going to do?'

'I've saved a bit. I might move to Florida. Soak up some sun. I've had it with this place.'

'Well,' Bill said, 'I hope it works out.'

He reached to get a dollar out of his wallet and Tommy stopped him with a hand. 'It's on me.'

Bill stood up. 'Thanks, Tommy. Merry Christmas.'

Tommy waved it aside. 'How long is it you've been out? Two and a half years? Stay lucky, Bill. Move on. There's a great big world out there. You can get lost in it.'

'Yeah, I'll think about it. So long, Tommy.'

But he knew he never would leave New York. It was in his blood. And he lived with the hope that one day he might see his daughter again.

CHAPTER 28

JANUARY, 1950

Mary was due home any minute now. Knowing how she was addicted to strong tea, and how she always liked several cups as soon as she arrived home, Bill filled the kettle and put it on the stove. He heard the key clicking in the lock.

'Hi, Mary!' he called out, brightly.

There was no reply and, when she entered the kitchen, he saw her face was pale and drawn and her eyes were red and glassy, as if she'd been crying.

'Oh, no,' he said. 'One of the patients died? Not Mrs Graylich?'

She always took a patient's death badly. Her sadness usually lasted for the early part of the evening, at least until she'd drunk several cups of the darkest brew and until Bill had commiserated with her. Only then would she snap out of it.

But tonight she stared at Bill with a mixture of fear, confusion and hurt. Then she took a newspaper from her bag and placed it on the table. The Manufacturers' Hanover Trust Bank, in Sunnyside, had been hit and he was being blamed for the robbery. His photograph and the headline 'WILLIE THE ACTOR STRIKES AGAIN!' was emblazoned across the front page. So, Altieri had got clean away.

Mary's voice was tremulous and quiet when she spoke. 'Everyone saw the papers today. They recognized you.' She tried to stifle a choking sob. 'Are you Willie the Actor?'

Bill was numb with fear and self-loathing. This was the moment he'd been dreading. He loved Mary. She was like a sister to him, and now she was going to suffer because of his crimes. He had to convince her it was all a mistake, if only to give her some hope for the future.

He looked her straight in the eyes, and said, 'Willie Sutton is my half-brother. We look very much like each other. I swear that's the truth, Mary.'

She wanted to have faith in him and gazed steadily into his eyes. Only a buzzing sound from the refrigerator disturbed the silence.

'I swear it's the truth. I wanted Willie to give himself up. He wouldn't. And how can you turn in your own flesh and blood?'

'Oh, Eddie!' she cried. 'Why didn't you tell me?'

He shrugged. 'Guess I was ashamed of Willie. He's brought nothing but disgrace to my family. If my mother were alive...'

He sighed and shook his head, as though unable to comprehend the magnitude of his half-brother's crimes. Then he heard Mary's sharp intake of breath and saw the decisive look that burned in her eyes. 'Eddie, I think you'd better see the Nursing Supervisor, and tell her what you've told me. They're all talking about you. At the moment, they're unsure what to do about it, but...'

Alarm bells rang in his head. Any moment now one of the staff might contact the police. He had to get out of here. If it wasn't already too late...

'She might have left for the evening,' Mary said, as Bill crossed to the door. 'Why not leave it until the morning?'

'I'm not going to Farm Colony, Mary. I'm going to look for Willie. I know the sort of places he frequents. I must talk to him, persuade him to give himself up. It's my only chance to carve out a peaceful life for myself. I'll only be a minute.'

He left her looking dazed and apprehensive, and dashed upstairs. Hurriedly, he stuffed his money into the bottom of a bag, crammed clothes on the top, zipped it up, grabbed his coat and rushed back to the kitchen. Mary sat at the table. The kettle started to whistle. Bill turned it off.

'I may be away for two or three weeks,' he said. 'So here's a month's rent in advance, just in case it takes longer to find him.'

He put some dollar bills on the table, money he'd earned legitimately. With this gesture, he thought she might carry on believing in him, in the knowledge that he planned on coming back. And it might delay her from going to the police. She might even manage to persuade people at Farm Colony that he was really Eddie Lynch.

'Goodnight, Mary,' he said, as he slipped into his overcoat. 'I'll be back as soon as I can.'

She looked up at him, her eyes moist. He could see her inner turmoil, the desperate struggle to retain her faith in him.

'Goodnight, Eddie,' she whispered. 'I hope you find Willie. I'll pray for both him and you.'

'Thanks,' he said, hurrying out the back door. As he stepped into the yard, the icy wind seemed to predict his grim future, back out in the cold. Life on the run again.

Mary's house had been his sanctuary, a place of warmth and security. Now he'd be dodging in and out of the shadows once more, constantly looking over his shoulder. He cursed his stupidity. He should never have tipped Altieri off about the bank.

He hurried towards the bus stop. His only hope of getting off the island was by bus across the bridge to New Jersey, then back to Manhattan via the Holland Tunnel. If staff at the hospital had alerted the police, they'd probably be watching the ferry terminals into Brooklyn and Manhattan.

He caught the bus outside Halloran Hospital. He was the only passenger. The loneliness of the empty bus heightened his feeling of defenseless isolation. He desperately needed a crowd in which to lose himself. And the darkness outside, as it crossed the bridge to New Jersey, accentuated the eerie gloom of his journey, while the bus rattled and shook, buffeted by the gusting wind.

It stopped on the New Jersey side and a three passengers got on, followed by a cop. Bill quickly closed his eyes and let his head drop on to his shoulder. He could hear the cop talking to the driver but couldn't hear what they were saying. Any moment now he expected the cop to come walking down the aisle to tap him on the shoulder...

He heard one of the passengers clearing his throat noisily. He wished he could hear what the driver was telling the cop. He didn't dare to open his eyes.

The gears of the bus ground noisily and the vehicle started to move off. He kept his eyes tight-shut for some distance. When he opened them again, he saw they were heading in the direction of the Holland Tunnel. Whatever the driver had told the cop, he was off the hook.

When he got to Manhattan, he felt he had no choice but to check into a hotel for the night. He selected a small, anonymous-looking one near Grand Central station, the type of establishment utilized by out-of-town salesmen. He wore his most confident grin as he approached the desk clerk.

'John Mahoney,' he said. 'I believe my company made a reservation for me.'

The clerk searched through a bundle of index cards, slowly shaking his head. 'Can't find your name, sir. Which company you with?'

'The Boston Safety Razor Company.'

The clerk pursed his lips and shook his head again.

'There's been no reservation made in that name, sir.'

Bill feigned annoyance. 'This is the second time my company's done this to me. And I suppose you're fully booked.'

'You kidding?' the clerk said. 'This time of year?'

'In that case, I'd like to book a room, and I'll pay for it now. I have a busy day tomorrow and an early start. If you could make out a receipt to John Mahoney of the Boston Safety Razor Company, so that I can reclaim the amount...'

'There an address?' the clerk asked.

'Just Boston, Massachusetts'll be fine.'

'Will you be having dinner, sir?'

'I've already eaten,' Bill lied. There was no way he could risk sitting in a hotel dining room when his picture was on the front page of all the papers. He paid for his room and made for the elevator.

'I hope you have a comfortable night, sir,' the clerk called after him.

In the classified section of the *Brooklyn Eagle*, Bill found a furnished room to let in a predominantly Puerto Rican district near Flatbush Avenue.

He hurried on over to the house and rang the bell. It was answered by an elderly white-haired lady who seemed to be staring at him but not into his eyes. There was something strangely unnerving about her expression but he couldn't put his finger on what it was.

'Morning, ma'am,' he said. 'I've come about the room to let. Is it still available?'

'Yes, it is. And your name is..?'

'John Mahoney.'

'I'm Mrs Marsden. The room's at the top of the stairs and it's the first on the right. If you'd like to go up and take a look at it, I'll wait down here.'

As he entered the dark hallway, he noticed the landlady fumbling for the handle to close the door. And when she spoke again, she looked to where she thought he stood.

'I won't come upstairs, if you don't mind,' she said.

He realized Mrs Marsden was blind. He couldn't believe his luck. There was no way she could identify him as Willie the Actor.

'Be back in a minute,' he said, and hurried upstairs. The room was a little on the small side and the furniture looked secondhand, but it was adequate. He hurried back downstairs.

'I'd like to take the room, Mrs. Marsden, if that's agreeable to you?'

Her head was slightly cocked to one side as she listened intently, vetting him through sound. He felt slightly vulnerable, wondering if there was something in his voice that might betray his character, something that a sighted person might miss.

'Whereabouts you from?' she asked.

'Newark,' he told her. 'I have a sales job lined up, selling elevated shoes. D'you have any other guests in the house, Mrs. Marsden?'

'I have two others. Both Puerto Rican gentlemen.'

She didn't see Bill smiling, but she sensed the warmth in his tone.

'My mother was Spanish. I'd quite enjoy talking in her native tongue once more.'

'Good. Well, Mr. Mahoney, the room is eight dollars a week and I'd like it fortnightly in advance, if that's all right by you?'

Bill counted out sixteen dollars and slipped them into the landlady's hand.

'Thank you,' she said, and tapped the door beside her.

'This is my room. If you need anything, don't hesitate to knock.'

CHAPTER 29

APRIL, 1950

Bill felt secure in his room at the boarding house and spent hours talking to the Puerto Rican tenants, who accepted him as half-Spanish, and wouldn't have dreamt their mild-mannered fellow tenant was a wanted criminal.

Yet, he still felt nervous whenever he ventured further than his immediate neighborhood. He hated using the bus or subway, so he risked buying a brand new Chevrolet from a dealer on the upper West Side. He had the owner's license made out in the name of John Mahoney, then spent hours in his room laboriously forging the state stamp in the driver's license, trying out varying shades of blue ink until he was satisfied that he had a reasonable facsimile.

Bill knew his money would eventually run out and there was a vague plan forming in the back of his mind. These days he carried a .32 automatic in a holster on his waistband which he'd bought from a criminal associate in the Bronx. His plan was in its nascent stage. If he could pull off just one more successful robbery, then this time he really would hit the trail for Mexico and put the past behind him.

He couldn't work alone though and needed someone he could trust. He decided to give Tommy Kling a visit at his restaurant, but Tommy never showed up. Bill didn't like using any restaurant or bar too frequently, preferring to remain an anonymous stranger wherever he went. On Sunday April 30th, he decided to risk one more visit to the restaurant, knowing that Tommy never worked on a Sunday and always ate just after midday.

That was when things started to go horribly wrong. He was parked not far from Bergen Street station, just a few blocks from his boarding house; but when he tried to start the Chevy, the ignition gave a feeble click and he suspected there was a loose connection to the battery. He raised the hood and checked it but everything seemed to be in order.

He glanced at his watch. It was almost midday. Now if he wanted to reach Tommy in time he'd have to catch the subway. He locked the Chevy, bought a newspaper, and caught a train to 42nd Street. He sat in the back seat of the last car, facing the rear, avoiding any seats running the length of the car, so he didn't have to sit facing a row of passengers.

When he arrived at the restaurant, it was twenty-past twelve. Tommy was nowhere to be seen. Bill ordered bacon, with pancakes and maple syrup, and two fried eggs, easy-over. His energy was being sapped by constant worry and he felt he needed sweet and stodgy fuel to help him through the day. After his meal he drank two cups of coffee. By now it was almost one o'clock. Either Tommy had been and gone, or he'd finally made it to Florida.

Depressed by the feeling that time was running out, Bill walked back to the subway, mulling over the problems of finding an accomplice. He would have to frequent some of his old haunts and hang around with the criminal fraternity again. This was risky. Sometimes it was hard to tell the criminals from the undercover cops. And he was one of America's most wanted men, so no doubt the FBI were also out to get him

On his return journey to Bergen Street, the back seats in the rear subway car were occupied, so he was forced to sit facing the centre aisle. As he raised a newspaper in front of his face, a strong sense of being watched assailed him.

It was like a sixth sense, the uncanny feeling that a pair of eyes was staring at him through the paper. He dropped the paper slightly and, sure enough, there was a young guy of about twenty staring intently at him. Bill shifted his position, sitting slightly to one side. He pretended to be reading, but was trying to see out the corner of his eye what this young guy was like. He was comforted by the fact that he was wearing black suede shoes and a colorful, striped windcheater with a number on the front. He didn't look remotely like a detective, more like a hip young guy who frequented dance halls.

At Bergen Street, he got up quickly as the doors slid open, as though he'd almost missed his stop. So did the young guy and followed him out. Bill tried not to panic. Maybe this was also the young guy's stop. He took the stairs two at a time, rushed out into the sunshine and hurried along for a couple of blocks.

He could see the young guy was still following him, on the opposite side of the street, but by the next block he had disappeared. Bill stopped and looked around for him. He was nowhere to be seen. Although it was warm, he experienced a grave-treading shiver, like a kick in the spine.

Jesus! He was becoming paranoid. He stood perched on the edge of the sidewalk and took another look round. Everything seemed normal. People were going about their business, enjoying a leisurely Sunday. He walked on until he reached his Chevy. He unlocked it and raised the hood, to see if he could sort out the battery fault. He became so involved with the mechanical problem, he quickly forgot about the young guy and didn't notice the two cops standing behind him.

'What's the trouble?'

Bill almost banged his head on the hood. He straightened up and squinted into the faces of the young cops who stood with their back to the sun. 'Having problems with the battery, I reckon.'

'Let's see your owner's license,' the cop demanded.

Bill got the paperwork out of his jacket pocket and handed them over. He was relieved to see the cops were more interested in the bill of sale than the forged license. He knew that automobiles were checked in this neighborhood as a matter of routine. Auto theft was a rising crime.

Diverting their attention from the driver's license, he pointed to the bill of sale. 'Can you believe that? Brand new Chevy, less than a month old, and already it's developed a fault. They don't make them like they used to.'

The cops stared at each other. One handed Bill back his papers.

'Seem to be in order,' he grunted.

The cops walked away. Bill wiped the sweat from his forehead with the back of his wrist, stretched under the hood and began tinkering again. He checked all the connections. Still, he couldn't find the problem. He got in the car and tried the ignition, just in case he'd righted a loose connection without knowing it. It clicked again. Still nothing.

He got out to take another look under the hood. The two cops and a man in a blue serge suit were striding across the road towards him. He knew the man in a suit was a detective, he could tell by the belligerent yet defensive walk, a demeanor that was prepared for a confrontation.

'You'd better come to the station with us,' he snapped.

'Why? What's wrong?'

'You look like Willie the Actor,' one of the cops said.

Police Headquarters was not far away on Bergen Street,and the cops walked one either side of Bill, the detective following behind. As Bill was marched in to the police station, the young guy in the suede shoes was leaning against the front desk, talking to a sergeant and looking pleased with himself.

So in the end, Bill thought incongruously, it was a young hip-cat in suede shoes that had brought Willie the Actor to his knees.

As soon as he was through the doors of one of the interview rooms, a lieutenant, the two cops and the detective started firing questions at him. At first he denied he was William Sutton, but when they got the fingerprint man to take samples, he knew it was just a question of time.

Now it would be over. No more lying, cheating, hurting the people he loved. No more going into hiding and waiting for the sharp rap on the door. No more fear. The big escape was well and truly over. And he realized that all his life he'd been attempting to escape from himself as much as the authorities.

The fingerprint man had left to check the prints. The lieutenant frowned thoughtfully and sucked his teeth.

'Have you frisked this man?' he asked the others.

The way they exchanged looks, he could tell it had been overlooked.

'Do it now!' he snapped.

'Stand up!' one of the cops demanded. 'And lean over the desk, legs apart.'

The cop ran his hands from Bill's armpits down to the bulge on his waist. He slid the .32 automatic out of its sheath and laid it on the desk. They all stared at it. The lieutenant fixed Bill with a gloating, triumphant look,

'Well, well, well. Now, empty your pockets.'

Bill took everything out: pack of cigarettes; book of matches; bunch of keys and wads of banknotes.

'How much is there?' the lieutenant ordered.

'Six thousand dollars.'

'Why didn't you bank it?'

'It's never safe in a bank.'

All the cops in the room exchanged looks and started to snigger. The fingerprint man burst into the room and pointed at Bill. 'That's William Sutton!'

The lieutenant's eyes glinted. 'And that's all the proof we need.'

CHAPTER 30

MAY, 1950

Warden Klein, of the Long Island City Jail, put Bill under constant surveillance prior to what would be a lengthy trial. A guard was on permanent duty outside his cell, the bars of which ran from floor to ceiling.

Early on a Monday morning, Bill scribbled some pencil notes in the margin of an exercise book, but the guard's hacking cough made it difficult to concentrate. He looked up and caught the guard's eye.

'Sounds like you might be coming down with a cold, Jim,' he said.

The guard shrugged and smiled. 'It was our baby's christening yesterday. We had quite a party after. I think I smoked and drank too much.'

Bill continued making polite conversation for a while, then he picked up a copy of *The Grapes of Wrath.* 'I hope you won't think me rude, Jim, if I carry on reading until my lawyer gets here.'

'Sure, Bill. Don't mind me.'

He recalled the beatings he took from the cops before his sentence to Sing Sing, and reflected on how different things were now. His non-violent felonies, and his daring escapes from Sing Sing and Holmesburg Prison, had made him something of a celebrity. The newspapers portrayed him as a latterday Robin Hood. He noticed that even the cops and guards seemed to treat him with grudging admiration now.

Not everything was plain sailing. He had asked Warden Klein if he could have a typewriter and a fountain pen and these had been denied. He knew the warden suspected him of possessing the same powers as Houdini, but he was aware that it would be a lot harder to escape from the Long Island jail than from any penitentiary.

He resumed reading the Steinbeck novel, reflecting on how much tougher the lives of the squatter families were than America's most wanted man. At least he had three square meals a day and any book he cared to read.

He heard the rattle of keys and looked up. His lawyer had arrived.

'Morning, Mr Herz,' the guard said, unlocking the cell.

The lawyer was heavily-built with dark, curly hair, and was surprisingly agile and boyish for such a large man in his mid-forties.

He chuckled pleasantly and acknowledged the guard, 'You look like I feel.'

The guard laughed politely and locked him in. He sat opposite Bill and his smile vanished. It was down to business.

'When you were caught,' he said without any preamble, 'you were packing a gun. If a man has a gun on him, this suggests he has every intention of using it.'

'I've never fired a gun in my life,' Bill protested. 'But when I robbed those banks, I carried one. You think they'd have handed over the money if I'd threatened them with a baseball bat?

'And I was carrying the automatic when I was on the run because if I was spotted on the street by someone, I could threaten them, then run for it. If someone came towards me, I'd already made up my mind to shoot above their head.'

The lawyer stared impassively at him, wondering whether to believe him or not.

'Look, Mr Herz, throughout my entire record you won't find a single instance of my firing a gun at anyone.'

'And what if you'd been in a tight corner? Would you have fired at a cop?'

'Those two cops who collared me in Bergen Street, they weren't sure if I was William Sutton or not. I could have shot them both and made a run for it. But I didn't. I came quietly. *You* know I did. And *they* know I did.'

Herz nodded thoughtfully. 'Okay. That takes care of the gun. Now let me ask you: prior to your arrest on Bergen Street, did you ride on the subway?'

'Yes. But why is that relevant?'

'Some young guy by the name of Arnold Schuster popped up from nowhere, contacted the papers, told reporters he spotted you in the subway, followed you, then tipped off the cops.'

'There was a young guy who sat opposite me on the subway, got off at the same stop and followed me down the street. He must have tipped them off, because when I arrived at Police Headquarters he was standing at the desk, looking full of himself.'

Herz took a newspaper out of his case. The front-page picture showed the suede shoes kid triumphantly waving a Willie the Actor 'wanted' circular in his hand and grinning at the camera. He wore a smart, light-colored, double-breasted suit. He had obviously dressed for the occasion.

'That's him,' Bill said. 'Good-looking young guy.'

The lawyer gave Bill a wry smile. 'The cops tried to keep this one quiet. Wanted to take all the credit for themselves. The two who arrested you on the street have been promoted a grade with a thousand-a-year increase.'

'I hope they still get it. I like to think someone's going to benefit from this.'

'Whether they do or not is not your problem, Bill.'

Bill nodded solemnly. 'I know. My headache's going to be proving I had nothing to do with the Sunnyside robbery. As I said before, I'm not pleading guilty to that one.'

'I don't expect you to. You don't have to prove you're

innocent. You're innocent until the District Attorney proves you're guilty. Don't worry. I'll see you get a fair trial.' He broke into a smile. 'Now, I have some good news for you. You've been front-page news and her mother's told her all about you. Apparently she was shocked at first. But now she knows who you are, she wants to see you.'

Bill felt his heart pounding. 'Not Jenny?'

The lawyer nodded and smiled, indulging in his own amiability for a moment. 'She'll be along at three this afternoon.'

Huge tears of joy welled in Bill's eyes. Embarrassed, the lawyer searched for his pack of cigarettes.

Time loitered annoyingly that day. He could no longer concentrate on reading. He was too excited. Every so often little tremors of nervousness fluttered in his stomach. What if she despised him for being a criminal? Herz had assured him that she was longing to meet her father. What if she had second thoughts on meeting him? What if she didn't like him?

These thoughts bombarded him. To fill in some of the gaps about his family and more prosaic worries about his appearance, he questioned his guard at length, but didn't take in a word of what he was told.

Another nerve-wracking half-hour had passed, and just when he felt he couldn't bear it any longer, he heard the door opening at the end of the corridor and footsteps walking towards his cell. He stood up.

And there she was!

Gazing at him between the bars of the cell, with an air of curiosity and expectation.

'There you go, Miss,' the guard who accompanied her said.

The rattle of the keys unlocking the cell doors sounded like the sweet tinkle of wind chimes. Bill was transfixed as his daughter walked timidly into the cell and stood before him, shy and uncertain. She looked into his smiling eyes and felt weak at the knees.

She had imagined this meeting for hours and days and, now it was real, she was slightly at a loss. Slowly she held out her hand. He grasped it as if she was made of delicate porcelain and gave it a gentle squeeze. She was leaning slightly towards him with her head slightly cocked, offering him her cheek. A frisson of fear snatched at him. What should he do?

As he kissed her, he fancied she smelled of sunshine and rose petals, just as she had when she was a tiny baby.

The guard re-locked the cell. 'I'll be just a little way along the corridor.'

Bill flashed him a grateful smile. 'Thanks, Jim, I appreciate it.'

Jenny sat down and Bill slid on to the edge of the bed opposite her and gestured helplessly with his hands.

'Last week you were nineteen,' he said. 'I didn't forget. I've never forgotten your birthdays. It's just… I was in a tight jam. I wish I could have gotten you something.'

'This visit is the best present I've ever had.'

Her sweet smile, her innocence, and the loving way she looked at him, compounded the remorse he felt, and he began to stammer, 'I… I'm sorry… Not much of a father, am I? A criminal.' He gestured hopelessly at the cell walls.

'I don't care what you've done,' she whispered. 'I love you because you're my father. I'll always stand by you.' She added defiantly, 'I don't care what you've done.'

'Thank you, Jenny. Thank you.' He swallowed noisily. 'I just wish I could have been a better father.'

'You're not a bad man. I know you're not. You've never harmed anyone.'

'That's not true. Most of the guys I worked with died violent deaths. And I lied to your mother. She had no idea I was a criminal. I'm glad she remarried. I really am. And has he been a good step-dad to you?'

'He's been wonderful.' She stared at him, as though

photographing the moment. 'But you're my father. You always will be.'

She fumbled around in her handbag and brought out the telegram he had sent her when she was two years old. He wiped the moistness from his eyes as she held it out for him to read. He knew the words off by heart.

"LOVE AND KISSES TO MY DARLING ON HER BIRTHDAY. LOVE. DADDY."

'You kept the telegram all these years.'

'Mom kept it for me. She gave it to me on my sixteenth birthday. That's when she told me all about you. All those years up until that time, I thought you'd left us, walked out on us. It came as a great shock, knowing that it wasn't through choice you'd left. I wish she'd told me the truth much sooner than she did. I could have handled it. I know she meant it for the best, but...'

'You were only three months old when I began my sentence. Your mother came to visit me, and we both agreed that she wouldn't tell you until you were older.'

'But if she'd told me, I could have come to visit you. By the time she told me, it was too late. You'd escaped by then.'

Bill's voice was almost a whisper now, 'It was you we were thinking of, Jenny. Schoolchildren can be very cruel. If they'd known your father was a jailbird...'

Her eyes flickered defiantly. 'I told you, I could have handled it.'

'I don't doubt it,' he gave her an affectionate smile. 'When you were very young, and you asked about me, how did Louise - your mother - tell you?'

'She said lots of kind things about you. She said it wasn't your fault. You were a loving father, but you had problems.'

'What kinds of problems?'

'Health problems. She said it wasn't your fault. You didn't know what you were doing - that you were a lost soul. We used to pray together that one day you'd regain your sanity and adjust to living a normal life.'

'You know, Jenny, what your mother told you wasn't so far from the truth. There must have been something seriously wrong with me to do what I did. I used to have long conversations about it with the prison psychiatrist.'

A frown creased his forehead. 'But since escaping from Holmesburg, I did manage to go straight. And I didn't do the Sunnyside bank robbery. You can believe that, can't you?'

She nodded fervently.

'But whether they find me guilty or not is academic,' he continued. 'The past sentences they dished out'll run for the rest of my natural life. Maybe I can achieve peace of mind, find a way of paying back society for the things I've done, but I'll never be able to walk with you in a park, take you to a restaurant or the movies, do any of the things that I've dreamt about.'

She looked intently at him, her eyes bright and passionate.

'I love you,' she whispered. 'I'll always stand by you. I'll always come to visit you.'

He could see the tears welling up in her eyes. She moved impulsively and sat next to him on the bed, letting her head fall on to his shoulder. She started to shake and he felt the wetness of her tears through his shirt.

'I love you, Dad,' she sobbed.

He put his arm round her and, with his other hand, smoothed her hair. 'I love you too.'

She had called him "Dad", and he smiled to himself. For the first time in years, he was truly content.

He waits in the shadows not far from his old man's store. Any minute now the cocksucker'll come along, then...fuck him...lights out. Kiss the world goodbye, pal. He hates fucking stoolies, and anyone who puts the finger on Willie the Actor deserves what he has coming to him. Jesus H Christ! Guy's a fucking hero. Should be fucking decorated.

Tension building now as he fingers the gun in his pocket. His breathing rapid and shallow. When he thinks about the fucking little creep who put William Sutton away, he feels a burning inside of him, a sensation not unlike the time he pissed razor blades after he'd been with that little whore from Newark. Fucking bitch! She'd be next on his list.

First he has to deal with the fucking cocksucking salesman. Maybe he'd take his old man out as well. Nah, on second thoughts, leave the fucker to mourn for his creep of a son. Now, the fucker's parents weeping at the cemetery, a dark rain-drizzled scene full of black umbrellas like the movies, he almost gets a hard-on.

He checks his watch. Cocksucker should have been home hours ago. Probably in some dancehall boasting to his friends how he put the finger on Willie the Actor. Acting like a big-shot. Just some fucking little creep of a salesman. About to get his one-way ticket to Blackoutville.

He hears a noise from the end of the alley, the clatter of a garbage can. He sees a streak of white fur and grins to himself. He likes cats. They take shit from nothing and nobody. They live for themselves. That's how it should be.

Then he spots him. The fucking squealer is crossing 9th Avenue. Any minute now he'll walk down 45th to his home. And he has to pass the alley. He can hear him approaching now. Whistling some nigger tune. Fucking asshole!

He steps out of the alley and sees the startled frightened expression on the cocksucker's face as he aims the gun at his head. He waits a moment. Wants the fucking cool cat to know he's going to die.

'This is for Willie the Actor,' he tells him, then pulls the trigger. A loud bang and the bullet gets him in the eye. Guy goes down with a fucking great hole where his right eye was, just a fucking black tunnel now. He leans over and lets him have it in the other eye. Another fucking black hole.

He straightens up, pockets the gun, and vanishes down the alley.

Bill was woken in the middle of the night by the urgent pounding of footsteps. Familiar rattle of chain and keys.

Clank of cell door opening. He blinked the sleep from his eyes as the lights came on and found himself staring into the face of Warden Klein. Usually it was a benign, avuncular face; that of a friendly football coach. Tonight it was filled with disgust and he looked at Bill as though he was an insect he'd like to squash.

'On your feet,' he snapped. 'And get dressed. Man from the DA's office wants to question you. And he has detectives with him.'

Bill dressed hurriedly, nonplussed as to why he was being roused in the early hours. While he dressed, the warden read him his rights with grim reluctance, 'In a case like this, Sutton, you have a right to speak with your attorney first. You also have the right to remain silent while being questioned under these circumstances...'

Bill thought about his lawyer who had been the one unlucky enough to be present in court while he was being arraigned, when the judge had appointed him as his defense attorney. George Herz wouldn't make a cent out of what could be a long involved case, yet he was putting as much effort into defending Bill as if he'd been a rich client paying thousands of dollars. He was even giving him cigarette money out of his own pocket.

There was no way Bill was going to inconvenience him. 'I'll talk to the detectives,' Bill said. 'No sense in dragging Mr. Herz out of his bed in the middle of the night. I'll waive any legal rights I have.'

'Okay. Let's go.'

Bill knew that something big must have happened because he was taken to the warden's office where he was greeted by the hostile stares of three men who looked as though they'd like to lynch him. The warden introduced them. 'This is Thomas Cullen, Assistant District Attorney, and these are detectives Morrisey and Smith.'

'Sit down, Sutton,' the assistant DA commanded.

Bill sat in a chair which had been placed at a right angle to the warden's desk, facing the assistant DA, who sat on a high-backed chair, smoking a pipe with a sickly-sweet aroma. The two detectives stood, one either side of him, both with their hands deep in their pants' pockets, juxtaposed like book-ends. The warden crossed behind Bill and sat at his desk.

Bill sensed there must have been an important new development with the case, but he was confused. Why this meeting at 2am? He wanted to ask them what was going on, but something told him it was better to remain silent. He waited, knowing they were using the silence to unnerve him.

'I've just come from the scene of a crime,' one of the detectives began. 'I've seen dozens of shootings in my time, but this was one of the worst. Young kid shot through each eye. Guy by the name of Arnold Schuster, the guy who identified you on the subway, the guy who provided the info that subsequently led to your arrest.'

Bill froze. It took him a moment to comprehend what he was being told but, as the realization hit him, a sickness gripped him deep in his stomach and he tasted bile at the back of his throat.

'Which friend of yours did this?' Cullen demanded.

'This is - is - inconceivable. I - I have no friends who would do anything like this,' Bill stammered.

The detectives laid into him verbally, taking it in turns to bombard him with questions.

'This looks like a revenge killing. Which one of your gang did this?'

'I don't have a gang.'

'Don't lie to us, Sutton. You didn't pull the Sunnyside job on your own. Who were you working with?'

'I didn't do the Sunnyside job. I'm pleading not guilty to that one.'

'But there's only one person with a motive for wanting Schuster dead and that's you.'

'I had nothing to do with it. I've never worked with violent men, hoodlums or trigger-happy scum. I never had time for them. Check my record. You won't find a single instance of a gun fired by me, or anyone I worked with.'

'Maybe not in the past, but now you're facing the prospect of rotting behind bars for the rest of your days, maybe you wanted to get even.'

'I swear to you, I'm not a violent man. Check with the prison authorities, all the time I spent behind bars, I never once had a fight or hit a man. I haven't had a fight since I was twelve years old.'

'But you might respond differently if you could get someone else to do your dirty work for you. And shooting someone between the eyes is the traditional method the underworld uses to dispose of informers. Who was it, Sutton? Who did this hit for you?'

'No one. I don't know anyone who could commit such a senseless crime. A youngster like that. I had nothing against him. I swear I didn't.'

'He was the guy who put you away, Sutton, and you're trying to tell us you had nothing against him?'

'That's right. I had nothing against him or the two cops who apprehended me. Like, I've nothing against the DA's office for prosecuting me. I've never had anything against the judges who sentenced me, or against the guards...'

Cullen, red-faced with anger, interrupted Bill. 'Save it, Sutton!' he snapped. 'After this, your love affair with the public's over. The newspapers'll crucify you for this. They'll be howling for blood. And any jury during your trial's always gonna be aware they're dealing with scum. A hoodlum.'

Bill looked down at his lap. His hands, which were clasped together, were shaking uncontrollably. He forced himself to calm down and looked up at Cullen. 'How could killing this poor kid have helped me? Don't you think I would have known it would go against me with any jury?

'This kid's picture's been in all the papers. He's been using his sudden fame to plug his father's merchandise. Probably some hoodlum got angry and behaved irrationally...a psychopath. All I know is I didn't have anything to do with it. And I don't know of anyone I've ever associated with who would.'

An image of Dutch Schultz burst into his head and everyone saw the uncertainty in his eyes. One of the detectives pounced. 'Why the hesitation, Sutton? Who were you thinking of then?'

'Dutch Schultz. I once worked for him, collecting for his Harlem numbers racket. He was a vicious killer. But he's dead now. I don't think even he would have done a thing like this. The senseless murder of a civilian. There'd be no gain. Only a psycho could have done something like this.'

The two detectives grabbed chairs to sit on and Bill knew it was going to be a long interrogation. They grilled him for another two hours. Finally, a little after four in the morning, his interrogators had had enough. They knew they wouldn't get anything more out of him. And there was a reluctant feeling growing inside each of them that he might just be telling the truth.

The guard returned him to his cell. As soon as the light went out, he lay awake on his bed, tormented by guilt and self loathing.

Just a good looking kid. A youngster. His whole life ahead of him. And what about the living? The agonized suffering of the parents, sobbing their hearts out. Their aspirations for their son wiped out because of...Willie the Actor. He was responsible. Everything he touched. Tragedy. Death. Despair. He was cursed. Responsible for the grief he brought everyone.

In the morning, he tried to write a letter of condolence to the boy's parents. He felt morally responsible for the death of their son and he wrote five drafts, trying to explain about how he'd had nothing to do with the crime, but felt responsible somehow. But he knew deep down the parents would be quite rightly repelled by any communication from him and, after completing the fifth and final draft, he read it through and then tore it up along with the rest.

CHAPTER 31

JUNE, 1950

It was stifling in the courtroom, and the trial was long and often tedious. It also had its lighter moments, which came as welcome relief.

'Detective, when you asked the defendant why he didn't bank the money, what was his reply?'

'He said, "It's never safe in a bank".'

The laughter that rang through the court went on for too long and Judge Farrell had to rap his gavel long and hard until it died down. Bill's quote probably didn't merit such a reaction, but it came after the DA's office had called so many expert witnesses to the stand to give what seemed to be unnecessary evidence, everything from ballistics to the layout and architecture of the Sunnyside bank.

Bill's remark made headlines the following day. As far as Willie the Actor was concerned, he was now treated by the Press as good entertainment value and his reported escapades were written as though he was admired for his audacity.

After the murder of Arnold Schuster, before the trial began, the Press condemned him as a vicious hoodlum. But, a week into the trial, John Mazziotta, a psychotic ex-convict, shot a striptease artiste from Newark, claiming she had poisoned him with her unclean body. Ballistics identified the gun as the same one used in the Schuster murder and Bill was back in favor with the Press and hundreds of young kids who had elevated him to hero status.

His worst moment during the trial came when Mary Corbett was called to the stand. He leant over and whispered to Herz, 'Don't question her. Whatever she says will be the truth. She doesn't know how to lie.'

'But what if her testimony hangs you?' Herz asked.

Bill shrugged. 'Then I'll hang. But I don't want her to suffer any more than she has already.'

While Mary Corbett gave her evidence, she caught Bill's eye and he smiled reassuringly. She hesitated, unsure whether to return his smile. The DA was already on to his next question. 'On the day of the Sunnyside robbery, what time did you leave for work?'

'I start work at seven, so I usually set off at six forty-five.'

'And was the defendant still at the house?'

'Yes, he was.'

'What was he doing?'

A slight hesitation before she answered, 'As I left the house, he was putting on his overcoat.'

'So, he was preparing to go out?'

'I think he was. Yes.'

'Had you any idea where he was going?'

'He often went out early. He was going to start his own business. He was looking to buy a small luncheonette, or something.'

'And you believed him?'

'I had no reason not to.'

Bill wanted to shrink in his seat, to disappear. He felt unworthy of Mary's friendship. She had trusted him and he had fed her nothing but lies. He caught Herz looking at him, and he knew the lawyer wanted to cross-question her. Bill shook his head.

Mary was on the stand for almost an hour. Her worst moments came when she was asked about the night after the robbery, when she returned from Farm Colony and confronted Bill about it. The DA was astonished that faced with such damning evidence as the newspaper photograph, she had still given the defendant the benefit of the doubt. A faint trace of derision crept into the DA's tone, and Bill hated him for it.

Eventually, Mary's evidence came to an end, and the judge looked expectantly towards Bill's lawyer.

'No questions, your honor.'

The bank manager was one of the key witnesses. When he was asked if he could identify anyone in the court who had robbed his bank, he immediately pointed an accusing finger at Bill.

'That man there,' he said. 'He was one of the robbers.'

Herz questioned him, 'Prior to the robbery at your bank, do you ever recall seeing William Sutton's picture in the newspapers in connection with other robberies?'

The DA leapt to his feet. 'Objection! I can't see that this is relevant, your honor. Counsel for the defense is implying that the witness picked him out because he saw his picture in a newspaper. Whereas my client has already stated that he recognized the defendant as one of the men who robbed his bank.'

'Your honor,' Herz said, rising, 'since the Sunnyside robbery, my client's picture has been in the newspapers on scores of occasions. I'm just trying to find out if the witness may have been influenced by the publicity.'

The judge raised his hand. 'The witness has already made a positive identification, and I see nothing to be gained in trying to use tactics to discredit him. Sustained.'

Two other bank employees gave evidence and identified Bill as one of the robbers. After they left the court, Herz sighed deeply and turned to stare at his client. Bill could see the doubt written all over his face.

Bill gritted his teeth. 'I swear to you, this is the one job I didn't do.'

But he knew he was beaten. The jury retired, and returned to the court after only five hours, and he knew the verdict would be "guilty", so, when he heard it pronounced, it came as no

273

great shock. He felt nothing. He was numb. After the rollercoaster emotions of the past month, all he wanted to do now was sleep.

Back at the Long Island City Jail, the guard unlocked Bill's cell and ushered him in and chuckled, 'Bad news for you, Bill, but good news for the warden. He can't wait to see you sentenced. Twice he's postponed his vacation because of you.'

'What did he do that for?'

'Worried in case you might do a vanishing trick.'

Bill smiled faintly. 'You kidding? Think I could pick a lock with a book? The warden thinks I'm Houdini.'

The guard laughed as he locked Bill into the cell. 'Well, at least he'll be able to sleep easier now he knows you'll soon be in a state penitentiary.'

Bill fell back on to his bed. He was exhausted, but there was no way he could sleep. He was too wound up. He stared up at the ceiling, but his eyes were fixed on the distance beyond as he thought about his future. Today was the start of the rest of his life, and the rest of his life was going to be like it was now. A never-ending walk towards the future, where the scenery never changes.

CHAPTER 32

JULY, 1950

It was almost time for sentencing and Bill's lawyer came to the jail to explain the complicated procedure.

'It's far from straightforward,' he said, offering Bill one of his filter tips. 'The judge has to take the other crimes you've committed into consideration when sentencing you. And your previous convictions have to be proven by the DA so that the judge can be absolutely certain you are the same William Sutton who was convicted of robbing the Philadelphia bank and the Rosenthal Jewelry Store, et cetera.'

Bill's face broke into a grin. 'But how can there be any doubt I'm not the same William Sutton?'

The lawyer shrugged and offered Bill a light. Bill leant forward and drew on the cigarette. The tobacco seemed mild compared to what he was used to and he stared at the filter.

'These days, people are saying they're healthier,' explained the lawyer.

Bill raised his cigarette and examined it. 'Maybe I'll get used to it.'

'Anyway,' the lawyer continued, 'the law has to be absolutely sure. After all, when you escaped from Holmesburg, you were pretty keen to deny you were William Sutton. So now the onus is on the DA to prove you are who you are. When you go before the judge, he'll ask you if you're the same William Sutton. You can either admit it or deny it. Or you can remain silent and force the burden of proof on to the State.'

'This is crazy,' Bill replied. 'What the hell would I gain by denying it or remaining silent?'

'Well, you'd maybe gain an extra two or three weeks at Long Island Jail.'

Bill blew out a cloud of smoke like a sigh. 'Did you know Warden Klein has postponed his vacation twice because of me?'

Herz looked puzzled. 'What's that got to do with anything?'

'He's treated me fairly. And he worries about me escaping. Why don't I just admit everything, then the warden can get a good night's sleep and get to Florida?'

'Are you sure that's what you want?'

Bill nodded. 'I'm certain.'

'Okay. But please don't forfeit any of your rights just because of the warden's vacation.'

'Why should I deny I'm the William Sutton who broke out of Sing Sing and Holmesburg? Three years ago, the papers pinned the Brinks robbery on me. If they want me to admit to that one, they can go to hell.'

'Somehow I don't think they will. They've got enough on you to...' Herz stopped speaking and inhaled deeply on his cigarette.

Bill finished the sentence for him, 'To put me away for the rest of my life?'

His lawyer stood. 'Oh, I think you should know. Loads of young kids hero worship you. You're a popular guy. Now church leaders are saying how worried they are that some of these kids will try to be like you.'

Herz saw the twisted expression of pain on Bill's face and he almost wished he'd kept his mouth shut.

'That's terrible. I wouldn't want that to happen. If I write a statement for the newspapers, can you see it gets to them?'

'Sure. I'll have a word with the warden.'

Warden Klein came to see Bill the following day. He was

carrying a newspaper, and looked worried.

'I didn't upset you by making that statement, did I, Warden?' Bill asked.

The warden shook his head emphatically. 'Of course not. I wholeheartedly approve. But your lawyer told me that you intend forfeiting your rights because of my vacation. I find that a little disturbing.'

Bill smiled. 'I'm not giving anything up, Warden. Go ahead with your reservation. Going anywhere special in Florida?'

'Wife and I'd like to see the Everglades.'

'Well, I'm sure you'll have a good time.'

The warden stared at Bill for a moment, trying to work him out, then handed him a copy of the *New York Times*. 'Here's what they printed.'

Bill took the paper and began to read.

'CRIME DOESN'T PAY, ADMITS SUTTON'

'William Sutton, the self-confessed bank robber known as Willie the Actor, yesterday admitted to a lifetime of failure. He said, "They said I was the best. But what is the result? I'm 50, and I've spent most of my adult life in prison, or in hiding. Many people think I have a great deal of money stashed away, but this simply isn't true. I'm penniless. Even if it were true, what good would it do me? If I take into account the prison sentences still outstanding, then I'll probably spend the rest of my life in prison. The Press has named me Willie the Actor, but Willie the Failure would be more appropriate. At 50 what have I got to look forward to, except the rest of my life behind bars?"

'Sutton, throughout his trial for the Sunnyside bank robbery, claimed he was innocent, but a jury reached a unanimous verdict in less than five hours and he was found guilty. He is due for sentencing tomorrow and is likely to face the prospect of another twenty to thirty years added to his original sentences.'

While Bill read the story, Warden Klein spoke softly, 'I can't figure you out. With your reputation I expected plenty of trouble, but you've been the best behaved prisoner we've ever had. You've abided by all the regulations and I've never once heard you complain.'

Bill looked up from the paper. 'You know, Warden, when I came here, I didn't think you'd put me outside to cut the hedge.'

The warden gave a deep-throated chuckle, 'You're a paradoxical guy, Sutton. I think if you gave me your word not to escape, I think I could trust you to cut the hedge on the outside.'

'Yes, you could, Warden,' Bill agreed, with a twinkle in his eye, 'but you know I'd never give you my word not to escape.'

During the sentencing, Bill admitted he was the same William Sutton who had robbed the Rosenthal Jewelry Store and the Philadelphia Bank, and was the same William Sutton who had escaped from Sing Sing and Holmesburg Prison. The idea of denying it, or throwing down the gauntlet and challenging the DA to prove it, struck him as absurd. And now he had nothing to lose, his sense of humor seemed to go into overdrive and he viewed the proceedings with detached amusement.

Judge Farrell sentenced him thirty years to life to run consecutively with all his other sentences; as far as he could see it meant he would be due for parole somewhere a century into next millennium! As Bill worked this out, a wry smile spread across his face, which Judge Farrell noticed.

'You find something amusing in this, Sutton?'

'Yes, your honor.'

'Well, you won't be so amused if I sentence you for contempt of court.'

Bill was stunned. What difference could another six months added to his sentence make? Hearty laughter broke out from the court reporters. The judge blushed scarlet, as he recognized his blunder. He cracked down his gavel, hard, several times. 'Clear the court. Immediately!'

The trial had taken weeks, and the time had crawled slowly by. Now, the flow speeded up. Everything was done and dusted and they wanted Bill out of the way. The newspapers rounded off his life with news of his sentence. And that was that. Now, he'd be yesterday's news. A forgotten man. With one exception. At least, now he had a loyal and loving daughter who intended visiting him as often as she could.

That same day, handcuffed to a guard, he found himself on his way back to Sing Sing. In the stifling atmosphere of the meat-wagon, Bill attempted conversation with the taciturn guard. 'This will be my third visit to Sing Sing.'

The guard grunted.

'You were supposed to say "and your last".'

Silence.

Bill stepped down from the meat-wagon as soon as they arrived at Sing Sing and a guard stepped forward to greet him. 'Hello, Sutton, welcome to your new home for the next hundred and thirty years.'

'I'll try to live up to it,' Bill grimaced. He could tell by the guard's expression that he didn't get it.

From somewhere deep inside the prison, he heard the slam of a steel door.

EPILOGUE

1976

One of the guards patted Bill warmly on the back. 'Good luck, Bill. Any plans?'

'Just take each day at a time.'

'Best way.'

The gate opened and, for the first time in twenty-six years, he was staring at the outside world. He blinked, as though he'd been deprived of daylight, and his eyes watered. Up on the hill, silhouetted against the late afternoon sun, Jenny's distant figure swam into focus. She was leaning against the door of her car. She waved to him and he waved back.

Without a backward glance at the penitentiary, he began walking up the hill. His knee joints ached and his chest wheezed, but it felt good to be alive. As he got closer to her, his stomach fluttered with excitement. She had been true to her word and had visited him regularly, but somehow seeing her in the real world was like a dream, someone else's dream. He couldn't quite believe it was happening to him.

He had wept tears of relief when they told him he was being paroled, the pent-up tears of all those long years.

And, during all that time, she had been the most loyal daughter any father could wish for. She had brought her husband, Frank, on occasional visits, and her two little girls, Elizabeth and Lauren, when they were a bit older.

Now they were grown up and might soon have families of

their own and he would become a great-grandfather. That thought made him speculate about the rest of his life and how much of it was left? He brushed the thought from his mind. He promised himself that he was not going to look to the future. It was the enjoyment of the present that was important; the 'here and now'.

As he drew nearer to Jenny and saw her face, radiant with happiness, he knew this was a moment that would live with him forever.

1	2	3	4	5	6	7	8	9	10
11	12	13	14	15	16	17	18	19	20
21	22	23	24	25	26	27	28	29	30
31	32	33	34	35	36	37	38	39	40
41	42	43	44	45	46	47	48	49	50
51	52	53	54	55	56	57	58	59	60
61	62	63	64	65	66	67	68	69	70
71	72	73	74	75	76	77	78	79	80
81	82	83	84	85	86	87	88	89	90
91	92	93	94	95	96	97	98	99	100
101	102	103	104	105	106	107	108	109	110
111	112	113	114	115	116	117	118	119	120
121	122	123	124	125	126	127	128	129	130
131	132	133	134	135	136	137	138	139	140
141	142	143	144	145	146	147	148	149	150
151	152	153	154	155	156	157	158	159	160
161	162	163	164	165	166	167	168	169	170
171	172	173	174	175	176	177	178	179	180
181	182	183	184	185	186	187	188	189	190
191	192	193	194	195	196	197	198	199	200
201	202	203	204	205	206	207	208	209	210
211	212	213	214	215	216	217	218	219	220
221	222	223	224	225	226	227	228	229	230
231	232	233	234	235	236	237	238	239	240
241	242	243	244	245	246	247	248	249	250
251	252	253	254	255	256	257	258	259	260
261	262	263	264	265	266	267	268	269	270
271	272	273	274	275	276	277	278	279	280
281	282	283	284	285	286	287	288	289	290
291	292	293	294	295	296	297	298	299	300
301	302	303	304	305	306	307	308	309	310
311	312	313	314	315	316	317	318	319	320
321	322	323	324	325	326	327	328	329	330
331	332	333	334	335	336	337	338	339	340
341	342	343	344	345	346	347	348	349	350
351	352	353	354	355	356	357	358	359	360
361	362	363	364	365	366	367	368	369	370
371	372	373	374	375	376	377	378	379	380
381	382	383	384	385	386	387	388	389	390
391	392	393	394	395	396	397	398	399	400